Letters from Yelena

Guy Mankowski

Legend Press Ltd, 2 London Wall Buildings,
London EC2M 5UU
info@legend-paperbooks.co.uk
www.legendpress.co.uk

British Library Cataloguing in Publication Data available.

ISBN 978-1-9090391-0-0

Set in Times. Printed by CPI Books, United Kingdom

Cover design by Gudrun Jobst www.yotedesign.com

Author photo © Mark Savage

Independent Book Publisher

PRAISE FOR GUY MANKOWSKI

**The Intimates* – one of the recommended titles in New Writing North's Read Regional 2011 Campaign*

'a clever conceit and a compelling narrative'

Edward Stourton, *BBC Radio 4*

'An intricately wrought and enchanting first novel... a measured, literary piece of work as hauntingly evocative of its setting and characters as Marilynne Robinson's Pulitzer prize winner *Housekeeping*.'

Abigail Tarttellin, Author of *Flick*

'[Guy's] ability to construct and develop his characters is formidable and the execution of this skill certainly added to the compelling nature of the book.'

The View from Here

'the book is unusually stylised for contemporary fiction, set in a glamourous, affluent world that seems to be decaying from within... [Guy's] background in psychology has a strong influence on his writing, which is rich with thoughtful, self-analysing dialogue... '

Culture Magazine

'Writing letters is actually an intercourse with ghosts,
and by no means just the ghost of the addressee but also
with one's own ghost, which secretly evolves
inside the letter one is writing'

Franz Kafka, *Briefe An Milena*

Dear Margaret,

It must have been strange to hear that you're the last hope I have of getting to know my mother. I suppose this is especially strange given that you never met her.

I know I became a little emotional when we met and I'm sorry about that. But I felt I needed to explain the lengths I have gone to, to try and find out about the mother I barely knew. The fact that I have even visited places she once mentioned in off-the-cuff remarks, in the vain hope that I would find some trace of her there, I know may seem quite ridiculous. It's been a journey that has taken many years. Recounting all this led me to feel a little overwhelmed by it all, so I am writing now to apologise and to give you some of the necessary details I neglected to mention that day. Perhaps also to explain why owning my mother's letters would be so important to me. I have been searching for my mother for many years, and it seems that the letters we discussed are my last chance of finding her.

Some people never feel like they truly know their parents. And just because a child comes from you, it does not necessarily mean you know them either. They are distinct. Never was this more true than with my mother. She always seemed far away from me. Even in her old age she remained a mystery. I never got to know what made her tick; what led her to lead such an unusual and extraordinary life. And exactly why she endured such difficulty. I would have done anything to hear the truth from her directly, but she was never a great talker, always too formal, too reserved. You would think a mother who'd been a Principal ballerina would have had many stories she'd be only too ready to tell her daughter. Not my mother.

It was only during her final days that she admitted how little she'd ever opened up to me. I presumed that her pain had imbued her with silence. It was too late for me to ask why together we had not felt able to overcome that silence, but she did at least offer me some hope. She told me she had only ever opened up to one man. A writer called Noah, who she had written to during her career as a ballerina. After her death, I came to realise I could only make peace with her if I found a way to get to know her, a way to understand her. I contacted the few names that existed in her address book, but the people who did offer to meet me had little to share about her. They depicted a closed, cautious woman, a woman full of contradictions and secrets. A woman who seemingly came alive only when she was dancing. Her ambitions, her desires and her sufferings had always remained completely her own. Except, that is, when it came to Noah.

I don't know what happened to the letters my mother received from this Noah. I suspect that she lived and died wanting to keep the contents of them completely to herself. But then one day, three years after her death, I found amongst her belongings a single postcard signed by him. The contents of the postcard offered me little, but at least it gave me his surname. It required the services of a detective over the course of two years before I was able to finally track him down.

He was now a reclusive and very elderly writer of some repute, living in a large house on the south coast. I wrote to him, and his reply suggested that he felt intrigued by the woman who was so desperate to meet him.

When we met he gave his memories of my mother, even to me, with some reluctance. I got the sense that their exchange had somehow been sacred, and that he wanted to keep it that way. When I mentioned the letters she had sent him though, his eyes lit up. 'Yes,' he said. 'Your mother revealed herself completely in those letters. It was as though she finally made sense.' He then confirmed that he had in his ownership a small box of letters that my mother had sent him during her lifetime. Towards the end of our conversation he admitted that he had become an 'almost totemic' figure to my mother during her life, for reasons he still could not quite fathom.

Feeling so close to the prize, I asked with some trepidation if he would allow me to read the letters. But unsurprisingly, he expressed reluctance to do so, saying they were often very intimate. When I explained that these letters were my last hope of ever getting to know her, he finally admitted that he had made a promise to protect her letters for all his life, and he simply couldn't break it. I tried reasoning with him and imploring him and eventually, just as I was leaving, he said that he would leave the letters for me when he died. It seemed there was light at the end of the tunnel. Even if I would only reach it with the passing of this frail but considerate man.

I am so glad now that I taped that conversation with him. I could never have imagined the contents of the tape would be required as evidence. I only taped the conversation because I did not want to forget any scraps of my mother that he might offer up to me. When I saw his obituary in *The Times* a year later I began to try and trace the letters, which had automatically passed into my ownership. I soon learnt that all of his work, including the letters, had become a part of his literary estate. An estate, which you yourself manage.

It was disheartening to hear that he had not legally entrusted the letters to me before he passed away, though I can understand this. As a creative type he did not seem *au fait* with the legalities required in such a case. He probably thought I could just turn up and claim them back by asking nicely. Which is why I was so grateful when you agreed to meet with me and hear the contents of the tape, and even more grateful that you subsequently agreed to find a way to ensure that the letters are entrusted to me.

I understand that the contents of the tape are currently being verified. I hope that the promise this man made to me will allow you, in time, to alleviate my desperation, and offer me the letters my mother once sent him. It is the only way I can foresee that I can make my peace with the mother I barely knew.

I eagerly look forward your response.

Yours sincerely,
Natalya Christensen

Dear Natalya,

Please find enclosed in this package the letters sent from your mother to Noah Stepanov during their period of correspondence, which began just after she had graduated as a Principal ballerina. With the exception of a single handwritten note, which is referred to in the letters, I believe they do comprise everything she wrote to him.

Given the financial and emotional effort you have invested in retrieving these, I hope you now feel satisfied that all the letters from Yelena Brodvich are in your possession. Due to the fact that Mr Stepanov gave very few verbal interviews in his lifetime, the authenticity of his promise to you on tape took some time to verify, but that process is now complete. It is possible that in due course some objections might be raised if these letters do not become archived property, as they do relate to Mr Stepanov's literary estate. I trust that the two of us will remain in contact to negotiate that situation if and when it becomes salient.

I am glad I was able to be of some service to you. I understand that this whole enterprise has been personally taxing and you have undergone many sacrifices to reach this point. I can only hope that these letters will allow you to make peace with your mother in the way that you described.

With my very best wishes and regards to your family,
Margaret

Letters From Yelena

By Guy Mankowski

Dear Noah,

I dreamt of you again, watching me rehearse for the ballet. In the dream I am standing three or four feet from the other dancers. The door to the courtyard is open, revealing that bright shaft of the city. It is summer, or early autumn. There is a certain sequence of chords that plays every time, and though there is a melody there it is distant and vague and I can't recall it when I awake. I recognise it instantly though, every time I have the dream about when we first met.

The melody is haunting and expanding, and it plays over and over again, that same refrain. The other dancers stretch, and I compose myself. I feel the heat of your gaze on the back of my neck. We haven't spoken yet, but I already feel I know you so well, simply from your gaze. It seems to search for so much and find even more. I think I knew even then that eventually we would come together.

No-one could have told you I feel sure of anything as I nervously try to find my first position. The maestro seats himself at the shining set of keys in the corner of the hall, and looks over at me. The *corps de ballet* watch me expectantly, waiting for inevitable errors. At the entrance, the hired hands pass amongst the sunlight. The girls conspire amongst themselves. I flex my muscles. I am alone, Noah, so painfully alone that I feel sure that I cannot dance. Least of all now. But I know I must, because you are watching. Because however inevitable our union feels at that point, I still must prove it to you right now.

I return to a barren wilderness every time I begin to dance. I know I have told you before that no matter how many other ballerinas I'm dancing with, I feel sealed apart from them. They flit about me like excuses. Every one is a distraction from my movement, from my expression. They are all in competition with me; at least that is how it feels. At this point in the dream the feeling of loneliness becomes so acute that I always struggle to breathe. However much after the dance people tell me that I moved beautifully, I feel as if they are talking to me in a bubble and that I am completely insulated from how I felt at the time. The praise by then feels as if it belongs to someone else. Sometimes, in my dreams of dancing, I trip over and fall to the floor just as I begin. When this happens the other ballerinas simply dance over me, until my body becomes a bloody pulp twisting into the ground. My thin figure becomes bruised and damaged as their tiny, muscular feet pummel into me. I become as indistinguishable from the ground as sunlit dust is from the sky, while it quietly circles our movements.

I want you to know how I felt at that moment, as I began to dance and tried to dismiss these fears from my mind. At that moment the isolation isn't like it was when I first moved to St Petersburg from Ukraine. That isolation existed as a kind of hollow pain in the pit of my stomach. The soft thump of ballet pumps at the Vaganova Academy made for an aching and resonant sound, but they were washed with a kind of nauseous excitement, because I knew that I had finally escaped my stepmother. I knew that I had arrived at the point where I could begin doing something of worth, and so the pain was not unchecked. I had only ever felt fulfilled before that on the afternoons I'd volunteered at the children's home, but that had felt different, that had been a more nourishing, steady fulfilment. That excitement had twisted into something new by the time I moved from St Petersburg to England, where you would finally watch me dance. At that point, a new thought had started to consume me, like a parasite – the thought that I could never truly be a dancer, that I lacked the nerve. And yet here I was, hundreds of miles from my childhood in Donetsk, struggling with this new language, amongst a troupe of women more talented than I, wondering if I was always doomed to failure. A failure that now could not be soothed by even the paltry comforts of home.

I won't remind you of how long it had been since I had felt a kinship with anyone. The wilderness stretched from the brittle terrain of friendship, through the chalky turf of professionalism. Isolation skewered through the sinewy paths of intimacy and had now settled into every second of my life. As I tensed into the first position, I was living in exile. And yet the heat of your gaze meant that at that moment all the loneliness was erased by the thought that I could yet be saved from it all. As it was the first time you watched me, so it is in the dream.

This dance feels so different from any other, because you are there. Any beauty I manage to carve out in this barren place is not wasted because it is for you, and that is what I tell myself as the music starts. I sense you raise your chin, and I turn mine perpendicular to yours. The piano chords begin to roll, and their momentum soon overwhelms me as I start to move.

I don't look to you at any point in the dance and more than ever I dance as me. For once I do not feel removed from the dance. I give myself the room to indulge a little, a small emphasis here and there as I always imagined it should be, as I would never have permitted myself were the choreographer present. My *attitudes* are more elegant, my *adage's* more pointed. But with you watching this is not only permitted, but expected. Finally, I am dancing for a purpose. Though you will not review my dance for a broadsheet paper, and though it will not be festooned with stars on an infinite number of cheaply printed sheets, this dance has more meaning than any. I am creating a piece of work that stands outside of time, a shard of self-expression that for once is not futile, and gradually, above all others, you are seduced by my movement. I feel the weight of pressure on me, the gorgeous weight of knowing that just this one time I must be incredible. That I must create movements whose meaning extends beyond the realms of the mundane. At first I feel your eyes possessively pore over my limbs as they extend and contract. You consider the white flesh of my clenched thigh as I *plié*, and the flashes of my body that my outfit reveals as I stretch and gambol. I am inevitably mapped out, a good portion of me at least, for the duration of the dance.

That is why I thought it apt to tell you of this dream in the first letter I'm sending you. At our reunion three days ago, in that beautiful rose garden, we agreed to be completely honest in these letters. Meeting one another made our lives extraordinary. Perhaps that is why we agreed in these letters, the first we have ever written to one another, to chart what has happened between us since we first met. In doing so, I hope to discover what caused the remarkable events that followed our introduction. But I have another, more personal hope for these letters. I hope that through them we can also work out exactly what we are to each other now. However pure our union first felt, we have, in all honesty, taken each other through dark places that no-one could have envisaged. Through these letters I hope to illuminate these sunless corners of our lives. To illuminate exactly who you and I are now, as a result of what we have done to each other.

My letters to you, my darling Noah, will be maps, in which I hope I can be found. Like that time you once mentioned, when you saw a glimpse of me, naked in front of the mirror, through the open bathroom door. You said you had seen me, not composed, but unadorned. Physically and socially unadorned. And that is how I hope I will be in these letters and how I hope to find you in yours too. I have always struggled to be anything other than stiff and secretive, and even now I struggle to find the language to be open and intimate. But if I can at last do it with anyone – finally ventilate all the hidden compartments of myself – I believe it will be with you. I don't believe we could ever write in such a way to anyone else. I hope we can do this. If we are to supply any remedy to one another, for the ills of fate and circumstance, then I feel sure that it will be through these letters.

Towards the end of the dream the dance ends and I start to remember who you still are to me. Just a writer in a navy blue trilby, clutching a red notebook, who's been reluctantly granted permission to sit in on our rehearsal while researching his next book. A voyeur, that is what you are – by your own volition. A voyeur is criticised for granting himself access to something which he is not privy to. And in that case, in that context, that is what you are. And yet it is not so simple. Because I made a decision at the moment the maestro seated himself: to play the role of a seductress. Therefore, although it is demonstrably me who is under scrutiny, you have been stripped of the power of your role. And from that moment on, the two of us were absented from usual life.

You remain untainted in this dream, Noah, even with the self-flagellation our dreams are often stained by. After the dance has finished, you note that I am alone. The girls wipe themselves down with stiff towels, laugh conspiratorially amongst themselves. They remain cautious, if unburdened. Conscious of the sheen of sweat on my back I look over to you, exhilarated and relieved, and the door to the city opens a little wider. The stagehands spill out into the summer's evening, keen to encircle the girls. You catch my eye and give a little flutter of your hand, ironically, as if *you* have just performed for me. Which, I must admit, you have though your performance was complete the moment you sat down. You have your fetishes. I know that you are probably fascinated by our outfits, by the faint scent of makeup in the city air, by the sunlight on our skin as we pour outside. I see you begin to move outside – from a bird's eye view indistinguishable in location from me, and yet formally the two of us have not yet spoken and we could not be more apart.

I hope that you are intrigued by me, intrigued enough to want us to speak. But you do not yet know if you possess the dexterity to overcome my natural and cherished awkwardness. And just as you are preoccupied by my details, so I am with yours. As you step in my wake, as I move outside. The synchronicity of our movements is not set to music now, it's merely punctuated by time. I am fascinated by you, by your mysterious red notebook, the contents of which I can only speculate over. Outside, I sit on a block of concrete, and I hope I somehow stand out amongst my peers. The sky in that quarter of the city has an untrammelled pureness to its blue, reminiscent of the kind of world I later learn that you wish to live in. I know I have become furniture in that world merely by sitting just there. You have begun to respond to me a little, for what I threw at you in the dance, and for where I now sit, a rare stone amongst the jewellery shop of this city. I already want us to be splayed amongst it, for us to cover every corner of it together. I want my presence to be so evocative that it is indistinguishable from your vague fantasies, to be the most potent amongst them. I assume that role happily though, because I already need to be a part of your world. I accept a cigarette from one of the girls, because I know that I need my apparatus too, my levers and pulleys to pull you in. There is still paint on my eyes and skin, and sweat on my legs. I can feel the sheen from my exertions shimmer on my chest, and I see your eyes catch the glowing skin above my breasts at least once. They rise and fall in the corner of your eye, and I know your body registers every undulation. I don't want this vast vat of blue to ever fade from my eyes and the eyes of the other, now beautiful dancers. I want to embody this symbol for you for as long as I can, as I know you will draw from it during the dark and isolated moments that are still to come in your life. For a moment I suspend myself in my current state, and I sense the weight of meaning upon me; a beautiful, timeless weight. And for a moment I actually feel playful. I laugh with the other girls, and I'm not scared of them. I love them and everything around me because I know it all means so much. I love feeling important for once. I love to drip with meaning like this, to finally be a part of something timeless. I just know that in time you will come over to me, and only a few moments later you do. I feel your approach in the corner of my eyes. There is no hurry; I have never been so sure that something will happen. You consider me for a moment, perhaps balancing the weight of your fear against the loneliness you will later feel in your room if you do not speak now. And then, having made that calculation, you move over to me. And you are not yet able to meet my eye, as you ask, 'Would you like a light for that?'

With love,

Yelena

Dear Noah,

Thank you for your letter. Isn't it strange how two people can recall the same events so very differently? You say it was during the opening night party that my presence first had a great impact upon you; that watching me rehearse merely laid the groundwork for that. I can see how that party could have acted as a fertile ground, in which secretly planted seeds could flourish.

I remember the exuberant performance the *corps de ballet* gave as the guests began to arrive. Having the event in a lavish art gallery overlooking the river contributed to that excited, intense atmosphere, mirrored in the bodies of the ballerinas as they took to the floor. Their nervous energy commanded the guests' attention. Nine dancers with feather plumes, their athletic bodies clad in stiff tutus. This was their moment, tonight they had the attention of the discerning for those few fluttering minutes. The three Principal ballerinas in evening wear, who were stationed at various corners of the room, exchanged amused smiles as the dancers braced themselves to begin. And then the air was filled with the striking of strings, followed immediately by the quick, arching movements of lithe arms, legs quivering as they went *en pointe*. They exchanged glances as they darted around the room like small sparrows, destined one day to soar, a trail of talcum powder spinning in their wake. The men, enchanted and engrossed, gripped their champagne flutes harder. The women, knowing and composed, watched them with narrowed eyes.

I remember the unique sensations of that evening so precisely. I can still recall the excitement and relief I felt; its unusual potency moves me still. There I was, anxious, suspicious little Yelena, finally in England, at the launch party for the first ballet that I would dance as a Principal.

The windows of that high-rise gallery captured the city's vivid bouquet of colours, splashing amongst themselves as far as the eye could see. Below me were the intricate houses of the city, each holding such comfortable concerns. Thin strokes of purple and red dispersed amongst the ice blue of the summer sky, which seemed so wide and promising. The glistening arch of the bridge below us, visible in the expansive windows, the city's lights reflected in its concave frame, illuminated amongst the deepening dark. And inside, all around us pyramids of champagne glasses bubbling away like small gold fireworks. The long arched necks of the dancers, their hair pressed into precise buns, immobile as they considered the city they were about to enchant below. That gently insidious music that accompanied the *corps de ballet*, propelling each of us dancers in brief and sensational moments to move along with it – and in so doing to show hints of our potential. It was the first time that excitement had felt pure, unspoilt by anxiety. That excitement passed between the lips of each dancer as their performance ended, as if it was our secret. What a glorious night that was.

I admit it was at the launch party where we spoke enough for our unspoken pact to feel validated. After the rehearsal Eva, still bewildered by your presence, had asked if you would be coming to the launch. You looked me up and down and I smiled, bemused by the way you so shamelessly considered the quality of my presence. But I didn't mind that, and felt excited when I heard you turn to her and say you thought that would be a good idea. And at the launch, when I saw you enter the gallery, that sharp pang of excitement returned as I realised that a new chapter of my life was about to begin.

I could tell you wanted to believe that I always inhabited the world of glamour represented that night. I could tell you liked the idea that I represented access to that world. Perhaps I had been able to sense, already, that need the first time we met. I know you mock me for this, but I believe it is a ballerina's job to relieve the trapped tensions of an onlooker through their movement. We act as a conduit for the observers' unexpressed desires, the silent appreciation they may contain for anything; a lover, a river, a building even. I know you are amused by such pretensions Noah, but they are essential to me. Ballerinas make the vague, the fleeting, the contained into something physical and real. Do you think that we dance the same for every audience, just as we make love in the same way with each partner? Of course we don't. But during the moments that all fears are allayed and our pleasures expressed, we realise our obligation to commend the audience, or lover, for prompting that in us. And as if to prompt a fine display of myself, I knew how to present myself in the array for you that night.

It was only the thought of your presence which prevented me from feeling utterly removed that night. The dress rehearsal that had finished a few hours before had been a strangely flat, insular experience. But now it seemed that the glamour of the art gallery could light the evening ablaze for me. And you would supply the spark.

When you arrived, I saw your excitement at this glittering façade. At the strangely childlike ballerinas, awkwardly holding their glasses of wine and struggling to remember how to enjoy themselves. Their presence more potent than they yet realised. For them, the party was a brief respite from the pursuit of perfection. For me, it felt like a different type of excursion. I could feel myself adjusting to become the person I wanted to be in your eyes: indifferent, graceful, and quietly confident of my abilities. I stood in a triangle with Erin and Eva, the two other Principal ballerinas on this final leg of the tour. I saw Michael, the director of the ballet, come to the entrance as you ascended the stairs. He reached out to you and you looked up. In a flash I took in the trilby, perched on the crown of your head, concealing your dirty blonde hair. I absorbed the deceptive heft of your presence. The way that your ruffled good looks instantly lifted the room. Michael, effusive and ingratiating, anxious to find you a glass of wine. Impressed by your accolades and reputation, warming himself on your presence. If I chronicle what followed too exactly, it is because at night I have been practicing my lines.

Eventually, Michael brought you over to the three of us. Eva was wide-eyed, learning to be pleasantly surprised by the new role Principals could play on such a night. Erin watched almost maternally over the two of us, her severe beauty intimidating and commanding.

'Ladies,' Michael said. 'There is someone here who you must meet. This is Noah Stepanov.' Eva smiled, her head to one side. Erin squinted suspiciously. I tried to look pretty and not like an alien.

'This young man is something of an *enfant terrible* in the literary scene. His last book was about a modern day messiah, who happened to live on a North London council estate. But for his next work he has decided to use perhaps a more evocative setting. We are fortunate that it is going to be based in the world of ballet. I have permitted him to sit in on some of our rehearsals as he researches it. And Noah, darling,' he continued, 'this here is Erin, the Principal ballerina who'll be dancing the role of Giselle for four nights on the closing leg of the tour.'

'Hello,' she said, with a pinched smile. Most of the other ballerinas were terrified of her, but whenever I felt I might become so I always reminded myself of the time I sprained my ankle in rehearsal and how, without fuss, she massaged it in the wings before Michael noticed, whispering in my ear, 'Smile my dear, and he will never know.'

'And Eva,' he continued. 'One of our more promising soloists. Eva will be dancing her first Principal role for one night as Giselle.' Eva smiled intensely, excitable and tender. Sometimes, as we daubed ourselves in paint at the mirror before shows, she looked at me with frightened eyes and I'd hug her with one arm. She would always devour this comfort and her anxiety would immediately vanish. That night I felt appreciative of her kind and fragile presence amongst all the glassy stares.

'And Yelena,' Michael said, turning to me. 'Yelena is, I think we would all agree, the most exciting dancer in our company. She is dancing the lead role of Giselle for the two closing nights of the tour. And I am sure that her volatile, exquisite dancing will help us close this tour with a bang.'

I had never heard him speak in such floral terms, and despite the compliment could not help but dislike this flashing consideration of me.

'Yelena,' you said, getting it wrong.

'Noah,' I said, getting it right. A little too enthusiastic on the 'h'. Our eyes locked into one another's. I looked at you as though you had already taken me; you looked at me as if promising you would try. Up close the tilt of your eyelids and the slightly aggressive sensuality of your lips made you more feminine and tender than you had been in my memory. I saw then, in a way that I could not now, the manner in which you considered everything around you, me included, with a precise eye.

A few minutes later, once the group had drifted apart, I pulled out a flower from a bouquet at the wine bar and twisted it around in my fingers. As I did it, I felt childlike for the first time in a while. How could one man's gaze liberate me from my own personal wilderness? How was I now able to feel happy like a girl, while still looking like a woman?

Recently I had understood that, without pretence, I normally behaved the way most people might while they recovered from loss. In my spare time I always wanted to wall myself off and walk around the city or along the beach, and drink in cafés by myself. I hoped I did not act this way as a result of some perpetual vanity, or to imagine myself as the heartbroken protagonist in my own film. But I have always been drawn towards solitude, melancholy, removal. It has always been my way of buffering the world, or perhaps of digesting it – the way you would later digest, in your writing, all you had devoured with your eyes. As I twisted the flower I saw that all of those days of consideration had been merely training, to build my strength up for the moments that mattered. Moments like these.

I saw you hover behind me, and then collect at my side.

'Yelena, isn't it?' you said, getting it wrong again. I smiled.

'Yelena,' I corrected. You laughed. I felt pained by my disappointment of you. I liked your hands, so long and damaged. But I didn't like your voice, tripping over itself, not as resolute as I'd have liked. The process of negotiation, between the imagined and real lover, had begun.

'And you?' I asked.

'Noah. We were just introduced.'

'Oh yes.' I twisted the rose around on my nose.

'This must be an exciting time for you. All of that work, about to finally pay off.'

'We are not ready,' I said, flicking my eyes up. 'You see that dancer, Erin? She has always been ready. She plans everything far ahead. But Eva and I… it is our first time. We are not quite there yet.'

'But the question is, do you think anyone will notice?'

I laughed. 'To me, it doesn't matter what other people think.'

'It must do a little.'

I smiled. 'Okay, a little. It does affect things, obviously. It is nice to be complimented, and I still feel it when I'm criticised. But ultimately, it only really matters how I feel about it.'

'And how do you feel about it now?'

I was taken aback by your intensity. But you leant in, and seemed genuinely interested. 'That's quite a personal question,' I said, before realising in the echo of my voice that it was not.

'Forgive me, I'm a typical nosey writer. A complete voyeur, always interested in things that I probably shouldn't be.'

'But that is your job. And so,' I put the head of the flower on your nose, wondering idly if it would change colour at its tip, 'you must ask.'

'You are quite evasive.'

'You are quite over-familiar.'

'Are you queuing for a drink?'

'Will you get me one?'

You didn't even wait for an answer, disappearing on my command. There I was, alone again, drenched in solitude. I dropped the flower in disgust. How pathetic I am, I remember thinking. To think you can enchant a man just by using a withered flower. Do you think he has not seen flowers before? And suddenly my stepmother's voice came to me, and squeezed me around the abdomen. *Why must you act like a child?* it said. *Why can you not be like a real woman?* I felt my blood freeze.

It thawed a little as you appeared from nowhere with a flute of champagne. 'Here,' you said. 'Something to still your nerves.' I suppressed a giggle; hated myself for being so coquettish. And then I hated you for bringing this upon me, when my solitude had finally become a comfort. Moment by moment, you were already taking that old friend away from me.

'What makes you think I am nervous?' I asked.

'I know it must have been strange,' you said, surveying the burgeoning crowd. 'To have a man sit in the aisles, watching you all practice. I felt like I must have looked like some sort of... I don't know. But it was in the name of my book, and I had to remind myself of that. But being there, I learnt how readily ballerinas express themselves with their bodies.'

'But some of us,' I said, 'have forgotten how to really express ourselves with our bodies.' You pursed your lips, and I couldn't help blushing. I pointed out Eva, and felt a surge of confidence. 'Take Eva, for instance, her life is ballet, and she is yet to fully embrace adulthood. Her bedroom is still full of toys. As far as I know, she is yet to have a boyfriend.' I said it almost defiantly, as if wanting to mark myself as different to her. And then I turned, and could not read your expression. 'Listen to me, I am making it sound as if I am a woman of the world. When I am anything but.'

'I'm trying to place your accent,' you said, narrowing your eyes. 'You're from East Ukraine? Perhaps via St Petersburg?'

'I'm impressed. Did Michael tell you that?'

A pause. 'Yes. I sometimes like to make myself sound more cultured than I am.'

I laughed. 'And why would you want to do that?'

You shrugged, and I suddenly sensed the eyes of the other two Principals upon me. I knew they had already taken in the invigorating presence of your intentions. At that moment it was as if you sparkled. You verified me by being talented, intriguing, and shamelessly interested in me. Your body moved like a sunflower bending towards the light. Your movements, I could already tell, were suffused with a little desire. I felt the stares of the other ballerinas, softened to try and look friendly but undeniably laced with aggression. In that mad moment of happiness I decided to pursue my advantage. 'I need some air.'

'You must take your drink,' you said, confident and direct. 'For your nerves.'

'Are you not coming with me?'

'Of course I am,' you said, as if it that was obvious. Taking my glass I began to walk slowly outside, shamelessly enjoying having the eyes of all the soloists upon me. Step by step, moment by moment, leaving a trail for myself that I knew I would one day come to carefully retrace.

The city seemed to have moved closer to us as we went

outside. The distant silhouettes that I had first admired through the window had now expanded. A photographer leant out of the door, wielding his camera with studied abandon. 'A quick snap of the two of you?' he asked. As if we would obviously consent, you placed your glass quickly on a table and I felt your shoulder press against me. I looked up at you, wondering if you would wrap your arm around me, and as the photographer prepared I found my fingers pressing awkwardly into the small of your back. Many months later I would finally get my hands on that photo, with me bunched into you like a child. You, concerned and grinning, keen to play the part. Me, with the tips of my hair blonde from the summer sun, my nose wrinkled at the sudden attention.

The bulb erupted. 'One more?' he asked, gesturing at us to move closer to one another. At that moment I moved my head over the triangle of skin exposed by your open shirt, and you placed your arm around me. It struck me how natural it felt to move into your space. Caught in that moment of lust I felt sure we had betrayed what we would become. When people later saw that photo they presumed we had been together a while when it was taken; not that it was our first night together.

The dancers drew the photographer away. 'Have you been up here for long? I asked, as you took out a cigarette.

'I've moved around quite a lot. But recently, in the last year, I have started to feel at home here. And you?'

'People talk about "home" like it is a good thing. I am still running from it.'

'There isn't much more room to run. Much further and you'll be in the sea. Perhaps you should try and stop running?'

I laughed at the boldness of your implication.

'What are you running from?' you asked.

I'm running from silence, I thought. From being treated like a human punch bag. From being told I am disgusting, so many times that I sometimes even hear the voice say it at night. I even sense that she is in the room, saying it to me. But of course, I could not say that. So I shrugged.

'How long is the run of shows up here?'

'Only a week, and then four weeks of rest, and then… who knows where I will be?'

'Back to St Petersburg?'

'I can't,' I said, despairingly. 'I mean, I really don't want to go back there. I need to move on.'

You looked inquisitive.

'Why have you decided to settle up here?' I asked. 'Surely as a writer you can go anywhere?'

'You don't like it up here?' You considered your cigarette for a moment.

'No, I do. At least, I'm starting to. But I'm interested to find out why you do.'

'It's hard to say exactly. Part of it, perhaps, is that I was here as a student. I came with lots of ambition about what I wanted to achieve, and though in many respects I failed, this place still reminds me of that time, and so being here drives me forward. You see that row of houses on the other side of the river?' You traced out a haphazard line of elegant houses with your lit cigarette. 'When I first came here I knew no-one. I didn't know where in the city I wanted to live. But I used to walk down here, to the quayside, on Sundays when I had a moment to myself, and imagine living in one of those houses. I don't think I can leave this city until I've achieved it. They seemed to epitomise success to me.'

'I envy you. You're not shackled to anywhere, nor so uprooted that you cannot imagine a home.'

'You don't have to feel uprooted. Perhaps on your travels you will one day decide that somewhere is right for you?'

I decided to seize the suggestion. 'Do you think here is a good place to settle?' I couldn't look at you.

'I think you should probably stay here long enough to find out.'

'I might do. Perhaps. If you could talk to your famous

friends,' I said, waving airily, 'and find me a penthouse with a riverside view.' I peered over the edge of the balcony.

'Anything else?'

I smiled. 'A concierge. And an enormous bathroom, with a full size mirror. And a sexy Spanish chauffeur to take me to ballet rehearsal every day.'

'I know a Portuguese taxi driver,' you said, your eyes moving with mine. 'But I don't know about the sexy.'

'And you can come and visit me. And I can make you pancakes.'

You laughed. 'Why pancakes?'

'Because it's the only thing I can cook,' I said, feeling tempted to stretch my legs out on the balcony rail, but thinking better of it.

'So what you are saying, is that if I sort you out a home, and a toy boy, you will make me possibly burnt pancakes in return?'

'Exactly. Don't pretend to not be tempted by the offer.'

'I wouldn't dare,' you said.

I caught Michael's eye. He was flanked by three floating soloists, all framed by the doorway. 'Yelena, I am about to make a speech,' he called. 'Can the two of you come inside for a few moments?'

The two of us. I rolled it around on my tongue. You pressed your hand against the base of my spine and a tingle reached from there, knifing up through my body, and glistened around my cheekbones as we began to step inside.

The night ended at around ten. And although you left my side for a brief while, to congratulate Michael, and for a few worrying minutes to laugh with Eva, we remained close to one other the whole evening.

As a waiter drew my coat over my shoulders, I found you back at my side. You looked concerned. 'It is still light outside, how about we check out your future home before calling it a night? I've not been down there for a while.'

'Okay,' I said, trying to sound wary. I turned to look for Michael, as if to seek his consent, but he had already left, as if deciding that you and I leaving together was inevitable.

You kept your arm around me as you guided the way towards the elaborate staircase, and I wondered if your interest in me would disappear now we were alone, no longer garnering the attention of onlookers.

But nothing changed. I skipped ahead of you slightly, as if ready to dance, and you trod slightly impatiently in my wake. Already, I had grown to like this grumpiness, which I knew I could soothe if it suited me. I moved towards the bridge, and you took my arm. 'Where are you running to?' you said, forcing a smile onto your suddenly serious face. I feigned being dramatically pulled into you. I looked up, and you moved into my body. The wind passed overhead like applause, and I took in your fragrance. It felt natural to be close to your body. You lowered your head, and I suddenly felt very small, as if I had been sealed shut for years, as you kissed me. I opened my mouth, but only for a second. A sharp pang of pleasure darted through me. I closed my mouth and pulled away. 'Where is this house of mine then?' I asked.

As we walked over the bridge, the city before us seemed to settle into itself expectantly. The water below was still and dark, winding its way mysteriously out of the city. At the other end of the bridge we could see on the quayside women in sparkling dresses, purposeful yet lost, trailed by their woozy men. Once on the other side of the bridge you led me down half-lit alleyways, trying to remember how to find your way to those houses. There was one small, concealed entrance we would be able to use you said, but you had to remember where it was.

'Down here,' you finally announced, leading me down a small flight of stairs. I suddenly found myself in a brightly lit courtyard, surrounded by saloon cars. Looking around me I felt like Alice, having fallen into Wonderland.

Taking it in, I understood why, as a lost youth, these homes had been so significant to you. They clearly represented an enclosed idyll, a world of easy affluence that seemed impermeable to danger. Pale white apartments studded with wide windows, set above us by pillars, skirted the courtyard. The streetlamps in the yard tastefully lit our arrival, and yet were too delicate for the occupants of the apartments to be roused by our late entrance. Through the windows we could see flashes of the worlds these homes contained. In one, a chic looking woman with dark hair sipped a flute of champagne over a suited man, who was reclining on a white sofa. In another, we could hear the muted laughter of a dinner party, of chinked glasses, and we saw slim silhouettes pass through one another like ghosts. It was as if we had stepped into an enclosed universe of easy luxury. I could tell that you were still not quite sure why you had brought me here, after what had been only our first proper conversation. But the look you gave me suggested that with me at your side, for the first time you did not feel like an alien in this place.

'It is beautiful.' I said. You looked relieved.

'Have you seen the one you want yet? I couldn't guarantee you a parking space, but I'm sure there'll at least be a railing to chain your bike on. It wouldn't be very far for you to walk to the conservatoire.' You spoke as if you were selling me a lifestyle – as if you actually possessed the means by which to give me this life.

'That one up there will do,' I said, pointing out the home of the champagne woman. Such warmth emanated from those houses. Even the most opulent homes in Donetsk had always seemed so spare, so cold. It sounds strange, but I had never seen somewhere before that I'd have liked to have lived, somewhere I could imagine being. The courtyard gave me that sense of aspiration for the first time. I looked up again. I wanted to live in that home, stand at that window after a dinner party with your friends, wearing a glistening black dress.

Considering how I had drowned my past in the river below us, I imagined how triumphant I would feel. And that sudden flash of inspiration was all that was required to illuminate for a second how my current state of mind looked. Dark, dusty, and littered with half-buried skeletons.

'I'll see what I can do,' you said. You took my hand. You must have wondered if you had lost me at that point, but I felt a need to show that you had not. Usually flirtations are exchanges of variable temperature, with each party taking it in turns to push and pull. But here, so sacred did this link seem, that I was too cautious to test it, even gently. We had demonstrably come to this place as some sort of flirtatious joke, but the serious undertones of this visit had become quickly apparent. 'I think any of them would do,' I said. And then I realised the champagne woman was watching us.

I wondered where the evening might have taken us next, but I wanted to leave it on a high. At the ballet, at the launch party and in the glittering courtyard you had only ever seen me in glamorous settings. I didn't want to take you back to the squalor of my flat, and prevent you from imagining me as the woman I wanted to be. Perhaps I didn't want to yet see your life as it really was either. I knew my façade was important to you, but I think yours was equally to me as well. We had constructed certain images of ourselves, through our shared sense of possibility. And in that delicious shift of intimacy that life can occasionally offer, we had begun to build that world through our joint association with it.

You walked with me until we were a few streets from my flat. At times I darted ahead of you, and when I fretted over having caught my dress on a fence you told me that it didn't matter – I would look beautiful regardless. Usually I found it distasteful when men called me beautiful, especially if they didn't know me. But I was almost able to take the compliment from you. I was still aware of how little I knew you, but I could feel myself grow into the role of a seductress. And far from that role feeling fake, I felt it actually portrayed the real me. Emerging from the charred, frozen ashes of my childhood.

'I live two blocks down,' I finally said. 'But I think you've taken me far enough. I'm worried that you'll get lost on your way home.'

I wasn't.

'I'll try to flag down a cab,' you said.

We paused.

'I could get one now, and take you to your door?'

'There's no need,' I answered. 'It's fine, it's only a minute's walk from here.' I lingered, and smiled at the ground.

'I can't believe I took you to a stranger's courtyard. Why on earth did I do that?'

'I liked it.'

'We should have gone for a drink.'

'We can,' I said. 'Another time perhaps.'

'Are you free this week?'

'I should be,' I said, a little too quickly. 'Yes I am, this Wednesday night.'

It would be the first night of the week we would not be performing.

'Let's go out for something to eat then,' you said. 'It'd be good to see you again.'

I opened the clasp of my handbag, praying that I had not forgotten my phone. It was there. I handed it to you, feeling myself tense as you fiddled with the buttons and rang yourself. I waited for a moment, keen to move home before you guessed where I lived. Wasn't I insecure? After all that had happened. You waited, for an eternity, and I worried that the spell would break. 'Thanks,' you finally said, handing it back. 'Are you sure that I can't take you to your door?'

'Quite sure,' I said, and turned into the night. I stopped, darted back, and kissed you on the cheek.

'Goodnight Yelena.'

'Goodnight Noah,' I answered.

I don't remember the walk home, but I do recall the moment I opened my front door. Because at that moment a heavy shroud overwhelmed me, my shoulders shrunk, and I felt suddenly crushed. It was a feeling that in time I would come to dread, and it made it almost impossible to climb up the two flights of stairs. The vivid colour of our encounter had only made your departure a more black experience. As I walked it hit me how important the night had been, and it exhausted me to know that, as a consequence, much would soon be required of me. But I didn't feel adequate enough to live up to the sense of expectation. I suddenly felt so tired that I could barely open the door and clamber between the sheets, still fully clothed. As I closed my eyes I prayed that the feeling would pass, once sleep had taken me in its arms. Because I knew that if the pressure of expectation made me retreat, then I would never forgive myself. But at that moment I did not have the strength to even fear that was the last we could see of each other. I just had to hope that when I awoke in the morning I would have enough energy to dance again.

With love from,

Yelena

Dear Noah,

I remember the days that followed that evening so vividly. With the opening night in two days' time, I had to keep the thought of us stashed away in a treasure chest as the greatest test of my career lay ahead. Fortunately the darkness of that night had dissipated with the morning light, and I felt almost energetic when I awoke. It would be the first time I had danced as a Principal ballerina, and even if I would not be performing in the title role of Giselle until the following Monday, every minute was now part of the psychological preparation I needed to undertake. As you know, Giselle is the most coveted role in ballet. I would be playing an innocent young country girl, naïve to the dangers of falling in love, and also her ghost, resisting the lure of evil spirits and trying to save her lover's life. I had never acted, so I was sure Michael had cast me as Giselle because he saw parts of my character in her. This aspect of the upcoming challenge was to make the next few days even more demanding – I was yet to know the personal demons I would be confronted with dancing as Giselle. I had longed to play the part as a little girl, but could not have envisaged what this might actually require from me. I had to embody the role, and thus every night I would be playing the part of a young woman destroyed by her love. I was not to know it yet, but surrounding me were other forces, quickly building, that I would soon have to contend with too.

I could not allow myself to ruin this opportunity by being

too lovelorn to make my mark. I told myself that I could enjoy the few hours of that Wednesday evening with you, cautiously perhaps, but that after that I had six more days in which I would need to be Giselle during every waking hour. On the nights I wasn't playing Giselle, I was the lead soloist; so in a way, I needed that evening with you, just to get through the coming week. During the final practice before the opening night my movements were nervy, and I was only sporadically able to lose myself in the dancing. Nonetheless, I found in myself a certain hunger, one that I imagine originated from this new and burgeoning sense of meaning in my life. This hunger told me that I could do it. After all, I had danced for you with what had felt like the weight of eternity on my shoulders. Nevertheless, I found myself in that sure state of mind only fleetingly. During rehearsals that day Michael accosted me, sometimes rather sharply, when I didn't get it quite right, particularly towards the end of sequences when my concentration began to falter. 'Don't travel on a *jeté*,' he would command, and I would curse myself for having messed up so close to an ending.

The opening night was completely sold out, and peering from the wings before the show the theatre looked like an expansive black hole. I couldn't imagine in a few nights commanding the attention of the whole room for an entire performance. After all, what gave me the right to take centre stage in such an extravagant setting? Despite all my commitment, I couldn't understand how I had got to this point.

That night, during my solo, I felt myself quivering. My body felt frail, my temperament too emotional. I must have looked as if I would fall at any moment, and yet somehow I kept it together. Afterwards people praised the dramatic element of my dancing, which had not been entirely intentional. However, Michael was not in a generous mood, and in the days that followed he pushed me harder than ever. I had seen that night the gulf between me and Erin as she danced the lead role. But she had also traced out for me the path that I would need to follow. While I still had no idea how I would dance the opening night, she was utterly in control. As I was reaching for perfection, she seemed above the idea of it, looking down upon it as something she could play with at will.

As soon as the curtain fell I ran up to her to tell her how wonderfully she had danced. It did not occur to me that in a couple of nights the critics' glare would be upon me, and we would be compared to one another. At that moment I simply wanted to express my joy at how beautifully Erin had performed. She was sweet and accommodating, and she looked relieved herself. In the papers the next day the critics were breathless with praise for her. And then it was back to getting my head down, and focusing on the areas that Michael felt needed improving. I had a few more days to do it, I told myself, and I always worked best under pressure. You were there though, Noah, at the back of my mind.

It was the morning before the second show that it happened. I often wonder, in retrospect, if until that point you had seen my composure at the party as how I usually am, and the anxiety that followed as some new, surprising development. I am sure you know now that is not the case. The placid, calm person you had met had simply been learning to play a role.

I arrived slightly late that morning; the tube had been delayed. I flounced over to Michael, full of weak apologies. But there was a trace of a smile on his lips, and it worried me. Stood in the corner of the hall, a sweater draped over his shoulders, he suddenly announced, 'I have a treat for you all.' As he said it he looked glaringly over to me. I realised how different his character was now he was no longer in a room full of luminaries. There, in the doorway, was Alina. She dropped her bag with a formidable clatter, and tore off her hair band. In that very moment, the world I had started to cautiously assemble shattered instantly into a thousand pieces.

We stood mute, in a rough semi-circle. Erin and I exchanged

looks; even she struggled to look composed. 'Alina Volodov,' Michael continued, 'is fresh off the plane from St Petersburg, having recently played Masha in *The Nutcracker* at the Mariinsky.' Eva looked down. 'She was, originally, going to be another Giselle, and now we are looking to create a new role for her as a soloist. Get yourselves warmed up, we will work out the details over the next few days.'

I looked over at Alina, her face tilted to one side as she looked curiously back at me. Her expression was one of amused rivalry.

Alina was settled in St Petersburg by the time I first moved there. She was already a soloist in the days that I was homesick, malnourished, and unable to make a mistake without silently cursing myself. She had never missed an opportunity to demonstrate her superiority over me. On one strange and difficult day, I had asked her advice on a routine and she had replied with a certain approach which she had said would meet with the choreographer's approval. Little did I know that the day before I had arrived, the choreographer had told the already assembled dancers that that approach was the one thing he did not wish to see. It had been my first chance to flourish and put the pain of those difficult days when I had first arrived behind me, but Alina had knowingly sent me into a humiliating situation, and my dancing had so enraged the choreographer that I had been consigned to the wilderness for the whole of that first season.

Alina had initially made me believe she was receptive and warm, someone I could turn to, only to later use that trust just to obliterate the competition. As a result I had sunk lower than I had ever been, lower even than when I had first come to St Petersburg. She was the last person I wanted to have competing for my role, at this most important moment. Especially at a time when hope had finally began to come into my life. I felt that if anyone on earth could push me into a state of dejection, even madness, it was her. That icy sense of entitlement, that complete lack of scruples, that ability to charm so effectively that it seemed she had suddenly changed. The pressure I put upon myself was formidable enough, let alone the demands Michael placed upon me too. But the added uncertainty of her Machiavellian presence would surely be too much for me to handle.

The second night did not go well. Minutes before we were due to go onstage I passed by Erin's dressing room with the intention of wishing her luck, and saw her with her head in her hands. It seemed that the presence of a new Principal dancer from Russia, ready to take her role at a moment's notice, was too much even for her. That night she did not dance as I knew she could and Alina, in her makeshift role, danced with a drama that captured everyone's attention. My solo dance was technically fine, though a little stiff and unemotional. Afterwards, I found myself lingering backstage, waiting for the opportunity to hear Michael's opinion of my turn. Eventually, Michael came over and looked me up and down. 'That wasn't bad,' he said. 'But I want to see some of that volatile dancing which made me first take a gamble on you. Very soon you will be dancing Giselle and you must step up to it. If I don't believe you can do it, Alina *will* get the role.'

At that, the colour instantly drained from my face. Michael saw this, shrugged and said, 'This is how it is in the top flight, and you have to prove to me now that you are up to it. You are working on your faults, and I am aware of that. But I need to see some uniqueness. It can be done, even in a soloist role. You need to prove to me that I should gift you with the role of Giselle for the most important two nights. Or I will be making changes.' At this he glanced over at Alina, beaming as she removed her headdress. I couldn't believe it. Already, I had moved from having the lead role for two nights to having to prove all over again that it should even be mine. And Alina had only just arrived.

During rehearsals for the rest of that week, Alina and I

locked horns to fight for the lead role. Every second Michael was present she became more flamboyant than ever, and I wondered when Michael's enthusiasm for her theatrical dancing might wane. But if anything, he gave her slightly more room to shine as the week wore on. I couldn't express my frustration at this. During the one time I needed everything to make sense, this ghost from the past had thrown it into complete disarray. All I could do was remain focused, not take in the eyes upon me, and draw from my own experiences when dancing. In so doing, I found that I had a well of emotional experiences I could use whilst being Giselle, and I gradually started to enjoy the audacity of expression.

After a day of this, Michael's criticisms seemed to lose their bite, and then their frequency. But Alina was undeterred. Silently, I speculated whether she specifically wanted to take the lead role on the nights it was scheduled for me, even though Erin was at present looking the most vulnerable. After all, Alina knew she had usurped me once, and therefore perhaps felt she could do it again.

I focused all my energy upon staying strong. I surprised myself in that week, and learnt that I was not the delicate wallflower I had long thought I was. You had messaged me after the opening night, Noah, saying that you had been unable to come but inviting me for supper on the Wednesday. It had been enough to illuminate the first part of my week and inspire me to hold it together. I had something to look forward to. I remember that Wednesday morning, when the lead dancers practiced their big jumps during centre work. Alina shamelessly elbowed me out of the way to make sure she had centre stage, even though it was I who clearly needed to practice this most. Far from discouraging this sort of competitiveness, Michael seemed to relish it. I had to spend most of the rehearsal pushed into corners, trying to practice as best as I could and wondering when Michael would assert some authority over this madness. But he just stayed there, leaning against the piano in the corner, his eyes flicking between Eva, Erin, Alina and me with a bored nonchalance.

But finally Wednesday night came, and I felt that I had held off this new threat, at least for the time being. I felt a hollow thrill in my stomach as I realised there was now a little room for pleasure. It was not long until Monday, when I would have my two nights as Giselle, once Eva had had her moment. I was almost walking on air as I made my way home in preparation for our date. I had not been told Alina would be taking my role, and therefore could only assume I had proven she should not. I did not know what lay ahead of me, but I did know that I had now earned the pleasure of an evening with you.

With love from,

Yelena

Dear Noah,

I remember it took a day for me to reply to your invitation for supper. When I got your message I felt at that moment as if I was standing on the edge of a cliff, which was looming over a great, shimmering sea. The wind was blowing hard against my back and it was inevitable that soon I would be pushed off the edge. But I wanted to choose the moment when that happened, and only once I had worked out how best to fall.

I remember it was a cool and bright day, if not quite the English summer's day I had mentally rhapsodised over when living in the east. One night after rehearsal, I checked that I knew how to get to your house. It was harder to pinpoint than I'd thought it would be, but in the end I found it, towards the edge of the city, at the beginning of the suburbs. It was on the corner of a field that students often cut through on their way to the university, partially obscured by a row of willow trees. Only by taking the more elaborate route home did I see from the other side that it was in fact a deceptively large townhouse, with none of its windows currently illuminated. I wondered if you were perhaps writing in the dilapidated chalet that I had noticed in the corner of the garden, just visible from the field. I didn't stick around to find out. I was concerned you would notice me and reasonably enquire what I was doing there, a few days early. What is curious is that in the days leading up to our date, in my mind I had already walked through your house, and when I did finally come to enter it, it was exactly how I had thought it would be.

That night I managed to escape from rehearsal a little earlier than usual. Knowing that I was coming to your house, I felt as if I was carrying a heavy jewel that I had stolen from the other girls. The silence of my flat seemed to push me out into the city as I stood, the desk lamp illuminating the contours of my stripped body, in front of my full-length mirror. Anxiety had begun to grip me. I loathed the slightly comic curve of my torso, the long, helpless circles my arms tended to swing in and the wide gap between my eyes. But then I remembered my sister's advice, on the days we'd toyed with makeup as little girls: 'You don't need to do this, Yelena. Wear as little as you can, so people can see how pretty you are.' As I prepared for our date, her words returned to me. I left my face almost devoid of makeup, expect for a touch of red on my lips. I chose a simple, white summer dress and brown sandals. I was late already, but in no mood to hurry the experience.

Having walked through the soft summer's evening, I heard commotion the moment I pushed the doorbell. I haven't been on that many dates, Noah, unlike you. The building throb of uncertainty, that rising thirst for details, the peculiarly feminine reluctance to yield without sufficient cause. These are emotions that you will be unaware of. And again the voice of my sister, in later years, returned to me. 'You are the woman – the pressure is on him to earn you.' That was what she had said. At the time I had dismissed her words as archaic and sexist, but as I heard movement behind the door, they acted as a sudden balm to me.

You were wearing a crisp white shirt, the sleeves rolled up as if you had been mixing ingredients with your hands. You greeted me with a half-smile before looking nervously at the floor. As you ushered me inside I took in the Rothko prints, the statuettes, the stacks of fanned books. The large portrait of a semi-nude ballerina over the fireplace – should I have taken that as a warning? Music was playing in the distance, but I couldn't quite make it out. Steam moved in bulbous curls from the kitchen. I could hear a kettle singing. As we moved towards the cooking I saw the back door wide open, and through it the faded façade of your chalet.

As the risotto cooked you suggested we open a bottle of wine out on the patio, where you could still keep an eye on the steaming pots. As you made adjustments in the kitchen I picked around the charming relics in your garden – the small, algae lined fountain, the somehow brooding chalet. I moved over to its windows and peered inside. It was dusty, but draped over a wicker chair I could see a woman's blouse, which looked recently abandoned. For some reason I decided not to think about it. Until we sat down together we remained in our separate universes, trading features of our new roles.

I saw for the first time the uncompromising terrain of dating. Each person has learnt enough about the other to assume the date could work, and yet the attending anxiety reveals aspects of the other far too intimate for a first encounter. We have to leave room for our accomplice to find their mask amongst this exposure. I was careful to appear remote, detached, but accommodating. You were clearly trying to hide how flustered and inadequate you felt, which made me feel more attractive. I took in tokens of your appeal, scattered around the house, each reflective of your creativity. It was suggested in the nude charcoal paintings lolling over one end of the couch; it was in the sheaves of writing pinned under glass jars. You asked how the season was going – I tried to make out it was just one occupation I had. The pots started to boil over and we hurried to spread their contents out on the table. You seemed relieved that I didn't want to be waited on, not knowing that a man had never even cooked for me before.

As we sat down together to eat, I realised how time experiences separation in such scenarios. While we talked I grew to know the endless chasms that can stretch out between one sentiment and another. It occurred to me that a date was perhaps nothing more than a matter of joining the dots. I could see you thinking that you constantly needed to have the next step of the evening ready to disclose. And it felt as if it was my job to calm that process, but more pressingly to validate it. That tension soon broke into a sense of expectation. An interesting question opened out on the fertile terrain, which we felt indulgent to remain on for long, so charged was each moment with awareness of the next. In coaxing one another through that it occurred to me how quickly the two of us took our mutual attraction for granted. I found pleasure in the rolling momentum, which we took it in turns to hurry and suppress. In so doing I temporarily forgot the appeal of your fragrance and the curiosity in your eyes. But when such charms hit me – between one wry observation and another – they were completely disarming. Gradually, as the plates started to clear, it became apparent that there was laughter in the air, laughter that was now unburdened by fear. Indeed, the two of us had found enough fertile patches in the conversation to return to at later dates. That generous sprinkling of promising moments was the glitter that would soon illuminate our relationship.

The flirtatious energy remained as you took the plates inside and fussed over the hot sauce for the pudding. I was stood at the entrance to the chalet, wondering if I could venture inside when I heard you draw closer. You pressed a glass of wine into my fingers – slightly steamed by the heat of the kitchen. You lingered as our eyes held one another's. Your eyes darted to my lips, and the moment I raised my chin you kissed me. I cupped your ear in my hand and giggled, kissed you back as your hand darted down the suddenly thin fabric of my summer dress. The tang of white wine was on your lips; the sun bloomed overhead. I felt it nestle in my back and I laughed. 'Our pudding, I'll burn that as well!' you said.

'Then fetch it quickly,' I answered. 'And we can enjoy the last rays of the sun.' I sounded imperious, and you shouted something inaudible back. 'Can we eat on the steps of the chalet?' I asked. Inside it I had seen a typewriter, and the notebook you'd had with you when you first saw me dance. I was intrigued by the thought of its consequence, and what it might reveal about your life. On your way back you momentarily looked concerned. 'If you like,' and then, 'of course.' You handed me a bowl of caramel tart and ice cream, at once hot and cool to touch. A dish I would never have allowed myself to enjoy normally, and yet here – in this role – I was able to. I realised I had now shed my role as a seductress; it had slipped away and revealed the real Yelena for the first time. You knew nothing of the self-loathing, of the isolation, of the silence of my past. It didn't need to exist anymore. Your intense, flashing gaze told me it was unnecessary now. But I promised myself I would tell you about it one day, if only for my own sense of integrity.

You asked me how I really felt in the city. I said I still felt pretty lonely, and I wondered if I was ready to dance as a Principal. I told you about my need to please Michael, about Alina, about how desperate I was not to go back to the Ukraine with my tail between my legs. That I felt on the edge of achieving something momentous, but that there was little evidence as to why. And then I asked how you felt in the city, and what was happening in your world. In snatched, self-conscious sentences you told me that an eccentric uncle had left you this house three months ago, which had forced you, for financial reasons, to return to the city that you had lived in as a younger man. 'Hence the state of disarray.'

Over the last crumbs of tart, as we looked back at the house, you told me about the progress of your book. You said the breakthrough of your second novel had been a pleasant surprise, given that it had been written mainly to satirise a certain genre of 'cutting-edge' fiction. 'I wrote it in a fit of despair at my life, as a desperate attempt to do something of meaning. For years I had worked in dull bureaucratic jobs, and writing had been my escape. My first book had been written under another name as a bit of a trial run, but my second one had instantly gained a lot of coverage. After years of frustration and hardship it brought me the kind of lifestyle I had always wanted. One which gave me the room to write. Now I suddenly find myself as a full-time writer, but I've done no groundwork to understand that role. And I'm still learning to be domesticated, and yet I have this great big house. It's so strange.'

You said you still felt like an outsider in the city, as if by returning you were outstaying your welcome here. But that as time went by, you were rediscovering what you had first loved about it. I asked how, with no-one telling you what to do, you had developed the rules by which to govern every moment of your own life. You looked at me as though there were years of consideration tied up in that question. 'I am still learning,' you said.

The bottle of wine was almost at an end. As its effect began to take hold, you amused me with your impression of Michael, lizard-like and effete one minute, then a kind of camp Nazi the next. You had him down to a tee, the slightly leering gaze which crawls up your face as he considers you, the twitch of discomfort that whips around his shoulders when he momentarily realises how disingenuous he is. I found myself laughing so hard I almost fell off the rickety rail I was perched on.

We passed the rest of the bottle of wine between us, like guilty schoolchildren. I saw that in fact having the freedom to run your own life gave you room for small decadent pleasures, which another's rules could never encompass. You showed me that I didn't need to see decisions as an unending pressure, that in time they could be a cause for celebration. I saw how addictive you found it to make me laugh. Once I began you didn't want me to stop, and you quickly went on linguistic flights of fancy, surreal and imaginative that had me giddy with the absurdity of it all. Through the sheer dexterity of your words, Michael suddenly became a meerkat in a gilet, clambering sleazily up a ballerina's leg one minute, kicked disdainfully off the next, and then suddenly asserting his homosexuality the minute he was addressed. Given the hesitant start to the evening, it felt great to find that groove with you. Suddenly the evening felt ignited with a sense of spontaneity. We drained the last of the wine, and you asked if I was ready for the grand tour. Throwing off my shroud of caution, I said that I was.

The house was like a dusty jewellery box, its many compartments still hidden even to you. There were grand drawing rooms, decked in mahogany and rich leather, lined with ancient glass cases all containing antique books. There was a dining room with a long oak table, surrounded by portraits of woodland scenes, like something out of the first act of *Giselle*. 'And this,' you said, pulling open two high wooden doors. 'Is the pool room, where my uncle gambled away the last of his inheritance with his many alcoholic friends. I don't even know what half of these pool cues do.'

I felt as if I had entered a C.S. Lewis novel, as if Toad of *Toad Hall* could come bounding into our company at any moment. The house resembled the most charming turn of the century English fantasy, every detail evocative of some new eccentricity. As you kicked a gramophone to life, I tried to show you the trick shots I remembered from my teenage days at the local pool hall. As the second bottle of wine flowed, we placed some of the antique statuettes on the table and tried to play crazy golf around them with the snooker balls. 'We'll tear the felt!' I said.

'And then I won't have to maintain it!' you replied, passing the bottle.

We found the cigars your uncle had hidden in a cabinet, and on top of them his old poker cap. With a Cuban cigar smouldering between your teeth, you kept scores on the chalkboard – Y versus N. As the wine began to take hold I danced with the pool cue, singing huskily along to the jazz numbers you played. I berated you, with wandering hands, whenever you started to cheat at our customised game, snooker balls flying noisily onto the wooden floor. In the corner of the room you played the role of decadent barfly, cradling a bottle of wine in the tips of your fingers. I played the role of a gangster's moll, serenading you with torch songs, the façade only broken by me occasionally coughing on cigar smoke. 'Finish that bottle before you take the shot,' you said.

'Are you trying to get me drunk?'

You muttered something about it being your only chance of winning, as you fiddled with a Nina Simone LP.

'I said, are you trying to get me drunk?'

As if about to address an errant child, you set the record down, and came over to me. I looked up at you, my mouth opening as I laughed, embarrassed at having said it. As you kissed me I dropped my pool cue with a clatter. For the first time, with my nervousness having vanished, I felt lust surge through me. The feeling was almost unrecognisable; it made me giddy and weak. You kissed me harder and our mouths opened. You pushed me up against the pool table. I giggled, but you suppressed that slightly feverish sound as you kissed me again, harder. I felt the strap of my dress fall around my elbow, our waists pressing into each other's. 'The neighbours will see,' you whispered. 'Shall we go upstairs?'

'Bring the wine,' I said. That lust swung inside me as you led me up the stairs, into a room filled with canvases, books, and a messy bed. The rich sun tumbled through the broken shutters. I felt a round throb rise in my middle, which spread through my torso as I stepped over to the bed. After setting the wine down by the bed, your every step acted as percussion, forcing my desire to build. I wanted to be placed so far within your world that I'd be irretrievable, and I kissed you as if seeking from your lips the very essence that would keep me there. As you kissed me your fingers explored the straps of my dress. I pushed you back onto the sheets and then reached behind me, unzipped the dress, and let it fall to the floor. Except for a tiny slip of fabric at my middle, I was completely exposed and yet I felt strangely empowered. Our eyes fixed upon one another, yours ablaze with curious lust. I unbuttoned your jeans, urged you to lean back. I felt a new urge, one I had never experienced before – the need to please. Carefully, as if your body was too refined to ignore, I unbuttoned your shirt and eased it from your back. Our lips closed again and I reached down to find you. And then, as sunlight spilt onto our faces, there was that glorious moment as I found my body with yours and you eased, determined and yet tender, inside me. That clamouring moment when our bodies assured one another's that the pleasure was only going to build. I draped my arms around your shoulders, and felt my hair stroke your face. Your eyes clamoured over my breasts and the slim delicacy of my shoulders. I leant back, the sunlight splayed through my hair, and you gave me a look of such tenderness and resolve, that I knew something had just begun. And I looked back at you, as if slightly afraid of what you might be about to unleash from me.

I'd never made love to someone so quickly before, Noah. That night we only revealed shards of ourselves, the type of glistening shards one usually reveals to a stranger in passing. There was that exhilarating sense of reckless disclosure, and yet there was something more elemental between us too, which we then began to build from. Our consummation in one sense was sudden, forceful, but within it there were shades of tenderness we both knew were too rich to neglect. And yet in that bright flash of sensuality we had satisfied one another with the present and with promises for the future. I saw the way that your eyes greedily took in my body, which I wanted to give generously to you. Not as a stranger would, as an indulgence, but more as a promise. I had never seen my body in that way before, but that night, for the first time, I saw its power. And in that look, I saw that you knew I had presented you with a gift too magnificent to be consumed in one evening. That you would find it almost indecent to neglect that truth. And then I prised my body from you, not yet ready for the state of intimacy that we would soon enter into so readily. I wanted you to feel that you would have to work to experience that again. So many men, I knew, might have their curiosity satisfied by such an encounter, but I knew you were not one of them. Not with your mental cravings and your creative insatiability. Until then my body had always been a foreign object, bent into shape for a stringent purpose, using bad temper and relentless hunger. It had never before been a tool of pleasure, an object of appreciation. Merely a long, pale curve, wan and fragile; hardly a plane on which a man could find himself. But from your starving expression, which betrayed how rarely you had felt such sensations, already I knew it would soon become just that.

I moved over to the other side of the bed, but you came over to me and firmly took the flow of my hair in your hands. You pressed your body against me, and though you did not see it, I felt you had given yourself to me then, more completely than I had given myself to you. Your eyes searched me for confirmation that you were not alone in what you felt, but I held back. I knew that in so doing you would be forced to make the room to express your feelings, and through that confirm them. 'You make me ravenous,' you said. I leant back, and pulled the sheets around my body until I knew its concealment would frustrate you. In the night you would have to reach out for me, so you could detail the next portion of your private map of Yelena. And when that time would come, I knew I would turn to you in the dark and embrace you.

With love,

Yelena

Dear Noah,

I'm sorry for my delayed response to you. There are some good, and some rather less good reasons for this. The most important reason is that I found parts of your reply very difficult to read.

I admit that with these letters we are trying to achieve something brave and perhaps also foolish. When we first agreed to do this, I felt inspired by the sense of possibility. I felt inspired by the thought of mapping out the wilderness inside me. In theory, I knew that it might sometimes be painful to do so. But practically speaking, I did not know the extent to which that would be the case; hence my delay. Although you did not intend your last letter to cause me pain, it did. And at times, in the last few days, I have feared how this process might irreversibly disturb the finally stilling waters of my mind.

Please do not be frustrated at me for admitting this. Both of us knew that this process would not always be easy. I hope it is not impulsive of me to think that in time I will reveal things about my past lovers, which you too will find it difficult to read. If I am to properly tell my story that time will inevitably come. And when it does, I will not shy away from the truth. Because you have shown me that honesty is essential if we are to achieve our purpose. And to be honest, I have refrained from replying sooner because if I had done so I would have written to hurt you. And I know that I must write instead to impart the truth, which is an entirely different matter.

I didn't realise how soon it was after Catherine left that you and I met. I knew that you and Catherine had a passionate affair, and that when she suddenly vanished from your life, without reason or warning, it caused you great upset. I knew that this pain caused you to isolate yourself, as at times I have had to do in my life. Catherine sounds intriguing; and I must admit that your description of her caused me some jealousy. She sounds mysterious, empowered and wilful. In many ways, the opposite of me. Like a force of nature; untroubled by self-doubt, completely focused in realising her desires. Although the thought of you lustily entangled with her causes me pain, I know that her abandonment set the stage for me. Her lack of commitment caused a void in your life, which I was soon to fill. It meant that when we met you were finally ready to love completely, as you never would have been permitted to with her. It comforted me for you to write that you never felt such devotion for anyone as you felt for me. For you to say that intrigue pales in comparison to love, with all its permanent realms, that only grow more distinct and detailed with time. And when I occasionally loathe myself for what I lack, I think of this.

You mentioned that as a writer, it bothered you to think you could not express yourself absolutely through the written word. Do not think of that again. It is not our fault that the world's social conventions force us to relate to one another only sporadically, and in such fragmented ways. It is part of our bind, on our trawl through this partial, compartmentalised world. Put aside your frustrations at the subjective nature of life. Trust me when I say that your hunger for an objective, definitive world is nothing more than a mute protest. To me, the world's beauty comes from its evasive, slippery quality. From the futility of trying to pin down petals, which whip and whirl in the wind. Because when you do catch one, it finally all seems worth it. And that is what we are trying to do with these letters. And if we do not manage to catch any petals, we should be mindful that it was still an admirable way for two people to spend their time. That it was beautiful to live in flagrant disregard of reality for the short period that we were writing to one another.

I find it so fascinating that I am beginning to gain a reputation as a ballerina. If only you had seen me in my youth, at thirteen perhaps. I do wonder what you would have made of that underfed, sulky little girl in cheap Western makeup. Her bruised little thighs poking out of a tiny skirt, her face constantly screwed up at something small. She desperately wanted to be a ballerina one day, she knew that much. But she wanted it in such a hostile way that it didn't seem very likely to happen.

My mother died when I was six. She was a flighty, small town girl, idealistic and naïve. She was English, and she ensured that I was raised speaking the language that she loved as well as Russian. This meant that although I retained a slight Ukrainian accent with some English words, my dialect did not possess the usual plummeting vowels that most Ukrainian bilingual's possess. As you know, my Russian background was not easy to detect. If anything, I spoke with a slight County Durham accent, for that is where she was raised. As a student, my mother studied English literature, and one of her first legacies to me was to pass on her love of this language. I collected and treasured English words as another child might collect stamps, and I delighted in writing and speaking the language at every opportunity. Whereas I found Russian to be a restricted and proud tongue, I found English delightfully exact. I seemed able to express myself better with it. English represented my mother, it was artistic and expressive. Russian represented my father; purposeful and determined. This was perhaps the reason I wrote my diary, from the age of eleven, in clipped and vibrant English.

My mother met my father at university, and moved with him

to his homeland in Ukraine to start a family. I don't think she had expected to stay there as long as she did, but his business began to flourish and she found herself drawn into nursing his mother through her final years. She was dutiful and protective of his mother, just as at times she could be over-protective of me. I think she felt I was not tough enough for the world, and she wanted to hold me back from it slightly. Tragically, she did not outlive her mother-in-law by very long. She was hit by a bus while out shopping with a friend. I remember the hysteria in her friend's eyes when she came to tell my father what had happened. My father had been utterly devoted to her, and her death caused a rupture inside him, which he never recovered from. He lost the will to fight after that, perhaps he felt there was nothing really to fight for now. I remember the utter confusion I felt about what had happened to her; it seemed no-one could give me a proper answer. Her sudden disappearance left a void in my life, which was never fully addressed. I think perhaps that my love of England became an expression of my frustrated love for her.

My mother's second legacy to me was ballet. She started dancing late, and I often wonder if she encouraged me to begin early so that I would have it all my life. When I was five she took me along to the local folk group, which danced at the village hall. I think they hoped she would become more involved, but her focus was only on nurturing me. She saw that I had a talent before anyone else did. I think she wanted me to have the glamorous, and in her eyes artistic life she never had, and I have always strived to fulfil that wish of hers. I can only imagine how she would have felt if she'd have known that one day her daughter would dance the part of Giselle.

It seems hard now to imagine how she would feel about anything. She has retreated into time, become idealised. She no longer feels like flesh and bone, but like a half-forgotten dream, one that I feel perpetually guilty for not fully remembering.

The only video we still have captures her as gamine and fragile. A sunny, natural happiness shines from her face, which does not seem strong enough to deal with it. I look most like the mysterious woman on that video when I am upset or ecstatic. In it she is standing in the living room of her and my father's first home, and my sister and I are still dots on the horizon. My father is picking out the notes of a slow waltz on the piano and she is dancing lightly along to it. Even to my eyes, she looks green. Many times I have feared how this waiflike woman would have reacted if she had seen what was to happen to her two precious daughters. I don't know enough about her to know if she possessed any fight. But the fight I have found in me, when my back has been against the wall, suggests that she would have done. She certainly would not have taken what happened next lying down. I know she would have fought with every ounce of strength in her body. Either way, without our mother, life suddenly became very difficult.

Nine months after she died, Bruna Zlenko discovered my father. Bruna met him during the sale of some offices that she part-owned the lease on, when he was first starting a business with my Uncle Leo. Bruna wiped the dust from my father's eyes and promised to raise his two daughters if he kept her in return. At first it was little more than a contract, born out of my father's desperation. He felt utterly overwhelmed at having to raise Inessa and me alone and Bruna seemed like a solution, albeit not a particularly romantic one. But over the years Bruna gained a hold on him, and she became almost a wife to him. He feared her, but he became convinced he needed her in a way that I could never quite fathom.

Bruna could not have been more different to my mother. She had a flat, almost feral face, and a naturally downturned mouth. Her eyes were always narrowed and she was quick tempered. From an early age my sister and I proved that we were tenacious enough to fend for ourselves, and that my father was capable of filling any gaps, but it was this essential truth which started the troubles. Bruna knew that her best chance of keeping my father was to convince him that his daughters needed extra attention. Without finding such a role to play, Bruna would have had little chance of keeping a man like my father – an enterprising and handsome businessman. At first, my father was reluctant to accept that his daughters were especially troublesome, but battered by Bruna's persistence he eventually acquiesced and at least outwardly accepted that Inessa and I were difficult children. Any of the usual misdemeanours reported by the school took on a sinister edge when Bruna relayed them. I have always found the tendency to colour information in that way a rather sickening trait. Bruna knew that Inessa and I had a natural intelligence that would one day render her presence redundant. And knowing that, she loathed us from the start. She knew it would be one hell of a challenge to prove to the world that we were useless. Her way of doing it was to constantly talk down our abilities to our father, and to seal us off from him enough so that he could hopefully not realise the truth. At first she was only able to do this by pretending it was done out of affection for my father, who seemed permanently weary from work. Consequently he allowed Bruna to have more access to us than she should have done.

Unfortunately, the more she learnt about us, the more she found reason to despise us. Her ability to distance us from him gave her many opportunities to express her venom. I don't want to go into this too much, Noah, not because I won't tell you, but because – and I hope you understand this – I have fought so hard to escape what she did. Bruna was given an almost free rein in raising us, and over time she found very inventive ways to express her hatred of us. She created a secret culture, away from my father's eyes, in which she constantly bullied, taunted and abused us. With my father leaving early every morning to work, Bruna would wash and dress us, arguing that my sister in particular was unable to do this well enough on her own. (Thinking of my sister now I realise how laughable this is, for she is a successful businesswoman, tactful and assertive, and unscarred in a way that suggests great resilience.) Bruna was so able to convince my father that she was a problem that she was still bullying Inessa to wash and dress even when she was six and seven years old, well after she would have been able to do this alone. By that age, I would be getting ready in my own room, but that part of the day would still be traumatic for me. I could hear Inessa crying in the other room, and at the back of my mind painful, glowering memories of the times Bruna had beaten us preyed upon me. On a few occasions, which I was too young to properly memorise, she sexually abused us, after her ritual mocking of our bodies got out of hand. This culture of abuse gave Inessa and me a sense of worthlessness that it has been difficult to shake, particularly for me. I wonder now when she learnt to do this so proficiently.

I can only think of that time as one long smear of pain, which obscured the rest of my childhood. I struggle to recall the abuse exactly, but at the back of my mind I remember periods of unendurable pain. The way her attention would often focus on my little sister, and the way she would enjoy it if I tried to stop her. The hour or so that Bruna had with us in the mornings were periods in which I constantly feared the ways her unhappiness might be expressed. As time went on, I'm sure Bruna saw those early morning routines as a brief reprieve from her own inadequacy, her time to express all her anger and frustration at the world on two little girls. And yet she did it carefully, so that my father was just about able to convince himself that nothing untoward was going on.

It was not that my father didn't care for us, merely that he did not know how to express his love in a day-to-day manner. He deeply wanted to believe that Bruna had our interests at heart, and so overwhelming did he find it to make a living and also deal with the loss of our mother that he did not have the strength to face up to what was really going on.

From an early age his love was manifested through his ambition for us. After my mother died, he continued taking Inessa and me along to the local folk group, which met on a weekly basis. I used to love him taking us there; I adored all of the colour and the laughter and the singing. It was like a new world; so separate from the drab reality I was growing used to. It was my escape. It was probably only a simple hall with very little decoration, but in my eyes it represented happiness. Even though the dances only took place in the local village hall, there were good links to local ballet schools and I was talent spotted at seven and began ballet soon after. My father, perhaps seeing somewhere to finally put his love for us, worked extra long hours (thereby giving us more time with Bruna) to pay for the classes. At this stage he'd focused so absolutely on his business that he was starting to make very good money for us, even if we rarely saw it. By nine years old I was practicing in long sessions at least three times a week, sometimes five. After school the day would begin for me in a way. When most children wanted to play, I found I only wanted to dance. When I danced, people used words like 'gifted', 'special' and 'talented'. I forgot all about Bruna and was able to escape her. Dancing became my world. When I was part of it people fussed over me and praised me. When I danced, I finally felt like I had value.

But it remained difficult to retain any sense of value in the home. As my father's business took off, Bruna's leash over us was tightened, and before long she had found an opportunity to use it. My father would often return home from the office after dark, extremely tired. Like any young daughters we would instantly rush up to him the moment he opened the front door, and want to have his undivided attention. But one evening Inessa jumped into his lap just as he was beginning to eat the limp, cool dish Bruna had made him. His plate went flying, along with its contents and my father was scalded with hot coffee. Amongst the ensuing chaos Bruna decreed that from now on Inessa and I would never disturb our father when he came home from work. My father was too tired and overwhelmed to resist the decision, as Bruna had pounced during a window of vulnerability. But Inessa or I could not have possibly predicted where Bruna's imagination would take this new decree.

Inessa and I always had to be in bed early, but Bruna started to enforce the rule that the minute she turned our lights off we had to be utterly silent so as to not disturb our father. 'He must close his eyes,' she would bark, pointing a thick finger at the prostrate form of my father, dozing in the living room. 'He must be allowed to close his eyes.' Now I see in that statement a hidden message that I was too young to understand.

By then, Inessa and I were learning to adapt our playful, immature instincts to minimise the time we were punished for them. But two young girls, left alone in a room before they were tired, were always going to make some noise. One night, around a week later, I was playfully throwing a pillow at Inessa, who'd started to giggle uncontrollably. It wasn't even dark outside, and my father wasn't yet in his bedclothes. But the shout came through from the next room, 'If I hear another sound from either of you, then you will both be sorry.'

Strangely enough it was Inessa who took the order more seriously than I. She rolled back into the thin sheets and lay rigidly on her back, seemingly willing herself to not move an inch, let alone make noise. But in my naïve state I was less disciplined. I didn't honestly believe Bruna could punish us as she did in the mornings with my father just in the next room. At worst, I thought, it might make the following morning slightly more unpleasant and I thought I had found a little opportunity to now needle her. I couldn't have been more wrong.

Making fun of Inessa's sudden obedience, I threw another pillow at her head. It missed, and clattered over the bedside table. Inessa's rigid stillness was suddenly disrupted as she scrambled to quickly put it back into place. 'Yelena,' she hissed, with genuine disappointment resonating in her voice. It's a sound I still remember.

We didn't hear Bruna coming. But suddenly the door to our bedroom was open and, striding inside, she slammed the door shut behind her. She brought out a long steel key that I hadn't known existed and, her eyes darting between the two of us, locked the door shut. I must have looked as if I might scream, Noah. Scream out for my father, scream out in apology. 'Now would not be the time to make any noise, Yelena,' she said. And then, pronouncing each word slowly and carefully she repeated her strange statement. 'He must be allowed to shut his eyes.'

She started to move over to Inessa.

'No,' I said. A sharp wave of her muscular arm swept me into silence. 'Please Bruna – let me speak. I am so so sorry, but it wasn't Inessa's fault, it was mine.'

I instantly regretted the line of reasoning. Bruna sensed something in me, and looked over at Inessa's bedside table. 'It happened on Inessa's side. She must learn to be responsible.'

'Bruna, please.'

'Back on your bed, and turn around.'

Wondering if I should risk shouting out for my father, but suddenly aware of the thickness of our walls, I tried to make my way back to my bed. I remember taking in the length of my arms, the sheer heft of Bruna's presence, and bitterly lamenting that I wasn't stronger.

'I said turn around,' Bruna ordered.

As I started to try to do so, I heard Inessa begin to whimper. Bruna's attentions were no longer on me. She seized the pillow.

'I have told you both, time and time again,' she said, her voice lowered now, 'to keep your stupid noises to yourself after dark. Your father must be allowed to shut his eyes, if only for one second. I see I will have to make you remember.'

'It was my fault – ' I insisted, but my words were interrupted. Suddenly, and to the shock of even Inessa, Bruna gripped the pillow and wrapped it around my sister's little head.

'Bruna!' I screamed. Barely able to believe what was happening. I ran over to Inessa, whose legs were kicking from under the sheets, her young body trying to scream in protest. Bruna quickly adjusted her body so Inessa couldn't wriggle free, breathe or even move. 'Back on your bed.' she said, her voice rising.

I couldn't help it. I ran over to Bruna and threw myself around her shoulders, but with one swift swat she snapped me back against the wall. I hit my head on the doorframe, and fell to the floor, stunned. I can't remember how long I remained like that, pulsing and yet immobile. I remember from that position seeing only Bruna's great shoulders and bowed head, and as I struggled to compose myself I saw that Inessa's feet had suddenly stopped moving.

I screamed. Bruna got up. Inessa lay still. I realised I had no idea how long I had been lying there for, trying to get my stupid head together while my sister squirmed and tried to cry out. At every moment Bruna's shoulders had seemed to become wider and stronger, like she was a woman possessed.

This time Bruna didn't seem to object to the scream. Perhaps even she sensed that she had gone too far. 'Get back into bed, you stupid girl,' she said, pointing me rather half-heartedly towards my messy sheets. 'She's just fainted.' And with that she slowly made her way to the door, unlocked it, and moved back outside. I could hear my father shuffling around his desk and Bruna's plaintive, reassuring voice coming into play.

Neither my father, nor Bruna, ever came in to check on Inessa. As soon as Bruna was gone I rushed over to her, pushed the pillow from her face and pulled her into my arms. Those moments seemed to last an eternity. She is dead, I remember thinking. And it's my fault.

She seemed so small and helpless, and I couldn't imagine how she must have felt as she suffocated. It was my job to protect her from this. At that moment, my self-loathing was so strong I could nearly taste it. And then, one long minute later, Inessa coughed and her thin body squirmed back to life. As I tried to ease her shaking body back into the sheets, she didn't say a word. Neither of us did. I knew her bed had now become a prison for her. I am sure the two of us stayed awake for every moment of that night. Both in utter silence.

The next morning, Inessa and I remained mute. My father went to work, early as usual, and Bruna remained silent and quietly disdainful. She didn't react when she saw Inessa the next day, only pausing to order us to get dressed. Any reaction I had hoped I might see in her, relief perhaps, never materialised. Sometimes, the most powerful act can be no act at all, and sadly it was Bruna who taught me that.

From that moment on Inessa and I fell completely in line with Bruna's desires. Through our childish logic, I think we both reasoned that no harm could come of either of us if we simply did exactly what she asked. I was not to know that she wasn't acting out of a strong desire for order, that there was something deeper hidden inside her. Consequently, our obedience acted merely to delay her next violent act, not prevent it. Painfully, in retrospect it all makes sense. But then my mind simply could not grow and advance fast enough to counteract her.

In the nights that followed I lay stock-still in bed, in a faithful replication of Inessa's rigid position. The difficulty was that there would always be times when Inessa and I had to make some noise. However, I was determined that the noise would never come from me. Whenever I was tempted to get up, or speak, or even move around in bed, I only had to look over at my sister to remind myself of what I had to lose.

One night, I was foolish enough not to go to the toilet before bed, and rather than move at night, I wet the bed. I felt so disgusting, trying to ignore the water in my bed, but strangely I also felt a proud defiance, at being prepared to debase myself rather than give into her. It seemed righteous at the time.

But this was very short-sighted of me. Yes, Bruna would have to suffer the inconvenience of washing my dirty sheets. But what I did not understand was that I had finally presented her with her next opportunity. Any pride I felt at my self-restraint, for not getting up at night, was soon lost when Bruna discovered the sheets the next day with a hollow roar. I remember being surprised at the ferocity with which she ordered me to come to my room. Her back was facing me as she angrily stripped the sheets. I could not see her expression, only guess at its twisted aggression.

'Yelena. I cannot believe that you are too immature to even control your own body. This sort of behaviour is simply disgusting.'

'I'm sorry Bruna.'

'It is not me you should apologise to. I don't go out to work every day to pay the bills, do I? It's your father that does.'

I knew better than to ask her not to show the sheets to my father.

'He will just have to see what you have managed to do for himself,' she said.

I didn't beg. I felt as if the air was sucked out of my body. My father was the one person in the world I wanted to impress, wanted to love me. I couldn't bear to watch as Bruna took the dirty bundle of sheets into his study and showed him just what his eldest daughter was capable of. My father, who had always struggled with the machinations of the female body at the best of times, could only respond with a repulsed confusion. Nevertheless, he refrained from meeting my eye in the time that followed. His silence, and the complicit disgust within it, was far more hurtful to me than anything Bruna might have said.

If the mornings were poisonous, the nights under this new regime – where every word and action could be used to punish you – were far worse. Night after night was spent listening out for the movement of Bruna's body in the surrounding rooms, and far more rarely the shuffling of my father. My senses alert, I tried to reason a path through this unbearable atmosphere. Once or twice, Bruna would come into the room even if we hadn't made noise, and tears would begin to seep out of my eyes, though I forced myself to smile at her. Each time I could only guess at what she was about to do. I was so terrified of wetting the bed again, and giving her a reason to punish us, that I started to do just that a few times a week. This would provoke Bruna's anger – an anger that seemed genuine rather than contrived – and cause her to humiliate me in front of my father. But this simply made me more anxious and therefore more likely to wet myself again.

Perhaps due to some innate survival instinct, Inessa began to distance herself from me. Sensing that she and my father were starting to develop a bond, on occasion Bruna would come into the room and punish Inessa, or in the mornings hurt her, for some imagined crime or even worse for something I had done. Starved of sleep, and with no-one to turn to, the guilt started to well up inside me. I had to watch my every step at home, but school was a different story. There, I was able at least to breathe without worrying how loud the breath was.

At school we had two periods of free time, and during that period I was always especially quiet and withdrawn. I enjoyed drawing and writing during those classes where that was allowed; and in the others I was careful to remain studious enough to get good grades. It was the short break before the end of the day that was unbearable because I was aware that soon I would be back home again.

One afternoon, the thought of returning home became too much for me. I thought my head was going to split open, or that I might faint. With a terrible sense of foreboding – because I knew that any act of rebellion would cause my sister to be punished – I told my teacher I had a headache and I asked to be sent to the matron.

The matron was sympathetic, she seemed to sense that something deeper was afoot. 'You are very pale, young lady, and your blood pressure is rather high. I suggest that you lie down for a while until you feel better.'

The matron's chamber was quiet, and smelt rather reassuringly of lotion and bandages. As I lay on the stiff bed, I tried to calm my racing heart but my mind didn't seem strong enough to do so. Needing to stretch my legs and clear this storm from my head, I made my way to the unisex bathroom and there, in a discarded mug, I saw a man's unwanted razor blade.

I acted instinctively. I had no idea what to do with it, but all I knew was that I had to quell the bubbling in my brain. I needed to feel something, something other than fear. I needed to feel calm, and perhaps only then would I gain a sense of control over this pulsating sense of guilt.

I went into one of the stalls and sat on the toilet, pulled my knees up against my chest. Through the frosted window of the cubicle I could see children starting to race out into the playground, full of abandon and glee. I felt as if I was watching them in a film. I knew it was almost time to go home. The pressure in my head was too much – I had to get it out. I chose the tender, pale skin on the underside of my arms, and in a moment of pure resolve I sliced deeply, awkwardly into it. Almost instantly, the blood gushed out, as if grateful, and I felt such relief that I almost laughed. My brain sang in ecstasy, and I let it pour and pour, the poison in my brain exorcised by the bright red spurt of release.

I dabbed the wound dry, covered it with a stolen plaster, and pocketed the blessed razor blade. From then on, during that final break of the day, I would always find the time to visit the toilet, seal myself in a cubicle and let off a little blood. The relief I felt seemed the only way to I was able to become strong enough to meet Inessa, and walk her back to Bruna.

But throughout this time, Bruna continued to be a source of unexplained pain, and her bullying continued. One day, I was so angry and confused by her behaviour that I could not help but react.

I was eleven, perhaps a little younger. It was early morning, we were due to leave for school in about ten minutes, and I was almost ready. As usual, I was dressing with the door to my bedroom open so I could listen out for Inessa. Bruna was with her in the bathroom, which typically meant Inessa staying silent. But on this morning, something Inessa had done had particularly angered her. My sister started crying, and her crying was unrestrained, almost hysterical, and with panic rising in my chest I crept towards the bathroom.

'Are you okay?' I called.

'Do *not* come in here, Yelena. Stay in your room!' Bruna ordered.

'Inessa, stop crying, it's okay,' I called. But this seemed to somehow make Inessa worse. I heard a smack, and then what sounded like my sister being thrown to the floor. 'Inessa!' I cried. Nearing the bathroom, I saw Bruna approaching my sister, who was curled up in a foetal position on the floor. Bruna had not yet heard me coming, but Inessa saw me and reached out. I thought for a second that Bruna was going to kick her, and in desperation I grabbed a cheap vase my father had bought, which was on the shelf just outside the bathroom, and hearing me behind her she froze. Slowly, Bruna turned around, and as she looked down on me she began to laugh. That leering laughter, so casually smothering Inessa's crying, angered me so much. I clutched the vase to my chest. At that moment I did not know what to do with it – I think I was probably just threatening to break it. Bruna laughed. 'What the hell are you doing, you stupid little girl?' she said. 'You'd better stop it, whatever it is. Because you are making life very difficult for you both.'

But I could see from the curl in her lips, and the glimmer in her eyes, that I had already done enough to warrant a harsher treatment than we had ever endured before. I had taken the first step, and I knew I had to see it through. Although I was a good few feet away from her, I raised the vase above my head. Suddenly her eyes widened. Bruna was finally taking me seriously.

'Yelena. You will drop that now,' she ordered, her voice ice cold. It dropped to almost a whisper. She smiled. 'You know you're too weak to do anything, so don't even bother. You're just like your mother. A pathetic little girl.'

I stepped nearer. I couldn't bear her talking about my mother. She wasn't fit to even mention her; let alone in our house, our home, when she was making little Inessa cry. I could feel my heart thundering so hard, and it scared me. It was as if my whole body was one big heart, pulsing so hard that I thought it could burst out of my frame at any second. I wanted her to see how wrong she was, how she had got us all wrong: Inessa, my mother, and me. I met her eyes, and saw fear. And that fear, to me, was a triumph. For the first time in my life I felt unhinged. I knew that were I to stop now, she would beat Inessa and me to within an inch of our lives, and our father noticing would not even be a concern.

With a cry I ran at her, and brought the vase down hard on her head. It shattered with a satisfying sound. Bruna let out a hollow roar, and clutched at her eyes. My sister cried out, and scrambled into the bathtub. I had no idea what to do. Bruna flailed around for a steady surface. There was blood everywhere. Desperately, I scrambled around for a shard of vase to threaten her with. Inessa cried out for me to stop. Bruna struggled to get to her feet, as I held the shard over her like a knife. Nodding, as if she now understood, she clutched her face and held out one hand. And then, that hand clenched into a fist and she made a sudden swipe for me, with a scream that seemed to shake the walls. Somehow I ducked under it, but in so doing I slipped over and fell closer to her. Bruna rose up to grab me, and I raised the shard, trembling in my little hand, above my head.

'Yelena, you will live to regret what you just did,' she said, and moved towards me. Inessa screamed, and in that moment I flung myself forward and stabbed her with the shard, just under her left eye. It just punctured the skin, before shattering painfully in my hand. Bruna screamed, recoiled, and fell back on the cistern. I grabbed Inessa, who was crying with all the force her body could muster. I struggled to lift her from the bathtub, as Bruna clambered to her feet. I managed to push Inessa out of the door as Bruna lost her footing for one blessed moment. We fled as fast as we could. I could hear her shouting as I forced open the front door, and we ran outside.

It was autumn, and already very cold, but there certainly wasn't time to get our coats. I didn't know where to go, two half-dressed school girls at half past eight in the morning. But even Inessa knew that we could not be near Bruna now.

On my insistence, we trailed around the wasteland just behind the railway track for the whole day. I knew Bruna would not find us there, and I had no idea what else to do. And yet despite this uncertainty I felt a vague sense of achievement. I knew that what Bruna had been doing to us had been wrong, but nevertheless I should never have hit her. As a child, I felt there was no justification for that and I was finished now, even with my father. I knew I could not go home to her, or to school, where she would inevitably find us. The only answer seemed to keep us hidden for as long as possible, at least until my father came home, knowing that she would not hurt us in his presence. I would have to try and hope that my father did not hate me for what I'd done. I had never told my father before what Bruna did to us, for fear of reprisal if I did. For that day of homelessness Inessa was too young to fully understand anything, and as her supervisor for the day I was useless, confused and wracked with guilt. We sat on discarded tires, under the oily leaves of the abandoned depot, and played games. It was hard to stay out of sight for the whole day, and I kept us moving around amongst those wet, spectral trees. I told her fairy tales until I saw men in suits make their way to their cars parked just beyond the trees. We were wracked with hunger, but I somehow made sure that my sister and I returned at precisely the normal time from school.

On our return, I was shocked to find an eerily calm household. I remember feeling in a daze; perhaps it was hunger mixed with pure terror. For years I had endured these terrible mornings in Bruna's company without ever considering trying to escape.

We saw my father first. I didn't know what to expect, but to my surprise he wasn't angry. If he had worked out what had been going on, it must have been buried far too deep for him to yet reckon with it outwardly. He looked down on us as we entered, and his expression was unreadable. 'Your mother has been very worried about you two,' he said, strangely unable to look me in the eye. 'She said that this morning she slipped in the bathroom and hurt herself and the two of you had not wanted to go to school until you knew she was alright, but she insisted. Is that right?'

He paused. He could see that we were not fully dressed. We were missing our coats, and didn't have our bags with us. I can only see now how curious his reaction was, and what an odd family we had become. It was such a pathetic lie, and my eyes begged him to face up to the truth of the situation. At least that would make some sense.

I saw Bruna sat on a stool in the kitchen, an ice pack pressed against what looked like a newly bandaged face. I decided it was no use. 'Yes,' I said simply, and squeezed my sister's hand.

'I think it is too much for your mother… '

'Our *step*mother,' I said.

'… to look after you by herself in the mornings. From now on I will speak to Uncle Leo about going in later, and I will take it in turns to help you both before school.'

I remember the huge sense of relief at realising I was not

going to be scolded, that something had changed. In his own weak way, my father had to face up to what was going on. My sister jumped up in delight and my father looked down. I looked at Bruna, glowering at me from the kitchen, with a sense of triumph.

From then on, Bruna had to redraw the battle lines. She had to rethink how to get to us, as my father would see any bruises the following day when it was his turn to be with us in the morning. Though my father never truly addressed what had been going on during those awful mornings, he had, it seemed, finally seen enough to learn that he must intervene. He was too scared and mentally fragile to face up to the truth of the situation. Despite this, nothing had fundamentally changed.

Bruna started to approach us more cautiously, in a way I had assumed she was not capable of. I saw how subtle evil could be. There were times when she would make advances to my sister, enquiring about aspects of my sister's life so that information could soon turn into power. I was slowly growing to be more of a physical presence, learning to be better at manipulating circumstances so that Bruna was never alone with her for long. My father came to understand the rules of this new, unspoken arrangement, and he reinforced it even if he did not have the resolve to face up to a life without her. Bruna was still there, and so I had to stay alert for the next problem that would arise. Yet even more so, I had my dancing, and I knew that if I were to neglect it, I would be trapped with her for a long time yet.

With love,

Yelena

Dear Noah,

For the first time, I was starting to possess some confidence. My father has to take some credit for this, as he was supporting my dancing. Since my mother's death he had always struggled to find a way to care for us, but when he saw that I loved to dance, and that I was actually good at it, his loving and pragmatic side were able to combine. I think he also wanted to honour my mother's memory by helping me to become the daughter she might have wanted.

The evening classes in ballet were not cheap, and he was determined that I be trained only by the best. Inessa and I were never allowed expensive toys or clothes, but when it came to employing ballet mistresses no expense was spared. These classes became my life, and by twelve I was *en pointe*. Over the next couple of years the classes formalised, and became the backbone to a strict routine. With great difficulty a special schedule was devised for me, whereby I could finish my academic work by three and after that devote the rest of the day to Classical Ballet. Our Uncle Leo, who became the only other man in our lives after his divorce, often commented on this. 'Vasily, you make sure your daughter can dance like a butterfly,' he said. 'But if she developed a hole in the wing of her outfit you would be too tight to close it up.'

There were six or seven other local girls from more well-off families who were taught under a similar arrangement. I was conscious that I was by far the least refined of all of them, and yet I had to spend much of my time with them. They were bright and ambitious girls, and when I was short of equipment they would often lend me theirs. I remember once Iza saying to me, 'Why doesn't your father buy you a decent pencil case?'

'Because he spent the money on pointe shoes,' I said, and she looked at me with utter confusion. Why not both?

Though I felt slightly separate from these girls, this never became a problem thanks to Uncle Leo. He had gone to university in England, and he knew a lot about class and refinement. On the occasions I would be invited to these girls' birthday parties in their grand homes, he would drill me on social protocol before I left. 'They might have more pig tails than you, but never let them convince you that they have more brain cells,' he always said. He knew that without my mother, we were not going to get any reassurance from elsewhere. My father certainly didn't see the importance, but Uncle Leo would insist that social interaction was important.

Even if I was less refined, I was determined that no-one would think I was less talented. I made up for not having a silky ballet outfit through sheer hard work. I see now that I must have had some toughness of character to stick with my dancing so doggedly at that age. There was something else that had been placed in me, something I couldn't quite define. I already knew that through ballet I would find salvation.

My focus on ballet became even greater when I got into a school that specialised in education for the arts. I was initially delighted – it got me out of the house a little more, which meant more time away from Bruna. But I sensed a change in Bruna's demeanour regarding this development. She would have more power over Inessa again. Therefore, in a perverse way she would have more power over me the less I was around. My anticipation at having more time to dance was constantly shot through with fear at what this would mean for Inessa. Yet I couldn't confide these fears to Inessa, for her own sake, as she was trying to keep me at a distance too. She was coping by staying after school and studying hard, and telling my father that she wanted to spend time at his work to learn about business. My father initially objected, saying that an office was no place for a woman, and so my sister had to find a way to be useful to him – which in her own, prodigious childlike way she soon was – running errands and posting letters. Leo at first found this office hand an amusing presence, but on the times he dismissed her he was suspicious at how vociferously she argued for her presence.

Soon, Bruna started to voice concerns that having a young daughter with him at work would distract my father from making money. I began to despair – whatever developments occurred, Bruna had a way of clawing back power. I felt guilty that I was not there to protect my sister, and yet another voice told me that she was better off without me around. I couldn't get the night with the pillow out of my mind. On the occasions that I tried to bond with her, buying her makeup or something I thought she'd like, Inessa's reluctant manner betrayed that she was unable to forget either.

Although Bruna would scold me when I was home, there was less opportunity for inflicting any real pain with me leaving early and coming home late, as well as entering competitions on the weekend. I wanted to do ballet full-time, the other children at school seemed happy just to be outside of the normal system and enjoying their school days, but even then I was incredibly serious about ballet. One salvation was that my private lessons continued, giving me the opportunity to practice on the weekend. Even if those classes were full of endless repetition and refinement, and even if they were often painful, they became like a kind of religion to me. Nevertheless, after a long week it alarmed me to see the state of my feet. My toes seemed to want to fuse together, and I constantly suffered from bunions and split nails. Uncle Leo would sometimes slip me a painkiller before a competition –

but I was worried that I might be punished for taking drugs.

There were still very dark moments and for some reason my father remained unable to face up to Bruna and what she had clearly done to us in the past. I knew that Uncle Leo sometimes asked questions about her, but it seemed that even to him Bruna was off-limits with my father. I wondered if she had a hold on him in some other way. One day, when I had had to stay late at school, I came home to see that Inessa had a huge cut on her face. I asked me father what had happened to her, and without looking up from his desk, he quietly told me that she had just fallen over at school. Bruna bounded into his study, insisted that I start my homework and gave my father a thousand and one important jobs to do before I could make more of an issue of it. Although Inessa stayed quiet on the matter, I tried my best to make it clear that I would not tolerate these things happening. Over time, Inessa gradually became closer to my father; she knew that if she was at his side she could not be hurt. I on the other hand, did not find intimacy easy, even with my kindly Uncle Leo who I kept at a needlessly suspicious distance. I see now that the experiences of being alone with Bruna made me shy from company for many years.

The first person I began to get close to was my ballet tutor, Therese. She had only recently qualified from a French conservatoire, which impressed my father no end. Therese was a slim, pale young woman, with a resigned expression, her faintly blonde hair pinned up with a couple of pencils. She did not spot any great potential in me – she retained that slight air of self-preservation not unusual in ballerinas – but to me she represented another world. She had been a dancer of some note in her teenage years, though why she had returned to Donetsk after training in Paris remained beyond me. But her sojourn away had been enough for her to now become, in my eyes, very cultured and worldly. I devoured every detail that I could about her. The photos of the Champs Élysées above her desk, the *Vogue* magazines she kept in her drawer, the sparse way she used makeup. To my surprise, I started to enjoy dancing with her, as well as merely craving it. I had never really enjoyed anything before, Noah, strange as that sounds. As a result, I found myself dancing every moment I was alone, though I was careful to keep up to date with my school studies – lest any failure gave Bruna an advantage over me. But somehow I managed this rewarding compromise. Therese and I became close; she was like an exotic older sister that I wanted to emulate. When it turned out that she smoked, I seriously considered starting myself.

I was delighted one evening when Therese invited me to join her for supper. By this point I was fifteen, and the outside world was beginning to seem in reach. I was starting to form my own identity, which unsurprisingly was largely based around her. Like my mother, Therese adored all things English, and unlike many Ukrainian girls she insisted on expensive makeup and wore her hair in a Western style. I tried to replicate her in every way. Just as you may have seen glam rock stars as otherworldly creatures from somewhere better, I saw Western women. Words like 'London' and 'Paris' were imbued with such exoticism to me.

That night, after a brief ballet class, Therese drove me to a restaurant to meet two men who had trained with her in Paris. They were now dancing in St Petersburg and I was just utterly entranced. Young people from St Petersburg are some of the most fashionable and cultured in the East, and I instantly fell for their cultivated air of sophistication. Until then my romantic liaisons had been restricted to guilty encounters behind the railway lines with the older boys from the college, who occasionally saw my developing figure as something to covet. But this was something very different. I was told by one of the men that Therese had described me to them as her 'star pupil'. They asked if I had applied to a Russian academy yet, and I told them I had not.

'Therese,' one of them said. 'People will look upon you in a highly favourable light if one of your pupils, in your first year of teaching, is accepted into a Russian academy.'

This remark seemed to catch something in Therese and after that night, she began to train me to be accepted into the Vaganova, the most prestigious ballet school in Russia; even the world. This became her purpose in life, and I think she gave it everything she had. In Russia, ballet is a way of life, and normally girls are accepted into the academy as young as ten. But it would be possible, we soon learnt, for me to gain entry there to qualify for a ten month certificate as a foreign student. The prestige it would bestow on me, and upon her as my tutor, would be incredible. It would allow me the opportunity to go on and dance anywhere in the world. It seemed that Therese and I were now bound on a journey together.

My increased focus on dance gave Bruna new ammunition, and life at home became more difficult. Inessa was not quite the ally I had hoped she would be, and we were rarely on the same page. I knew that to get out of this situation I had to leave Donetsk the moment I could, and Therese was my ticket out.

Fortunately, my father supported this new venture wholeheartedly and paid for me to attend summer schools, which he knew would give me an edge over the other girls. These summer schools were wonderful places to me – whole buildings dedicated to teaching young people to express their creative side. It was an eye-opener to know that other people shared my passion; even if they often found pleasure where I found duty. I could not help but view the whole affair through slightly detached, ironic eyes, but I also discovered intriguing new parts of myself.

Yet something always held me back from embracing happiness. Experience had taught me that happiness was a delusional state. I must have constantly looked coiled, haunted. I sometimes wonder why no-one ever questioned why such a young girl was so reticent. I learnt that sentiments were not ordered as ideally as culture would let us know; people dedicated time primarily to their own concerns and welfare, with little time to look out for others. My resignation to this belief led me to find other people pretty unsavoury.

As my body began to develop, some of the boys at the school started to take an interest in me. Though I had initially felt pleasantly surprised, the sensation was to be short-lived.

One in particular, a tall and muscular boy from the city with a quizzical smile, started to pass me notes during quiet moments in class. I didn't dare tell anyone else about these notes. The contents of them were by turns flattering and, it had to be said, a little frightening. After a few weeks, I started to write him the odd note back, more out of boredom and slight curiosity than anything else. I hadn't yet ever felt romantically inclined, but in a moment of weakness, I agreed to meet him in a quiet place behind the log cabins after school.

When he arrived, there was an urgency about him that seemed to suggest I had promised something that I couldn't remember doing. For a while we sat and talked, and it felt good that someone was interested in aspects of my life that I felt were so mundane. Then he wanted to kiss me. At first I resisted, but gradually I began to relax. Then the moment came when he started to touch me. I felt the tension in me rise, and then to my horror, I began to wet myself.

'I have to go,' I said. 'I'm going to be late.'

'Where are you going?' he said. Just then, the wet patch on my trousers became visible and he began to laugh. On my way back to the dormitory I couldn't find my key, and in that awful moment a group of girls saw the wet patch on my clothes and began to openly laugh at me. I'd never felt so ashamed.

At about sixteen, Therese and my father agreed that I had won enough local awards to start applying to the Russian schools. Though the audition itself would not cost, the flights to St Petersburg most certainly would. For the first time, I had a goal on the horizon. I wanted desperately to escape this stifling town for the excitement of St Petersburg, and the elegant streets of Ulitsa Rossi, which housed the Vaganova Academy.

Eventually, I had to hear Bruna's thoughts on the matter. On one occasion, she snapped down the knife she'd been using and said, 'Yelena, you are too ugly and fat to be a ballerina. What makes you think you are so special?' Something shifted in her face as she said it, as if she had wanted to unload this thought for a while. I left the room, but Bruna was not to know that I went straight upstairs and cried. That evening, the razor blade came out again, the shock of the vivid red and the blessed sense of calm returned. I pulled the pillow hard around my face, desperate to not leak a single sound. Deep down I was terrified that she was right. On the internet, Therese had showed me videos of girls who had been accepted there. Their bodies had been so beautiful, flexible and disciplined. However many classes I undertook, and however much practice I did, I had still never been a member of a ballet school, and here I was applying to the best one.

After school, alone in my bedroom I would sometimes strip off and inspect my body in the full-length mirror. It gave me a curious sensation. For years I hadn't done anything to earn the body of a ballerina and yet, if what the other girls were saying was true, I had one. Yes, I still badly wanted to reduce the swell of my stomach and the weight at the top of my thighs. But I had at least got my mothers' neck, expressive eyes and long legs. Looking in the mirror it occurred to me then that this body was simply on loan to me for a few years, and I had to fight with every ounce of strength I had not to loathe it. I knew I had to learn to see it as an instrument. A lump of rock that I needed to chip away at in order to make the sculpture required. And yet this increasingly practical attitude to my body was very different to the way I saw myself, as a person. I felt that my Mum had abandoned me because I wasn't good enough, and that perhaps Bruna was the only one unafraid to tell me that. She simply treated me as I deserved. I was waging a considered war on my body, but a far more vicious war on my mind. Bruna was a factor I had to constantly consider. The blood letting helped, but then I started to live in fear that she might discover that too, and send me away to some asylum.

During practice, my determination manifested itself by refusing to leave the barre until I felt I had got it exactly right. At times I became frustrated with Therese because I felt she was too gentle, too timid with me. I knew that when I auditioned, at any moment I could be tapped on the shoulder, and have to leave the room instantly. The other girls would know what to be thinking of second by second, and yet I would not. As I strove to better myself, Bruna's voice became part of an internal monologue, taunting me. Often it would just laugh, the laugh ringing around my head for long into the next exercise. But I was damned if I was going to give into it. I watched every morsel that entered my mouth, and I practiced every moment that God sent. My feet sang with pain at the end of the day when I finally took to my bed. But I didn't have a choice, I had to escape that life. After a few months, Therese started to tell me that she thought I was doing well. And what was more, she felt I had a good chance of getting in.

The only way to get an audition at the academy was to send a tape of myself dancing. Of course, I made Therese tape me six or seven times before we finally made one that I felt was good enough. We eventually sent the tape off and one day after school I had a letter from the Vaganova inviting me to audition with them. My father was delighted, and not a little surprised, and he booked flights to St Petersburg for Therese and me.

On the flight over, I was barely able to speak. Therese tried to remember exactly what the audition would comprise. I would undertake a usual session at the barre along with all the other candidates, followed by some centre work. I must not allow myself to be distracted by the other girls, she said, however good they were. Although I had walked through this process in my mind many times, I had no idea how little mental preparation can replace the education of experience.

St Petersburg was bustling and overwhelming as Therese and I tried to find our way with our little bags. I felt awed by the austere buildings, their windows set high above the ground by stone pillars. Each seemed imbued with centuries of sacrifice and pain and yet around us young people nonchalantly chewed on fries and snapped one another on cameras.

The Vaganova was just off the manic Nevsky Prospekt, where screened Pepsi adverts sat opposite ancient palaces. It encompassed one long street, which stretched out just behind the compact majesty of the Pushkin Theatre. The academy filled the buildings on both sides of the street, which were painted in a majestic but slightly queasy shade of yellow. Inside, the halls of the academy were grand, but disarmingly blank. Despite the glorious chandeliers that hung from the ceilings, the building itself was filled with a curious, expectant silence. As I waited for my audition, I saw around me mums fussing over their daughters as they waited too. Although I felt fortunate to have Therese at my side, at that point I would have done anything to have had my mother with me. The academy had an aura that was so overwhelming, but my Mum, I knew, would have somehow made it all seem like an adventure.

Therese told me that the panel look at the physique of the applicants' parents as well, needing to see that they are slim and athletic, to ensure that their offspring will develop appropriately. While the mothers corrected their daughters' hair and drilled them with instructions, Therese looked vacantly at the ceiling, as if she had suddenly regressed to being a child. I suddenly felt very small, in my cheap Ukrainian gym clothes, and I wondered if Bruna had been right after all.

Therese promised she would meet me in the hall outside as soon as the audition had finished. As she left my side I hoped the next time she saw my face, it contained pride rather than shame.

I was part of a group of seven girls that were shown around the academy before the interview by the director. We were then given a five minute break before the auditions started, and in that time I shut myself in the toilet and tried to calm my nerves. In those desperate, jagged moments I told myself that this was my only option, my only chance. I simply had to make it good. There would be no-one to comfort me if I messed up, and no-one to blame but myself. I imagined how I would feel if I danced well and was accepted. It was too painful to imagine the alternative.

A few minutes later we were led upstairs into a great, high ceilinged hall. I saw that a black and white portrait of Nijinksy was looking over us. As I stepped into the room, I felt that my every footstep was clumsy. From watching videos with Therese I knew what the protocol would be – we would simply dance a usual class that the director at some point would come along and observe. The other girls seemed so much more assured than I at this point, and I wondered how many of them had already walked these historic floors. We each found a place at the barre. The door closed with a great bang, and then six members of staff, some carrying clipboards, came in and stood at the other end of the room. None of them smiled, they merely raised their heads expectantly. The girls consulted nervously with one another and looked to their feet, trying to find their first position. The maestro took to the piano in the corner of the room and one of the people, evidently the ballet mistress, ordered us to prepare, in brisk Russian.

The music began, and to my horror I felt suddenly overwhelmed by the turn of events. I missed the first step. Bruna's laughter returned to me. Not now, I told myself. I felt the ballet mistresses' eyes upon me, but a moment later I sensed that her attention had moved on. I could see the panel conferring with one another out of the corner of my eye, and then one of them motioned to the mistress. She ran over to the maestro, his music suddenly stopping before he began the piece again. It was only then that I saw, from the expressions on the other girls' faces, that many of the others had fallen behind too. I was relieved beyond words to see that the music had not stopped just because of me.

From practicing, I was used to sweating a great deal at the barre, but today I could already feel it pouring out of me and I had barely begun. I implored my mind to catch and then follow each instruction, to be agile enough to also show grace and flexibility in every move. As the music began again the mistress did not show us the whole moves, but merely suggested them with a flick of her hand. As we progressed through the *pliés* and the *slow tendus* I saw the mistress pacing around the room. Occasionally she would stop, and touch a girl gently on the shoulder, and they would scuttle out of the room. I focused on staying on top of the music, and straining to hear every word that was said. A few minutes later I sensed the mistress at my shoulder, and my body tensed as she leaned in. I could smell her expensive perfume. I closed my eyes for a moment, and when they opened she had passed me by. I had not yet been discounted, and I felt determined to carry on.

After a while the mistress motioned for us to leave the barre and move into the centre. I heard the panel mutter amongst themselves. Many of the dancers did not even look at one another as they prepared to start again. As I began to dance, I felt my body relax, and to my surprise I began to dance fluidly. My body became a little freer. I attacked my pirouettes, and they seemed crisp and confident. My mind had been sharpened by years of practice, and as the nerves faded my movements were as sharp as they had ever been. Once or twice I saw the mistress tap another girl on the shoulder. Some already seemed resigned to this, and almost relieved to finally bow out of the room. As the session began to draw to a close I knew that they would be looking for me to show endurance, creativity, grace under pressure. Yet I felt something tighten inside of me that wouldn't release just when I needed it to.

I felt their eyes scour down my back for telltale signs of restraint. I knew that I would need to display great poise during my big jumps as the class ended, and I desperately hoped that my body would not let me down. From one corner of the room, one by one we followed the music and in the final grand *jeté* I felt myself just reach the height required. During these routines I even started to put in little flourishes and expressions that Therese had always told me looked good. When the music finally faded, I realised my body was screaming out in pain. I had never felt more emotionally or physically exhausted in my life.

'Thank you,' the director said. 'Those of you that are still here have danced well. We will let you know our decision in due course.'

The flight home was unbearable. I was terrified that I would return back to instantly find a letter to say that it had all been in vain.

I waited, day after day checking the post, but there was nothing. Then, finally I came home from school to find Bruna waiting on the doorstep. I looked at her, and tried to read her expression, but it was dead. 'You didn't get in,' she said. I took the letter from her, my blurred eyes looking down to see the six or seven lines printed on it. 'Of course you didn't get in,' she said, and then she swept past me, laughing.

With love from,

Yelena

Dear Noah

For that next year life in Donetsk became an endurance test and I am still unsure exactly how I survived it. Therese was offered a job as a choreographer in England, which she immediately accepted. I had no option but to carry on training by myself, in the hope that I would be able to secure a second interview the following year. I knew that there were other places my dancing could have taken me, but I had had my sights set on the Vaganova. Getting in would teach me that I was capable of something special; that all the extra effort I had put in had been worthwhile. It would prove that Bruna was wrong. It would show my father that I had achieved something special, given all the investment he had put in. I also would be achieving something that I knew my mother would have been very proud of. This was to be my time in the wilderness, and I know you are aware of how difficult and yet necessary that time is.

In your last letter you asked me how I could have felt gratitude towards my father, despite his support, given that he didn't confront Bruna. I can see that when explaining the intricacies of how another family works it is often impossible to justify them. The truth is that only now do I see how weak and scared my father was.

For a few months I carried on with my dancing and schoolwork, and I tried to fight the bitterness festering inside me. Every day I would go to school and curse the ride there, the people around me, the mental prison that I felt trapped inside. I started to feel like I was suffocating, and worse that my moment had passed. That year taught me self-discipline, how to endure, and it gave me an academic fall back position. Those qualifications also started to prove that I was not as useless as Bruna said I was, and that gave me some comfort. The qualifications seemed to signify that in time I inevitably *would* leave this town. In moments we were somehow alone together, Bruna would tell me that given my father's effort I should feel ashamed for not having achieved even better grades. By then I had adopted a dismissive demeanour to her face, but later on that night I would often need to let off some blood just to get through the darkness. A rot was starting to creep over me, and I didn't know how it could be prevented.

Therese's replacement eventually came. Natalya Jalinski's impending arrival was announced a few weeks in advance, and having undertaken some research into her background I was surprised to find pictures of a bright eyed, waif-like woman, almost ethereal. She had not only trained at the Vaganova, but had also been accepted afterwards as a dancer at the Mariinsky Theatre in St Petersburg – where only the finest ballerinas are accepted. It looked possible that I suddenly could be back on track. Natalya would have skills and knowledge far beyond those Therese had possessed. But first I needed to convince her that I was worthy of receiving intensive training from her.

I was nervous about meeting her in person, but for once, my father was there for me. During a rare afternoon alone together he told me I shouldn't allow this setback to prevent me from pursuing ballet further. In the past few months he had seen his daughter change from someone stoical and driven to someone whose failure had started to corrode her. There had been times that I had cursed my sister, screamed in frustration at my father, and quietly threatened Bruna. Looking back, this time was a crossroads. Many people are not fortunate enough to go the right way, and I believe their lives can become one long bitter lament at having taken the wrong road. My father knew how pivotal this moment was, and he wanted me to meet this new and rather exotic sounding teacher at the first opportunity.

In the end I met Natalya on the first day that she began at the school. On entering the dance studio, I was surprised to meet a pale and slightly disconsolate woman in her late twenties. The first time I saw Natalya she was standing by the window looking over the school courtyard, with a rather melancholy expression on her face. It was only after the lesson that my father told me that injury had prevented her fulfilling her promise at the Mariinsky, and had pushed her towards a life of teaching instead.

As Natalya turned to face me, I saw that she wore her long, dark hair in a lose knot at the side of her head. As my father introduced us, Natalya looked at me with sympathy. I think she had already picked up on the aggression of my ambition, and I wondered if she thought it naïve.

On my father's insistence the elderly music teacher was summoned as I demonstrated my barre work. Although I was a little rusty I could see Natalya's eyes widen as I threw myself into the dancing. She lit a cigarette and inhaled it deeply as I went through the sequences, with her instructing me when to *plié*, *tendu* and *glissé*. My energy started to imbue the piano music, keeping up with the momentum even when she interrupted the sequence. After the barre work was completed I was sweating, and I suddenly realised I had given it my all. Still standing by the window, Natalya narrowed her eyes and lit another cigarette. 'Let's do some jumps from the centre,' she said, and before I knew it she was rushing me through from small jumps to the great, grand allegros, which require you to be at full stretch. My father pursed his lips, leant against the wall, and I sensed him refraining from speaking. Eventually Natalya waved at the teacher to stop playing.

'How long have you been dancing for?' she asked, moving over to me.

'Since she could walk,' my father said, from the back wall.

Natalya ordered me over to the barre, and as I went *en pointe* her hand brushed against the back of my calf, and against the small of my back. 'Neck up,' she said. I could smell the cigarette smoke as I tried to hold the position without quivering. 'Who told you to land like that?' she asked. Her fingers traced the straightening of my neck.

'Therese, my last ballet mistress.'

'Right.' Her hand brushed down my back, and I felt a quiver of electricity flow through me. I suddenly felt an inexplicable devotion to her. 'She sounds like bad news,' she muttered.

Eventually, when the cigarette had finished, Natalya resumed her position at the window.

'Well?' my father asked.

'Technically, Mr Brodvich, Yelena does have potential. But to be honest technicality is only a small part of being a ballerina. She has a great deal to learn, and she doesn't have much time in which to do it. You see, a ballerina doesn't only act the role, she also has to live it with her very essence. I don't know if it will be possible for her to do that with so little time.'

'Will you try?' my father asked.

Natalya looked me up and down. I raised my neck again, as she had just shown me how to.

She sighed. 'I've not decided yet,' she said and turned to face me. 'You can certainly dance, Yelena, but I need to see how you respond to the drama, the fire, the passion of ballet. Only then can I properly see if you have what it takes.'

I had no idea what she meant, but I was soon to find out. The Ukrainian National ballet in Kiev was about to open with a season of one of the most famous ballets, *Giselle*. To my delight, one day after a particularly quiet practice Natalya told me that she had secured tickets for us to go together on the opening night.

'I can only know if you have what it takes after I have seen your reaction to this show,' she said, rather cryptically, and she would not be drawn any further on the matter.

I didn't know at the time that my father had had to pay her a good deal to take this trip with me. The trip would require a fifteen-hour overnight train journey, with the two of us in one another's company for every moment. It would certainly be a great adventure for me, but I was yet to see what it would be to her.

On the train journey there, the conversation between us was rather halting. But this slightly withdrawn woman suddenly opened up when we came onto the subject of dance. It was as though through dance we were finally able to fully address one another. As she spoke, with flickering eyes that seemed to replay potent memories, I sensed that I had found someone with a similar soul – troubled, and yet strangely determined.

Natalya explained, while the world outside the windows grew darker, that *Giselle* is split into two acts. In the first act, the lead character of Giselle must play a simple and rather innocent country girl who's being courted by two men – one of whom she falls deeply in love with. But at the end of the first act she learns that he is engaged to another woman of noble blood, and as a result she dies of a broken heart. In the second act she then has to play Giselle's spirit, communicating with the living from the other side. She has to be ghostly, and yet loving too. Its demand for technical perfection, and also great dramatic skill, meant it was the ultimate role for any ballerina to play.

It was the first time I had visited a truly historic theatre house. The venue seemed to come directly from the pages of one of the fairy tales that my mother had often read to me as a girl. The Odessa Theatre was a circular, silvery grey building decorated elaborately with statues and pillars. Passing through the great entrance it opened out into a rich array of red seats and gold stalls. Natalya had seen her first national ballet here too, and as we took our seats I could see her start to become a teenage girl again, experiencing it all for the first time.

When the curtain finally rose it revealed a woodland scene. The Giselle who danced on stage was clearly an innocent, unworldly presence, and far more vulnerable than she is yet to realise. Her mother, who flits from a nearby cottage to watch over her, is protective of her fledgling daughter, because she believes her heart to be weak. I instantly saw shades of myself in the fragile and vulnerable Giselle. In the first act, Giselle was desperate to escape the restrictions of her home, and as the drama unfolded I felt as if it was my story that was being told through the performance. I shared Giselle's joy when a noble man came to her door and courted her. When a hunting party came to her village Giselle was in awe of one of the noblewoman's fine clothes, and she gratefully received a gift from her. At this point she did not know that this woman was already engaged to the man she loved. Her other admirer, a humble gamekeeper called Hilarion, found the sword of Albrecht, the man she loved, and in showing it to her confirmed his identity as an engaged nobleman. Giselle had refused her mother's warnings, which had implored her not to trust a man and fall in love.

Sat in the stalls, I felt something take hold of my heart as the reality of Albrecht's deception unfolded. Where she had first danced lightly, with a simple joy for living, she was now ravaged by betrayal. At this moment, the character seemed to tap into a fear that had existed inside me for a long time; one that I had never before brought to light. That vaulting feeling when you realise that the purity of any love you feel for another is not somehow over-arching. For all its virtues, it can be easily transcended by experience. I watched in horror as Giselle was torn apart by the realisation that her purity was of limited value. She tore at her hair, and the ruthless, wild momentum of the truth threw around her tiny body. I felt tears streak my face as the unfolding spectacle carved a place in my heart. Never before had I seen the power of performance at its most raw – its capacity to speak to us, without words, about the darkest truths not only of ourselves but others too. I had never guessed at how possible it was to make a public spectacle of private trauma.

During the interval I was mute. Natalya remarked that I looked as if I had seen a ghost, and in a way I had – I had seen a reflection of myself on stage, more nuanced than I could have written myself. I felt that Giselle had been written for me, that this evening contained in it a message from fate that somehow this play would come to mirror my life. At the close of the first act I also felt utterly terrified by Giselle's madness as she became undone. I was terrified that in dark moments I would become plagued by it too. Until now I had felt comforted by the fact that there had been little sign of this in my own life, and yet Giselle's fall from grace had been so sudden and brutal. Natalya had brought me here to show me the power of ballet, and she had certainly succeeded. As we found our seats for the second act I started to ask myself if I was Giselle, and the play mirrored my life, then what did it have to teach me?

The curtain rose to reveal a woodland scene at night, which was bathed in silver lighting. It didn't occur to me that Natalya might be watching for my reaction, examining me in every moment. In the distance, white lights flickered and faded away. Giselle floated onto the stage, her dancing unnerved by these illuminations. Natalya had told me that they signified the arrival of a horde of female spirits known as the Wilis. The Wilis, Natalya had said, were the ghosts of women who had been jilted at the altar. As one, they rose from their graves at the dead of night and encircled any man foolish enough to be in the forest at that time of night. I harboured a bitterness inside me for Bruna, and had always feared what that would lead to. I was afraid of what the Wilis would signify, and in this performance, my fears were being expressed. As they arrived on stage, countless ballerinas whose movements expressed their murderous intent, they illuminated my current fears.

They faded back into the silver light. Then, as the stage lights dimmed, Albrecht arrived on stage and laid flowers at Giselle's grave, begging for forgiveness. I felt my body tighten as Giselle returned to the stage, now dressed in white. I watched as she readily forgave the man who had betrayed her and as the two of them, haunted by their bond, began to dance again. I felt like something inside me was being drawn out – thin as a gossamer thread, yet strong enough to never break. I was realising something about love that my immature mind had never understood before; that the world we live in rarely gives us the means by which to fully express our love, with all its myriad intricacies. Sealed apart from her lover by death, Giselle was required to connect with him from a spiritual place, but somehow, in some illogical way, Albrecht was able to sense that such a connection was being made. I thought that perhaps only in the greatest works of art can we recognise a mysterious process which transcends reason. And yet looking at the tightened expression on Natalya's face, I saw that each of us recognised that pain – the idea that it sometimes takes some elusive, ill-defined process to truly communicate how we feel. To see such resonant, grand and yet intimate sentiments expressed through dancing terrified as much as inspired me.

I need barely tell you, Noah, how accurate my fears of this play representing my life are. Like me, Giselle finds the bravery to interact again with those who have been the source of great pain.

The Wilis then returned to the stage, and building in speed they encircled Albrecht and forced him to dance. Led by their commanding Queen Myrtha, they caught him in their relentless pull, forcing him to mimic them. It was then that Giselle arrived on stage, and begged Myrtha to spare him. She refused, but Giselle was not to be dissuaded. She resisted the pull of the Wilis, and the temptation to be vengeful like them. She came amongst the Wilis and begged them to spare Albrecht, and her insistence, her devotion, eventually persuaded them to leave him and fade into the silver again.

In the final, delicate sequence, we watched as Giselle slowly returned to her grave.

When the cast came out for the curtain calls, I felt as if I was in pieces. I knew then that I had found my calling, and as Natalya applauded and cheered with the rest of them, I saw that the colour had returned to her face. I knew then that my destiny in life was to dance Giselle.

As we began to file out, I felt Natalya's hand at the small of my back. 'What did you think?'

'I don't know what to say.'

'Of course you don't, I could see how you felt merely by glancing at your face. Yelena, I would be happy to tutor you.'

I threw my arms around her and kissed her on the cheek. She laughed, but a moment later her body tensed, and I recovered myself.

In the months that followed I was utterly in awe of Natalya. I would watch, awestruck, at her huge jumps and soft, catlike landings. Due to the passion she evoked in me, I think she started to come to life again as well.

She helped me rediscover my love of dance, while also teaching me the true rigours of it. I learnt that although I had never been low on effort, I had suffered from a lack of necessary training. At my first audition I had tried as hard as I could – but ultimately I had been wrong to blame myself for the eventual failure.

Natalya taught me eight routines that became my bread and butter. I practiced them night after night, until I eventually started to satisfy her with my accuracy. My only goal was to impress her, and it gradually seemed that I was. Being in a new town, she started to need me as much as I needed her. After all, I validated her decision to spend a term teaching at some small Ukrainian town, after the glamour of her past. I made her sense of failure at having to teach disappear, because I made the value of her teaching clear. It was transforming my life, day after day, right in front of her eyes.

After a while I learnt those eight routines so well that Natalya and I moved closer to becoming equals. Sometimes, after a particularly long session, I would sense something in her expression. It was one of admiration, and slight envy. I saw, in the widening of her eyes, that she was witnessing something for the first time. Natalya started to use words like 'talent' and 'ability' when talking about me, words which before I had only heard used for others. Then one day, Natalya started to say that she was sure that this year I would get into the Vaganova.

Although it was only words, I kept this wonderful secret to myself. Natalya gave me confidence – not a confidence I had pulled out of myself, but one that she allowed to bloom from the barren soil of my inner self.

I needed to ensure Bruna was unaware of this development. If for some reason I was forced to be alone with her, it felt like a kettle had started screaming in my head and I had to instantly relieve the tension. I had no-one to talk to. Although Natalya was a confidante in one sense, I had no idea how to share my problems at home with her. So with these thoughts bottled inside me, even small, tidy little cuts allowed me to feel replenished; it transformed my state of mind just to see that small jet of blood spiral into the sink. When I danced I was able to ease the pressure out through my arms and legs, through the sheer thrill of moving to music. But when that release wasn't there for me, the fear of Bruna caused me to reach for the razor blade time and time again. I knew that I would struggle to get lead ballerina roles if I hurt myself much more and choreographers noticed scars on my body. So in effect I had to be dancing enough so that I was rarely around her, and so not scarring my body anymore. Dancing took me away from that destructive mindset; it drove me towards something safer.

By that point I had gone so far beyond hoping for acceptance. I had felt so battle-scarred by pain and disappointment that I didn't dare hope. I dared not even believe that Natalya might be right. Natalya started to film my performances, and one day told me she had sent off a videotape to the Vaganova. I normally would have been angry at not having chosen the contents of the tape myself, but by then I trusted Natalya absolutely. A few days later a letter confirmed that I would get to audition for them for a second time; a rare occurrence, I was told. Natalya promised she would be there for me from the moment I entered to the moment I left.

That year I went to audition with a very different feeling from the sense of wretchedness I had taken there the year before. On the flight over, Natalya was an entirely different person to Therese. She found the occasion exciting, and told me that I was entitled to this, perhaps even that it was overdue. I got the sense that she herself had been preparing for this trip together for some time in her own mind. She spoke to me in a matter of fact, personal way, which she never had done before.

'This is your opportunity to show the world just what you have,' she said. 'I wouldn't have taken you on if I didn't think that you would get in this year. You are exactly what they require, it was just that last year you were unable to show it. There will be girls there dancing, who through no fault of their own do not have the key attributes that you possess. You are physically very fit, athletic, flexible – all the things they like. You have dramatic skill too, and these people are the best in the world for recognising potential. Just go in there and show them what you can do.'

When we arrived, some of the other girls looked at me with new eyes, as if they could now sense something different about me. This time I liked the fact that I was one of the few who did not have a parent with me, but instead a young and beautiful instructor who seemed utterly devoted to my cause.

When the course director showed us around the academy he seemed to recognise me from the year before and said, 'It is not often that girls return for a second try.'

With Natalya at my side, this time I warmed up more

professionally. She wanted me to take longer over it than I thought necessary, but I see now that flexibility is so important. When I went in to audition I felt for the first time poised and assured. I wished that my mother could see me now.

Throughout the barre work I felt composed, finely attuned not only to what they would ask next, but also to how to do it confidently. I realised how underprepared I had been the year before. After the barre work, I noticed that two of the panel were keeping their eyes fixed on me. Many of the other girls seemed tired, covered in sweat, but I felt that I had barely started. When we moved into the centre, unlike the previous year, I did not feel anything constrained inside. In fact I felt as if some ugly edifice inside me had taken a huge, mortal blow, and was now crumbling in every passing second. I felt all of the skills I had gradually learnt whirl from my body, spin from my fingertips, and surround me with their colour.

'Thank you,' the woman said, as the music faded. 'We appreciate your time. You are now free to go.'

For the next three days Natalya called me every evening to check if I had received the letter. It was on the Wednesday that I came home from school to find my father holding an envelope addressed to me. It seemed that he had asserted himself this time, and stopped Bruna from intercepting it first. I looked at the small, crisp envelope, and my father called my sister down from her room. Bruna sat in the corner of the room on a wicker chair, her eyes steady and unwavering. In brisk, formal language the letter told us that I had got in to the Vaganova.

The first thing I saw was my father's face, which erupted in delight. Something wonderful had happened within the small walls of our home. An exciting sense of possibility had suddenly blazed into our lives. My sister jumped into my arms, and I saw Bruna slouch back in her chair, and the colour drain from her face.

I phoned Natalya to tell her straight away, not daring to think that she might not answer.

'Yelena?' she said, as the line activated.

'I got in!'

'My God, yes!'

She sounded utterly thrilled, and insisted that the two of us go out for dinner to celebrate. My father was waiting in the doorway, listening to our conversation with a smile on his face. When I'd finished on the phone, he brought out two boxes. In one, he said, was a present for Natalya. In the other, a present for me. A dress from Paris, saved up for and brought from France by Uncle Leo. 'I knew you'd get in,' he said.

In the half hour it took for me to get ready for dinner I was shaking so much that I was barely able to even apply lip-gloss. So much of life is taken up by working tirelessly for our goals, and often we do so simply because it distracts us from considering the alternatives. But at the moments when those efforts come to fruition, life at last begins to make sense. That sense of isolation I had felt for many years had finally allowed me to transform into something. I had validated the commitment my father had shown in me. I had validated the curious path I had taken to train my body. I had proven that the criteria I had developed for myself had been correct, even when there had been no-one to check it with. I had done something to set me apart, which my mother would have been proud of. After all of the pain and loneliness and hard work, I had been accepted into the place where many of my heroes had trained. I felt the walls which had slowly built up around me crumble away. As I left the house, I felt as if my emotions would torch the sky. From then on, I knew everything would change. For the first time I would be able to see the world not as somewhere to fear, but as an arena of possibility. Finally, I felt that my life had begun.

Love,

Yelena

Dear Noah,

I felt I needed to write quickly after my last letter, if only to thank you. I had indeed been worried about all I had disclosed in my last few letters. Ever since we met you have always been interested in aspects of my life which I had formerly assumed one never shares. When I first realised that our bond had developed in a unique way, there was always a danger that I might test it too much. I was concerned that in that letter I exploited your interest in me to the point that I might have destroyed it. After all, romances often require you to manipulate your own perceptions to some degree, in order to fit another's peculiarities. By shattering any illusions in describing my past openly, it occurs to me that I might jeopardise, rather than strengthen our relationship. Your reply, and confirmation that was not the case, meant a lot to me. I know we had agreed in these letters to try and map ourselves completely, but as with any correspondence the caveat had surely been that we would do so within the context we had known each other. Once I posted that letter, it struck me that I had recently blown apart such boundaries. Why exactly I wanted to do that I don't know. I can only hope it was for brave, rather than foolhardy purposes.

I'm glad you want to know about St Petersburg, and what happened next. But first you should know how liberating it felt, under the crooked shelter of adulthood, to admit my past to you. As a child, having to go through all I did, I completely lacked the confidence to express myself. I did not even realise I had a voice, much less that it might be valid. I feared that if I ever tried to properly speak out, no-one would believe me. Perhaps that is why my father was able to maintain the illusion that Bruna had never done anything that bad to my sister and me. Either way, by writing down what actually happened I felt that I had achieved a breakthrough.

My time in St Petersburg was important not only because it gave me the training that brought me to England and to you, but also because it was essential in sculpting me as a person. It brought me in from the wilderness, and made me palatable to the world. I feel I need to tell you about it so you understand how much I transformed whilst there. St Petersburg was the bridge between the childhood Yelena and the Yelena you later met in England. For you to understand the woman you met, I need to explain how she had become her – how recently she had learned to calm the turbulent waters inside her. But before I tell you about that, I must answer the final question in your letter. Yes, I did try and bring Bruna to justice before leaving Donetsk.

Having been accepted into the academy, I was suddenly in possession of a glimmer of confidence, but it possessed little foundation. I began to see that Inessa and I were in no way to blame for what had happened. On a logical level, I had known that for a while. But having had someone use me in that way, I'd come to reluctantly believe that I must be somehow lowly and inferior. Perhaps that is why I had been so ferociously ambitious, to try and scrub that feeling off me. But then I suddenly understood that Bruna had been trying to keep me down because she was scared that one day I would gain the necessary confidence. And now I had, it needed to be used.

I think when injustices occur – whether they are within a family or an organisation – it's most likely that the injustice can never be as elaborate as the construction society enabled it to occur within. So unravelling that injustice is always going to be hard, because you'd need to dismantle something that has been built very carefully. Now I know, you might well have to satisfy yourself with merely getting your voice heard. But I think our idea of justice, of making a punishment fit a crime, will always elude us in a world which insulates itself purposefully from the truth, often for some more partial and self-interested cause. So it was with Bruna.

I was reluctant to address this issue; but it was concern for Inessa's welfare without my presence that pushed me to. Part of me felt I should leave the situation alone; that I would only make it worse. And yet the logical part of me told me that I needed to act right now.

Bruna started to see to it that my father was always busy, so I had to insist we have time together, a meal perhaps before I left. And yet whenever the time for that event neared, Bruna always seemed to intervene. Through sheer persistence, he finally agreed to take me for a drink in a café that Sunday. I noticed that he kept this from Bruna.

When he drove me into the town that day, I remember looking over at him and wondering if I could really do it. Now that he didn't need to be strong for me, I saw him for the anxious, unsure man he had always been. As he parked the car, a layer of sweat glinted from his forehead, and I saw a slight tremor in his hands as they drummed upon the wheel.

He bought me a milkshake, and as silence descended between us I decided I couldn't miss this opportunity. It was then, as his hand clattered around a teacup, that I told him what had happened. At one point tears came into my eyes, even with me skirting over the details, but my father resisted taking my hand. As I looked up, he avoided my eye. The gap between the end of my sentence and the start of his was evocative of the years that had passed since the abuse. It ached and waned for an eternity, and yet the confession still seemed so raw and exploratory for me.

'Yelena,' he finally said. 'I don't know why you do this.'

I couldn't speak. From then on, his eyes stayed trained on

a portly woman at the end of the bar who was picking at a plate of chips. Eventually, the waitress came over to take our bill. We drove home in silence. The silence on his part did not seem angry, but deeply contemplative.

In the final days before I left, my father made it clear he would not discuss the issue with me further. Nonetheless, I felt a gulf gradually widening between him and Bruna. One evening as I was packing, Inessa came into my room and told me that our father had asked her about it. Inessa had been reluctant to confirm that all I had said was true, preferring instead to remain silent. She clearly feared being harmed in my absence as a result of this new intervention. I had not yet realised the weight of what is not said, and the importance a few words can afford. How silence can underline those words. I could not understand why Inessa had clammed up at the moment she could have ensured her own security, but years of abuse and endless bullying had taught Inessa not to act.

Strangely enough, without me saying anymore, in my final days I felt as if my father had started to turn, like a vast ship. There was a harsh negotiation going on, between the part of me wanting to leave and the part of me feeling guilty for abandoning my younger sister. If I felt conflicted, then Inessa's manner towards me seemed just as confused. She seemed to resent me achieving my ambitions, and yet deep down she also feared the effects of me staying. As a result, my relief was tempered with self-loathing because I had not been able to manage the situation better. When I finally left, my father and Bruna felt so distant from one another I knew it was only a matter of time until he finally left her. However, as a consequence of Inessa's silence, Bruna escaped any sort of punishment, and despite my best attempts, I was unable to take the issue further. Our family had developed its style of communication for subjects of great importance, and it was of little use now. The thought that someone could abuse vulnerable children and yet escape justice was agonising. As a result of growing up with Bruna I had grown used to injustice – but seeing it perpetuated even once I had found the courage to address it was too much. Eventually the issue became so poisonous that I had to force myself not to think about it. I didn't know if I had it in me to handle the challenges ahead, but I needed to start preparing for them.

That unresolved issue did not dampen my euphoria about finally leaving. Photos were taken for local newspapers, and people I had known for many years suddenly started looking at me differently. I felt a little sad to be leaving Natalya, but with a look of gratitude she told me that I had helped her find direction in her life. The pale, rather lifeless woman I had first met now seemed invigorated, even surprised by her new vigour. I caught the train from Donetsk and had to prepare myself for the toughest test of my life.

The Vaganova was unlike anything I had experienced. I feel it's important to explain to you how I handled it, because I had to suddenly develop new components to survive that time, and it's important you learn how recent they are. I believe I can never connect fully with you unless I have shared with you my darkest moments. Only by confessing them to you can I feel it possible you will fully understand me.

It felt strange to be arriving there this time knowing that I would be welcomed into the very heart of the institute. Having long harboured dreams of getting in I was completely unprepared for the highly disciplined, almost military environment. Strangers weren't allowed into the academy, and security guards stood at each entrance. I felt a silent thrill as they ushered me in, watching the most recent applicants linger just outside the gate. It all added to the sense that as a student here you were somehow different, special even. The price for this feeling however, was high. Utter dedication in every waking hour was demanded.

I was the only Ukrainian in my year, on a hallway surrounded by Korean girls. They were welcoming but clearly had a very different mentality to me, all of which reinforced the sense of loneliness I already felt. I shared a room with two of them, in which all my belongings were stuffed into one corner. A small window overlooked an unkempt courtyard, and behind it I could see a small square of St Petersburg sky. The halls were run by matrons who were strict women with a high sense of duty and expectation. As the matron explained on our first night – you stood when staff entered, you said hello to any adult who you passed in the corridors. I was there to become a professional ballerina, and that was all that mattered. Like the other girls on my hall I had never experienced discipline like this before. One of the Korean girls, whose sister had trained here, told us on the first night that any kind of individual expression was not only discouraged, but almost impossible. Any emotion or pain that I felt at any time was simply irrelevant. This was how the country had been able to make its ballet so famous. I was grateful for the warning.

Waking up in the morning I would immediately take my holdall and tramp slowly from the fifth floor down to the practice room. We began at nine and ended at six, sometimes later if we were rehearsing for a performance. We worked six days a week, often in repetitive classes where we had to stay at the barre for many hours, refining the simplest of movements. Our academic work was not allowed to suffer at any point and there was great pressure to stay on top of that as well. During the ballet classes, boys and girls often trained separately, and the pressure to get a repetition right could sometimes reduce a girl to tears. Though some tutors would try and reassure the students, others would have little patience for this and order them outside. If they stayed, the girl next to her might try to whisper her an encouraging word or two, but you didn't want to get caught doing this. Dedication to the task was more important than anything. Dreams of being a star pupil often met a quick and cruel death. This was not about sheer effort; the tradition of excellence had to be honoured at all times.

As time progressed I saw the unusual manifestations of this pressure on the students. They gradually turned from slight, elegant humans into walking works of art. Poised at all times, utterly focused. They retained a childlike enthusiasm and a singular dedication, as well as a pretty strong sense of entitlement. I was one of the eldest, and yet there was noticeably no outlet for my relative worldliness. The students merely supported one another in the moments when they could. When Sunday finally arrived we were usually too tired to do anything other than watch DVD's or go for pizza in the nearby square (hunger was a persistent problem, and we all waged our personal wars with it).

But even during those quiet times, the sense of history was ever present. It was in the framed pictures of Nijinksy that watched over us in the studios. It was in the sterile atmosphere of the canteen at lunch times, where a few slices of fruit were given to sustain you. It made you feel important, worthy of focused attention. It was a new feeling, and one I tried to welcome into the core of my being.

On the few occasions I was able to leave the academy I would often walk, pulling my tattered coat around me to protect me from the cold. I liked to take the short walk to the Church of Spilt Blood, and though I didn't feel able to pray there I found the powerful, orthodox sense of calm there nourishing. I would then cut into the Mikhailovsky Gardens, where performing musicians once drew in great crowds before it was banned. That perhaps explained the sense of absence that pervaded there. It was the start of autumn, and the secretive wind that swept around the trees confirmed that this was where I should be. Cast against the attainments of history, battling to assert myself. I would mutter to myself, and giggle amongst the trees, and wonder what I had done to bring myself here.

At night, a curious feeling would arise in me the moment the lights were turned off. I began to long for something, but

I didn't yet know what it was. The days were streaking by in a flurry of pain and expectation, but despite my newfound sense of purpose I still felt lost. Where exactly did I belong? I had only ever wanted to escape from home, and to do so I had needed a destination. But this was clearly not a new home, simply a means to an end. Sometimes, when tiredness got the better of me, I felt a pulsating sense of anxiety. Could I really get through these ten months? What was all this leading to? Sometimes I feared that having got what I wanted, I now felt more lost than ever. Being here didn't answer my questions, it only provoked me to ask new ones. But at least it was something. And at least I now felt able to ask questions, even of myself, with a clear and crisp voice.

Living with the other students, I was unable to employ my usual strategy of wilfully isolating myself in order to focus upon a goal. I saw that the next issue I had to address was how to endure, and perhaps even enjoy company. The difficulty was that Bruna was still a part of my inner audience, assuring me that any moment I would be found out. This made being sociable even harder, as I tended to feel that being in the company of others meant I was distracted. But I knew something must change, and so I started to try and develop a kind voice, which I used to nurture myself during the gruelling sessions and the nights of uncertainty. I began to self-medicate, banning myself from using words like 'failure', 'fat' and 'useless', and instead saying under my breath statements like 'well done' or 'keep at it'. Self-loathing was just too easy and I credit the Vaganova for making it redundant as a coping mechanism. I was determined to purge myself of all self-pity. Self-pity might have driven and nurtured me for many years, but here it would be of no use. I knew that I would never be naturally light hearted, but I could at least learn to smile and laugh. A ballerina may be exhausted and underfed; her toes may be bleeding, but ultimately all that is of no consequence. She has to learn to smile, because deep down she loves every second of what she is doing.

The more approachable I looked, the more the other students started to come up to this reticent stranger. The other girls had bonded with one another immediately, and I was determined I wouldn't be far behind. Ultimately it was my passion for dancing which brought me out of seclusion. Some of the younger girls admired my dancing and looked to me for advice. I felt so honoured that they had turned to me that I gave them all I could. Soon I learnt that they too could help me in ways I had not imagined. When all I wanted to do was be alone, they encouraged me to join them for films and I started to see this was better than isolation. We messed around with makeup, painted one another's nails, and practiced our *retires* on the radiators. Many of the girls could still only do this slowly, and with some wobbling. I taught them the technique Natalya had shown me – to take a sharp intake of breath just as you snap your foot into position. When it spared a couple of them the rod in our next session at the barre, they were very grateful for it. I soon found myself turning to these girls for laughter and comfort instead of bottling it all inside.

With some of the students looking to me for guidance, my instructors made it clear that I was towards the top of the class, with only a couple of the more expensively trained dancers ahead of me. I wasn't only becoming popular in class – a couple of the boys would insist on walking with me whenever we moved between lessons. The Korean girls saw this as more of a compliment than my European contemporaries, and they encouraged me to start wearing more makeup. I was still cautious around boys though. It seemed ugly to use my body for sex, when I felt its purpose was to dance. Relationships at the academy were discouraged, and that reinforced the feeling I already had that sex was wrong. My whole thinking about it was negative and restrictive. But some of the more mature boys at the academy helped me to gradually soften my perspective.

Inessa and I started to write to each other. She was not

very good at expressing how she felt in writing, but I guessed at her silences and tribulations. I hoped for the opportunity to get her away from home, but I knew that in time, she would be perfectly able to do this herself. She said she did not recognise me in the letters I sent her. She said it sounded as if my life had become very glamorous. Once she even said she wished I could have taken her with me.

Slowly, as my guard came down, I started to enjoy my new life. My preparation for the graduation dance, known as the Sdacha, became my welcome distraction. Teachers began to ask me what role I would like to dance in it; I would be prioritised along with Freijer, a catlike Danish girl who I grew close to when our joint ambitions presented us with similar challenges. I knew that a high percentage of pupils would not make it to graduation, but I didn't fear this. One day, my teacher Massine confirmed that he had picked me to dance the famous *pas de deux* from *Romeo and Juliet* with a young Argentine called Julio. I had never spoken to him, but I had admired his dancing for some time, and so I thought our partnership might work. I had reasons to be enthused.

Thank you for allowing me to share these hidden moments with you, Noah. By revealing them through a letter I feel I have excavated a period of time which otherwise would have always remained concealed. It's strange how when you open up to someone you assume your candour and their receptiveness will consistently endure. But writing to you today I see instead how miraculous it is if you ever get to reveal yourself at all; how many people must keep their stories supressed for the whole of their lives. So you allowing me to express myself more than once causes me to owe you a debt of gratitude that I don't think I can ever repay.

Love,

Yelena

Dear Noah,

It wasn't a dancer who first overcame my defences. Rehearsals for the Sdacha had just begun when I met Vlad, a man who flaunted his charms almost aggressively. Difficult as it might be, I feel I should tell the story of what happened with him. Otherwise a key part of who I am now will remain unmapped.

Although at that time we were all becoming more and more focused, a sense of excitement was also building. All the students were exhilarated to think that we would soon be dancing at the world famous Mariinsky Theatre. Amongst the elite in St Petersburg, taking your children to watch the ballet there has long been part of a cultural rite of passage. The Mariinsky is an elaborate building not far from the academy – its exterior a unique blend of blue and green, studded with white pillars. It would be the scene at which many of our ambitions would soon either be fulfilled or dashed.

As the date of the Sdacha grew nearer we started to hear about the many talent scouts from around the world who would be present at the performance. We knew impressing them would be key to ensuring a career in ballet. As if this was not enough to take on, as a result of my prominent role I was told that some local culture magazines were keen to interview me in advance of the show. The largest of these would also be interviewing two other dancers from the Vaganova for an article entitled 'Tomorrow's Stars of Ballet'. The journalist assigned to interview us was called Vlad, and when his name was first mentioned I noticed a frisson go around all those present.

It was on one particularly balmy day in April that I first saw Vlad backstage at the Mariinsky. Rehearsals had now transferred from the studio to the theatre itself, and I had just finished practicing. For the performance a special, sloping stage had been commissioned to match the floor we had all trained on. Looking out from the stage, the theatre itself was undeniably intimidating, with its infinite rows of red seats framed by gold stalls that rose to the grand ceiling. The centrepiece of the ceiling was a great chandelier, skirted by painted cherubs. The vast stage, teetering over the orchestral pit, directly faced the Royal Box. I was stood on the side of the stage, getting my breath back and taking it all in, when Vlad first caught my eye.

We held each other's gaze until someone called his name. As he turned to respond I took in his profile. He had a high, almost aggressive jaw line, further pronounced by the half-light backstage. He scribbled something in his notepad, and while he did so, people came over to him in a manner that suggested his presence was somehow validating. I was not sure exactly what it was that made people consult him so much, but when I later spoke to him I realised that every movement he made was imbued with an unusual confidence.

Freijer came over and told me that this young man apparently wished to interview the two of us. He was keen to see our dressing room, and Freijer and I exchanged amused glances. Throughout the interview I couldn't help but be detached and distracted, and at the time I barely noticed how this seemed to intrigue him and make his advances even more overt. The other ballerinas were vying for his attention, and yet I was treating him with total disregard.

Afterwards, the girls started to make their way to drinks at a nearby bar, and I heard the photographer ask Vlad if he was coming. He loudly said that he would if I accompanied him and...

Are you sure you want to know these things? I remember how badly it stung me to read about you and Catherine's past. I'll gloss over the parts that might be tricky to read, but you cannot ever be jealous of Vlad, Noah. The only important point to make is that for the first time, I genuinely intrigued someone; at least that was how it seemed. At some point over the course of the evening we ended up alone together, and he was keen for us to talk into the small hours. And not only talk. I had never known someone be so intrigued by my answers that they expressed a compulsion to chase the numerous implications within them. I felt helpless, overpowered. It seemed that everything about me amused, unsettled, intrigued him. I told him about Natalya and he wanted me to physically describe her: how exactly had she inspired me? I mentioned Donetsk, and he wanted to know all about my friends there, what the school had been like to live in. A pithy answer provoked some minor deconstruction of my personality, and yet however much I dismissed or belittled his attention, every time he implored me to reveal more I felt myself weaken. All the time he drew physically closer, and all the time I was made to feel that was natural, and not overly intense at all. He was masterful at seduction.

He had this very easy way of being tactile without seeming intrusive. Freijer took me to one side during the course of the evening. 'You know,' she said. 'He is quite a big deal. I know that he only seems interested in whoever looks to be the next big name, and that's probably the case, but he's making quite a name for himself as a journalist. You could do a lot worse than have him as a boyfriend.' I laughed the remark off, but there was no denying that his focus on me drew the attention of everyone around me. Suddenly, I was not only a promising dancer, but a talking point too.

At the end of the night he offered to walk me back to the academy. As he did so, I remember him expressing some jealousy towards me, which I found quite strange. 'You're going to be famous,' he had said. 'Aren't you?' I wasn't sure if I was supposed to confirm or deny this. At that moment his eyes narrowed, and I laughed to dispel the tension. 'If I'm not careful, you'll outshine me,' he said. I thought nothing of it. When he asked me if he could take me for dinner that week, I found myself accepting.

He met me at the Vaganova, and he seemed keen to see as much of the academy as was permitted. He had arranged for us to have a choice table at the Rossi restaurant, on the end of my street.

The conversation had a level of intensity I had never known before. The smile when greeting me seemed warm, but was somehow predatory too. The pauses between statements were never longer than they needed to be. He again pushed for details, but knew when to relent and give me space. All the while, everything was tended to – did I have the right kind of wine? I had never experienced how on a date a person can anticipate your next response, and always have something ready to intrigue you with next. I know that you don't like being reminded of another man's romantic cunning, but I didn't want you to think that I yielded to Vlad easily. I didn't think that the careful appliance of attention might be the actions of a slick salesman. Vlad had done his research on me, and had decided in advance that he was impressed, regardless of what I said or did. When I in turn enquired about him I always met a curious blank. I see now how clever that was – in not revealing himself he urged me to strive and understand him. By catching myself in the act, I would therefore think myself taken with him.

I didn't normally drink. But he made every offer of wine seem decadent, yet also perfectly natural. At the end of the meal, he suggested that we go for a walk. It was spring by then, and I had barely left this quarter of the city for months. It was late on a Saturday night, and the sun had just begun to descend behind the high buildings. I told him that I didn't know where we should go. I wasn't going to take him to the Mikhailovsky, that belonged to me. 'You mean to tell me that you live here, but have never seen the city?' he asked, as we made our way down the Nevksy Prospekt.

During that walk, St Petersburg reached inside me and took a hold of something, for the first time. We were passing the Kazan Cathedral and maybe it was the wine, but as we walked past, the two wings of the building suddenly seemed to spread out in an encompassing embrace. Its high pillars towered above us, solemn and patriarchal. The cathedral was bathed in a gold glow, and the city's lights flickered over its exteriors. It reflected them, resolute amongst the tides of history. Around it, vendors loudly announced their wares and I could hear eighties pop music emanating from a nearby car. The combination of the music's plea and the building's resolve was suddenly gripping. I felt as though time slowed to a pace in which all the sensations around me were absorbable. Advertisements bristled with colours and persuasion, capturing lifestyles most of us would never have. I thought how, regardless of the era, people were always sold dreams that they could never fully consume. They never ceased in their striving, they consumed ravenously and wanted lustily too. Vlad saw that I was moved by the spectacle, and he placed his arm around my shoulder. 'At last, you are fully seeing the city,' he said.

That night we walked down to the Admiralty Gardens, which skirted the great, ice blue River Neva. It was where our quarter of the city ended and the next province began. We came to the fountain in Alexander Garden, which spurted thin jets of silver in glistening arcs. All around the fountain couples clung to one another in the fading light. Vlad invited me to sit down on one of the benches, and as I did I felt part of a couple for the first time. We fitted in so neatly amongst the other nestling couples around us. In the dark I felt him reach to put his arm around me, and something inside me gave way as I leant against him. It had stood resolute for many years, but it had been eager to crumble so readily.

In the weeks that followed our romance moved quickly. His apartment, a chic, lavish affair just around the corner from me, became my second home. I did wonder as to what degree this affluence was a result of his achievement, or parental funding. On his wall was a pop art portrait of himself and his new business partner. Photographs of him at Spanish and English festivals emblazoned the wall, his eyes curiously glazed in each. On Sunday mornings there was the cleaner, who eyed him narrowly as he fussed over breakfast for us.

It was inevitable that I would want to seek out his company the minute I was free. After all, it came with such immediate rewards. He would often arrive to meet me laden with flowers. When I came for dinner there would inevitably be some small, wrapped present waiting on the table; a poetry book perhaps, with the sections that reminded him of me underlined. I had never been courted, and so being fussed over made for a pleasant change. Sometimes it seemed impossible for me to say anything he disagreed with. The only time his sleek, immaculate exterior became threatened was when he was in the company of somebody he felt was superior to him. In late night dinners, or moonlit walks, he was always the same: self-enclosed, eager to praise, and yet always resolute. For some reason I didn't find the sense of distance at all concerning, merely charismatic. I tried to address this boundary by opening up to him in a way that I had never done before. I told him a little about Bruna, and that I had always felt sure I would never be able to share these dark chapters with anyone. I explained that because of what had happened, I'd wondered if I would ever be able to have a relationship. He replied that we were simply very lucky to have found one another.

There was another Vlad, which remained out of reach. In his absence, my sense of excitement was maintained by his constant messages. He wanted to cook dinner for me on any night he could and show me off at social occasions, telling people what I did before he explained who I was.

Even now, I cannot trace the exact moment when he decided I was no longer worthy of his attention. Just as his immediate affection had seemed unearned, so too did his sudden disdain. I was too young to notice when someone liked me for what I was, rather than who I was. His messages gradually became terse, his disdain for me more apparent in public. It was as if he found it distasteful that I was not everything you'd assume a rising ballerina to be. I was unashamed of the fact that I had got to this point through sheer application. But Vlad had fallen for a package, so he felt cheated when it was not all as he had hoped it would be. At first he had found my lack of cultural sophistication charming, but it now frustrated him. If someone would mention an English band I didn't know, his brow would crease as if somebody had just vomited next to us. In my heart, I was still the same girl who had felt lost even in Donetsk, so I certainly did not have the confidence to apply myself in social situations here. I was not prepared to fake myself either, and so floundered in the middle ground. As a result, his messages suddenly dwindled, and he took much longer to reply when I tried to get in touch. It was a fortnight later when one of the Korean girls told me she had seen him having dinner with Freijer.

When I called him to ask if this was true, his phone was turned off. After agonising for another day, I called again the following evening. This time it rang out. When he finally answered his phone, his first words were, 'Come over.'

It's hard to dwell on the vaulting feeling that overwhelmed me when he answered the door.

'Is it true that you have started seeing Freijer?' I asked, as I stepped over the threshold. His eyes widened, and he grabbed his coat. He looked at me with an expression that I struggled to see as anything other than pity. 'Let's go out,' he said, ushering me back through the door and closing it behind him. As we turned I saw how quickly certain areas, once conducive to a bond of some sort, could be closed off. A couple of months ago he had urged me to treat his home as if it was mine. But now something had shifted, and like any spurned lover I was expected to immediately relinquish any intimacy with place as well as person.

'Why can't I come inside to talk?'

He pulled the coat around himself. 'You can do if you want. It's just, I thought you might prefer to walk and talk.'

'I'd prefer to know what has happened between you and my friend, Vlad.'

He continued walking, half a step ahead of me. We passed down a series of side streets, and I sensed him growing out of breath. 'Slow down,' I said. 'I can barely keep up.' It was only when we came to the canal that he finally slowed. 'Just tell me if you took her for dinner.'

He stopped, and leant against a rail. 'Well we went for dinner, yes. I don't see the harm in that.'

'You invited her out?'

'There were things she wanted to talk about.'

'What things?'

He opened his mouth, but nothing came out. He stood agape for a moment, looking slightly ridiculous. His aggressive sensuality was not attractive now, but somehow bohemian and distasteful. 'I don't know. You'll have to ask her.'

'So you're saying she asked you?'

'Yelena, what do you want me to say? I thought we were just friends, but we just... kind of hit it off whenever we saw each other.'

'And so you thought you'd follow that interest up with a date, without telling me first?'

'I've had a difficult year,' he said. 'Don't make this harder for me.'

I bargained and pleaded with him. What about all the gifts and flowers and meals, how could he so quickly change his mind? But he just looked at floor, and hugged himself, and said 'These things happen.'

It reminded me of the way Bruna had left me feeling; that no matter how much I developed, or what I proved to myself, I would always be beneath contempt. I felt so embarrassed by this turn of events. Everyone at the academy had known we'd been dating, and now everyone would see him with Freijer. I said this to him, but he just shrugged. I had never before known that feeling, of suddenly being unable to engage with someone who you'd felt close to. When you are wanted by people like Vlad, you can do no wrong. Everything you say is funnier and more interesting than what anyone else can say. But when they have consumed you, it is as if you have an aroma that is unbearable. And if you are unsure of yourself, it can serve to confirm your darkest doubts. Which is what began to happen the moment I left him, mute and inarticulate, his resolute air only temporarily bruised.

The raw hurt I felt made me curse my decision to be less introverted. Over the next few days I remained silent in class, and then holed myself up in my room when the day was over. The romance with Vlad had only lasted a couple of months, and I berated myself for having let it get so public during that time. It meant that my sudden introversion drew more attention, induced more gossip, but I didn't know how else to get through the day. The girls in the hall responded with unexpected kindness, wanting to distract me by inviting me to watch films with them. Afterwards, they would try and get me to open up. Others comforted me with the previously withheld knowledge, that he had a long history of forging public relationships that his vanity could not maintain for long. People didn't speak of Freijer though, and what all this said of our friendship. When I saw her in classes she was inevitably smiling, and sensing my gaze she would quickly turn away from me. I learnt to see her as just another member of the class but it was hard, as we would soon be performing in the same show.

I became acquainted with a new kind of silence, one very different from the type I had cultivated in Donetsk. This was the silence of emerging resolve, and the silence of a great city. In a strange way, I learnt to draw comfort from it, and see how this short relationship was of so little consequence given all that was happening to me. I knew I had to regroup quickly, as my graduation performance at the Mariinsky would be my one chance to impress people who could ensure my success. I knew that a good performance could see me being permanently accepted as a dancer at the Mariinsky. This would give me financial security as well as ensuring my career as a ballerina. Yet at this crucial hour I felt so flat and dejected.

I walked around the fringes of the city, as if hoping to find a place in which all this confusion made sense. But over the course of those many long walks I realised that answers could not always be found externally. I grew to know the uncompromising silence of the outside world and in abandoning my resentment, started to search for meaning inside myself instead. I learnt that within me there existed a labyrinthine world of my own making, which I was the architect of. I saw that I could seek infinite comfort from its textures, but I would never be able to share them with another. It seems strange now that such a shift in my worldview occurred from so brief a romance. But my life had been a wilderness for so long that the discovery of intimacy had seemed a belated invitation to join the real world. Now it had been snatched back, and I felt like I was an outsider again. It had briefly seemed that I might be able to exist in the limelight of people's attention, but this break up confirmed my suspicions that I would always exist on the perimeters. Knowing this, I developed a hunger for solitude that persists even now. Vlad would never know this, but by prompting me to seek strength from myself, he gave me the tools with which to finally become a ballerina.

I had been mentally preparing for my role in the Sdacha

for a while, but now I needed to perform physically too. I was not feeling very strong. My sense of confusion and anger was still very fresh, but I knew that I would be back to square one if I missed this chance. I had to find the strength to get over this pain and give the performance of my life.

People often talk about channelling despair and anger into a worthwhile activity. At that point, dancing became an aggressive distraction. Sensuous expression was not top of the agenda. To be considered for the Mariinsky, the next step was to dance well at the end of year exam. That was the only way to be one of the dancers that the director would choose for consideration at the theatre.

At the exam I consciously tried to channel my hurt and pain. At the barre I would continue to hold a position even when I had been told I could relax, just to show what I was capable of. I was simply refusing to fail. I was utterly focused, but it was at the expense of any self-expression.

I was told after the exam that although I was still being considered, I had not danced with enough versatility to guarantee anything. My next chance to prove myself would be at the audition for the theatre, where I would need to dance not only in front of my own teachers, but also the directors.

The days that followed were perhaps some of the hardest of my career. If I failed, I couldn't use Vlad as an excuse, I would have only myself to blame. This opportunity would not come again. The exam had taught me that at this level, focus, determination and precision were not enough. I also needed to display something special, something that set me apart from all the other girls.

I was told in advance that at this audition, I would be dancing alone in front of the panel. The night before I decided to walk around the city, although it was already late, and I was feeling tired. I wanted to try and reconnect with exactly why I was here. At first I replayed in my mind all that I had gone through, but that only made me feel more anxious. But as I was turning, rather disconsolately, back towards the halls it came to me. I was here because I was the girl who had sat in the stalls at the Ukrainian ballet and felt sure it was my destiny to one day dance the greatest role in ballet. All this was nothing more than a means to that end.

The nervousness I felt was hidden by years of practice. I wore a determined smile throughout the audition, and as I danced I gradually became looser, and the smile became more genuine. Afterwards, catching my breath at the barre, I was told I had danced well, but that unfortunately it was not enough. I needed a very good graduation performance and only then would I be considered.

I decided to simply stop feeling overawed by the Mariinsky. Seeing it merely as a theatre, an arena for opportunity, and for the first time I did not feel conscious of its history. I told myself that I would dance as I had always meant to – with passion, and hunger, and pleasure. I wanted people to be able to forget themselves as they watched me dance, to give people solace and a means of escape.

In the days leading up to the dance I developed a couple of habits that have always stayed with me. I put Juliet's music onto my ipod and I listened to it during every free moment – over breakfast, over dinner, and before I went to sleep. In so doing I grew to learn its nuances and love its intricacies. I stayed on the stage for longer than I needed to, familiarising myself with it, as if it was my own.

Backstage, the Mariinsky is a rabbit warren, made up of little intricate spaces and concealed chambers. Although I was sharing a dressing room with the other dancers, in my mind I pretended I was a Principal, and I acted with the focus that you'd expect of one. The time that I normally would have spent with the other girls I was on the next floor, where the haberdashers worked on all the beautiful costumes. I wanted to make sure my costume was exactly right, and we kept at it until it was perfect.

We were told that during the dress rehearsal there would be no time for repetitions or corrections. I was relieved therefore to see that out of everyone, I seemed the most prepared. Julio was utterly focused on the task too, and with him I danced as well as I ever had. Freed of the burden of an audience I was able to imagine we were alone in my room, or even that it was just a dream. After the dress rehearsal some talent scouts approached me. I took their cards, but did not allow myself to be swept away by their attention. After all, I knew it would soon evaporate if the Sdacha did not go well.

I told myself to enjoy this final flourish; that I deserved it. My father and Inessa flew in to watch the show, and it filled me with happiness to see them taking their seats at the front as the orchestra warmed up. Inessa looked overawed by the beautiful and historic surroundings, and my father had a look in his eyes that suggested he was quite overwhelmed to think that his own daughter would be coming on stage, here, at any moment. It was enchanting to see an expression on his face that I had never seen before, created as a result of my own effort. It made me feel more confident as I looked out onto the lavish array of rapidly filling seats from the wings. Before the show I sat backstage, listening to the building clamour of the audience. Our teacher came back to offer some last minute reassurance. I smiled at him, and he patted me on the shoulder.

I heard the *corps de ballet* enter the stage and I felt the soft thump of their feet through the floor. Eventually, the horns that heralded the close of their sequence began. A stagehand appeared at my door and nodded. I tiptoed out onto the stage, the lights instantly blinding me. I felt a murmur of appreciation fill my ears and I looked up and saw Julio enter from the other side of the stage. He held out his hand, and something inside me instantly spread out like wings. That night Julio was a wonderfully attentive partner, and if I slightly overwhelmed him with my jagged and unpredictable style, he was generous enough to accommodate it. I felt utterly in control of the moment, as if it was mine to manipulate and experience at will. My concentration was such that I felt time slow down to the pace I needed it to be. As the piece came to a close I felt a sudden ecstasy tumble through my limbs, and Julio's smile suggested he was relieved and happy too. As the audience rose to their feet in ravenous applause I felt as if I had suddenly closed the door to a painful chapter of my life and been ushered into another – one full of light and hope. The audience's applause came as an unexpected balm. This was what life was about. I would always know I could bury myself in that thrilling, visceral noise. We were called back for three ovations, and at the final one, some of the girls at the edge of the stage turned and applauded me. I felt tears slipping down my cheeks, but I always kept smiling.

Afterwards, I went backstage to find the dressing room filled with flowers. A representative from the Mariinsky came back and offered me a place in the company for the next season. When Inessa and my father came back they looked utterly thrilled – Inessa was actually shaking with excitement. It seemed that I had finally found my place in the world, and I could not have felt more relieved and gratified.

With love from,

Yelena

Dear Noah,

Of course I understand if you didn't know quite what to make of my last letter. If it seemed cruel to send you an account of my first heartbreak, I can only apologise. I never intended to be unkind, only myself. You said that you found it morbidly fascinating to read about Vlad, though it is not a letter you will probably read again. I can understand that. But I was grateful to read that you enjoyed the story of my graduation. It is a story that I often replay to myself, and therefore one I felt I had to share with you.

It is true that I do not dwell on my time at the Mariinsky. It's not because it was not important to me, more because it is not important to us. I was proud to have gained my certificate, and though I entered the *corps de ballet* feeling excited, it did not last long. I had drawn attention to myself with my graduation performance, and did not realise that consequently some people might want to knock me down.

However, the looks I got from some other members of the corps when I entered suggested that I was vulnerable. I remember I started compulsively tying and untying my pointe shoes, a nervous tic that had suddenly started. From the corner of the hall, a cluster of girls studied me, their hands on their hips. I looked back at them, trying to be impassive. Sensing this exchange, a girl with auburn hair came over to me, reached down, and neatly tied the ribbons of my shoes around my calves in one go. I looked up at her, pleased and surprised.

'Thanks,' I said. 'I'm Yelena.'

'I know,' she answered. 'I'm Alina.'

At that moment the choreographer entered. He was a slight man with a rather squat face, his eyes moved analytically over us. As we moved over to the barre I whispered to Alina that I didn't know how to play it for the first session. In quick, hushed tones, Alina told me the advice the choreographer had given the girls at a pre-season party the night before. I barely had time to thank her before the barre work began.

But when my moment came, towards the end of centre work, I found that everyone was doing the opposite to me. Whereas my dancing was full of dramatic flourishes, the rest were being very minimal and crisp. The music suddenly rolled to a halt as the choreographer snapped his hands. 'You,' he said, pointing at me. 'What is your name?'

'Yelena,' I answered.

'Everyone observe. This – ' he started to do an exaggerated version of my flourishes and turns, ' – is the last thing I want to see this season. If you want to find yourself at the back of the pack Yelena, continue to dance like this. Maestro, please.'

I looked over at Alina. She was smiling at some of the other girls, who raised their hands to their mouths.

I recovered from this inauspicious start, and learnt to be more selective about who I trusted. I worked hard, and after a year I began to feel a part of the group. I quickly graduated as a second soloist, and a few months later grew into first soloist roles. I slowly came to deeply love rather than fear that wonderful theatre. I expanded my repertoire with many of the most beautiful roles in ballet. I danced as all the fairies in *Sleeping Beauty*, and in some of the most testing solo roles from *Paquita*. The choreographer even began to praise me personally, particularly when I danced as Gamzatti in *La Bayaderé*.

Soon I was twenty-four, and more settled than I had ever been. St Petersburg had gradually become my home, although there had been little time for anything other than ballet. I had grown into the lifestyle and had found a way to make it suit me. Although it was the most famous dancers who were generally taken on tour, opportunities had started to arise to allow me to dance around the world.

For a while producers had been watching me, saying that I was ready for Principal roles. One day, after practice, I was introduced to the director of an English company, a rather unsettling and curious man called Michael. He had come to Russia to scout for talent, and had been ushered in my direction by our choreographer. To my amusement, he insisted on taking me out for dinner, and over a small bowl of pasta he enquired what role I most wanted to play.

Of course, I told him it was my ambition to dance as Giselle. He seemed to already know this. When I told him that the role had always thundered with personal meaning to me, he was not as impressed as I had expected. 'Ballerinas can over-identify with a role you know,' he answered. I argued that just as all dancers have their speciality, mine would be the personal dimension I brought to it. I told him that there were personal reasons that I felt capable of dancing Giselle. He waved his hand dismissively and said, 'I don't need to know.' But a couple of days later, I was delighted to receive a phone call from him offering me a place in his new company. Breathless with excitement, but trembling with fear, I accepted the offer to move to England.

By then I was used to intense application, and having danced my last at the Mariinsky, I focused all my energies on learning about English culture. I didn't have to try hard – the country had long existed in my affections. No longer needing to listen to the soundtrack of my next performance, I instead silently mouthed along to English speaking tapes over the course of that fortnight. England felt like the right place to go next, and I hoped that journeying there would enable me to reconnect with my mother somehow. As soon as visas were arranged, I found myself on a flight to Heathrow. The tour would take me all over your country for six weeks, closing with a week at a prestigious new theatre in the North East where we'd perform Giselle – with me in the title role on the final two nights.

Those six weeks felt like a breathless sweep across the dusty stages, service stations and dry wipe hotels of your country. As a child I had romanticised the land beyond belief, it seemed to me a place where it was possible to lay your delicate mark upon history. It was the land of David Bowie's glamour and pomp, in my mind populated with witty, arch Peter Cook types who placed themselves amongst history simply through the natural expression of their personalities. It seemed a land that lent itself to immortality, a place where a little serendipity could usher one into eternity. The ghost of my mother, and the ghost of Giselle, leant those six weeks an elusive, resonant meaning. When I was not focused on my next solo role, I was chasing spectres with my eyes across the moist, fertile land that span outside the train window.

During the occasional day off I went looking for my mother. Searching, rather desperately, for traces of a slight, pale woman I had barely known. Trying to imagine how she might have felt as a young woman, when my existence was so remote as to be negligible. Did she have the same thoughts I had? Was she prone to flights of fancy, awkward in social situations? I walked around and wondered how she might have looked, on the edge of the pack perhaps, trying to find her way into the world. At times, I felt tempted to try and communicate with her. I felt that she, and she alone would understand what I was going through at that moment. Sometimes, I couldn't help lamenting that I had never known my mother, and I worried what would happen if I ever became a mother myself. How would I know what to do? When to be there? I would have no-one to model myself on, I barely remembered her and there was nothing about Bruna I could look to.

There was a spirit amongst the English people that I

recognised as my own – perhaps my mother had passed it onto me, and it had lain dormant for many years. When we stayed in Manchester the company director took us for post-performance drinks, and many ended up in the city's Northern Quarter, knocking back vodkas and dancing to The Stone Roses until the small hours. During those snatched nights I felt freer than ever – as if it was now for the first time okay for me to openly enjoy myself.

Once we arrived in the north, I was taken to the house that would be my home for this final stretch. It sat just above a gentrified quayside, which reflected the city lights when the sky grew dark. It was my home for now, but after that I had no idea where I would go. A severe looking matron owned the house, and as she waved me into my room I suddenly felt very alone. I put my suitcase on the floor, and felt a kind of rising nausea within me. It soon collected, and knifed into a feeling of distinct sorrow as I suddenly realised I didn't have a home. It felt so odd to arrive somewhere and to have no-one to call, no-one wanting to know if I had arrived safely. By now I had grown used to not contacting Inessa, for fear of undoing any safety she had secured for herself. I felt unable to contact my father too, as I couldn't bring myself to accept why he had not done more to protect us as children. Although the hostess at the residence was warm towards me, I also knew that the smiles that ushered me into this room existed purely while I had a function to serve. I saw that once I stepped off the narrow precipice of hospitality afforded me as a Principal, I was utterly alone.

I opened one of my shoe boxes, in which I kept my most cherished possessions. They were all photos of people I had known in St Petersburg, along with the odd faded photo from my youth. I saw that almost all of my memories related to my work; that for me there was no life without it. I realised then that I had to learn to open up, to overcome my suspicions and move on.

I continued to unpack, but then gave up and looked out of the window at the city. In the evening light it appeared hunched, cautious, like the rest of the world – a shell that I couldn't work out how to prise open. It was then that a new fear set in, a fear you would see when you first saw me dance a couple of days later. I feel that what happened after somehow belongs to you.

But where was I before I plunged back into my childhood, and the journey that brought me to England? Yes, I remember now. I was in your sheets, nuzzled against you, only hours after our first date had begun, with my first performance as a Principal dancer only four days away.

Erin had danced exquisitely on the opening night of *Giselle*; however, her second lead performance suffered after the arrival of Alina. It was remarkable how much impact the weight someone's intention could have. Although Alina never said that she was pursuing the lead role, her every movement and expression implied that she was. As a result, by the third night she had been promoted to the role of Myrtha, Queen of the Wilis. Personally, I felt there could not have been a more fitting role for her to play, as Queen Myrtha has to be cold, aloof and resolute – no matter what. Even when men beg for leniency she has to still command her legion of female spirits to dance them to their death. Something told me Alina would be able to do this.

Although this casting made for a great performance, it also meant that as my first Principal performance approached, I became increasingly unsettled. She seemed to represent the ghost of anxiety from my early days at the Mariinsky. In her determination to prove herself a more worthy lead, she also represented the ghost of potential failure. It amazed me how fate could blend all my fears into one person.

During her final performance alongside Erin, Alina terrified me in ways that I could not have envisaged. On stage she was a dark, commanding force of nature. She conveyed the drama of the role by completely embodying it. As she danced men to their death it seemed she was acting not as a result of her own will, but as an agent of nature, as a pawn in a game that she had been unwittingly cast in. I began to fear that I would find it too overpowering to fulfil the demands of my role alongside her. I began to dread the scene in which I would beg her to spare the life of the man I loved, resisting her demand that I join the Wilis. I feared it would not only be the ultimate test of my ability, but the ultimate test of my character too.

I feared people like Alina, because I was jealous of their surety. I was reminded of her powerful confidence on Erin's final night in the lead role. During it, Erin looked completely overpowered by her, despite her usually unshakeable veneer, struggling to find her composure in the key scenes. On stage Alina ruthlessly asserted her presence, to the point that when Erin's Giselle resisted the Wilis it seemed an act of mercy on the part of Myrtha, rather than a triumph. I saw this, but more importantly Michael, and the audience, saw it too. I knew that if an established Principal like Erin could be unsettled by Alina, then one such as me could be completely dismantled.

Following Erin's second performance, young Eva was due to take the role of Giselle in the following show. But after Alina's dominating performance, Michael pulled Eva to one side.

'I am sorry,' he said, 'but it is my job to respond to what I see on stage. I have to be sensitive to who is on form. You will not be playing Giselle tomorrow night, Eva. Alina will.' And with that, Eva had suddenly lost her opportunity to play the ultimate role in ballet.

Although this only gave Alina one night as Giselle, with my two nights following consecutively on, I knew she would not relinquish the lead without a fight. That evening, I could only watch helplessly as Alina's performance commanded the stage. Any hopes I had that the dramatic demands of the role would be too much for her were not borne out. In the first act, she played a Giselle who was whiter than white, brutally ravaged by deceit. As the ghostly Giselle in act two she was spectral and yet formidable too. Eva was cast, malevolently perhaps, as Myrtha. Whereas Alina had been imperious in this role, Eva had no such surety. Alina's presence rendered everyone else as mere supporting fodder. It felt somehow violating to see Alina dance the role I was born to do, on the night before I was due to play it. I had no choice but to put my heart and soul into rehearsals the following day, to prove that I was still worthy of the role. But Alina did all she could to prevent me having my moment.

It was a Sunday, and the stress of it being the final leg of the tour was starting to show, but Alina's appetite for success seemed unaffected. She flirted with Michael, she hogged the floor, and she disrupted my sequences by laughing. I desperately hoped that my hard work would allow Michael to still think me as worthy of dancing Giselle, and that these tricks would not be enough to prevent me having my turn.

During those two days of practice, Michael seemed deeply contemplative, his focus switched constantly between Alina and me. For him, this was a quandary of the highest order. The theatre had only recently been re-opened, and it was essential that the company constantly garner the best reviews. The shows were sold out each night, but a dip in form would affect demand for the next season.

The personal importance of playing this role was beyond question. It would symbolise to me the possibility of triumph over doubt, failure, and even darkness. And so I approached that opening night like a warrior, ready to fight to the death. And in Alina, all of my adversaries – real or abstract, past or present – were captured in one person.

You once said that there is nothing more solitary than the act of creativity, but based on my own experiences I would take that sentiment ever further. I would say there is nothing more solitary than the act of achievement. That night, as I prepared for the first time in the brightly lit Principal's dressing room,

I felt completely alone. Though the room was festooned with flowers, I knew that at that moment their presence was entirely cosmetic. Michael had not confirmed the role was mine, but he had not confirmed a change in the casting either.

I knew that under the circumstances, when I went on stage I would feel more isolated than ever. Fighting tides of fear, wave by wave as they battered like the relentless movements of the Wilis. No-one would have a kind or comforting word to whisper in my ear as I took to the stage. Now, at the pinnacle of my achievement, I would have to draw from wells of strength that others did not know existed. That night, people would expect me to be the commanding presence. Alone on that stage, there would be no pause for corrections. If I made a mistake, I would be more visible than ever, under the brutal glare of the lights and the myriad eyes of the audience. If there were any small gaps in my performance, Alina would be there to pull them into gaping holes. And if I was to keep the role for another night, I would need to learn the precise whereabouts of my resources for the moment I needed them.

Although I feared I would be tested to my limit, I didn't yet know where my limit was. In the opening act, I was all too briefly the wide-eyed country girl, sprightly and innocent. In the scenes when Albrecht courted me, my heart went so readily to him. I danced as if buoyed by love; I tried to feel untrammelled by doubt. Dancing became an act of seduction, exactly as it was always intended to be. I was dancing to show him my vitality, how young I was, how I had saved myself for him. At that moment I fully believed that those aspects would capture him, and yet my sense of darkness never felt very far away. That being the case, I was still surprised by the sudden pang I felt in the scene where I learnt that Albrecht was engaged. Her other suitor, Hilarion, shows Giselle the badge on Albrecht's sword and at this moment Giselle is required to suddenly unravel. In that instant something in me unhinged. I suddenly felt very aware of all the women who had danced this role, and how they too had expressed the way it spoke to them. I felt as if I was summarising the pain of all women whose love had been rejected for one more worldlier, more sophisticated than her, the sickening moment when you see how purity counts for nothing. This was the altar on which young desire was recklessly destroyed, and as I danced on it I felt the pain pour out of me. Somehow, I was able to make public the private acts of humiliation I had felt in my past. In dancing to capture my own pain at that moment I expressed it, with total clarity, in front of all of those people. You were not there that night, Noah, and my awareness of that made the experience even more acute, because I knew that you would only get to see me dance as Giselle if I got this right. At the end of that first act, when I died from a broken heart, part of me was glad that you were not there to see it. It felt all too real. I felt the weight of experience bludgeon my twenty-four year old shoulders. I was all too aware, from the bottom of my heart, of how the world worked. That events do not go to plan but you soldier on, maintain your steely smile, and hope no-one has noticed your mistakes. Even when you know that they have seen it all, and that you have probably already lost. I had not made a mistake yet, but I dreaded the moment I would. As I withered on stage, and died from a broken heart, I was grieving at the thought of what would happen when Alina came on stage. And as act one ended, and the applause roared in my ears, there were tears in my eyes. I was already grieving for my inevitable demise.

In the second act, I came on stage as Giselle's spirit, awoken by Albrecht's love as he visits her grave. In this new persona I felt strangely calm, as if I had already lost in having had my heart broken. Albrecht returned to the grave to proclaim his love, his arms brimming with flowers. Then came the haunting *pas de deux*, where I forgave him for his deception. My partner was gentle, searching and receptive. I remembered how, as a teenage girl, I had sometimes wondered if it was possible to express a love that reached far beyond the day-to-day world we live in. In the intervening years I had never learnt if it was possible to do so, though I had suspected it was. Now I had to do it in front of all these people. I suspected that I would have to go beyond the limits of physical endurance in order to succeed.

The beauty of this dance was overshadowed by my awareness of the impending moment I had been dreading. The sharp stabs of music from the orchestra, which herald the arrival of the Wilis, headed by the brutal, uncompromising form of Alina. From where I was positioned on stage, it looked as if her narrow eyes had turned black.

The orchestra trilled and in a flood of movement the Wilis surrounded me. I experienced them as a whirl of white, their small wings flickering manically. My initial resistance of them was not dramatic, but very real. I tried to come to my senses, and remember the role I had to play. First of all I had to resist their insistence that I join them, and then I had to prevent them from dancing my lover to death. I suddenly had to summon all my strength to protect Albrecht from their fatal influence. I looked over at Alina, more severe, commanding and dominant than I had ever feared she'd be. From the stalls it would not have been possible to absorb the look of sheer ruthlessness that she shot me on stage. With a sharp wave of her hand she ordered the Wilis to dance my lover to death, and when I implored her to have mercy she did not even meet my gaze, did not even register I was there. I lay flowers at her feet, begging for her benediction, all the time knowing it was useless, like trying to speak to a hurricane. And then the music started, signalling the moment that I would need to dance to save my lover's life.

I felt too weakened, too chastened to dance, and at first I moved sluggishly. I suddenly sensed in Alina's eyes a look of dark triumph. The dancer playing Albrecht looked over at me, for a second moving out of time as he implored me to start dancing with his hands. And so slowly, far too slowly, I met Alina's eye. This was my moment to fight back, and at my first flourish I was sharper even than the orchestra. I visibly saw her retract in shock. And then, as I danced amongst the Wilis, begging each of them in turn, my strength started to build. I circled Albrecht, as if trying with mere movement to seal him from their bitter influence. I danced for my life. At the tip of the stage Alina looked nonchalant, as if at most she was bored by my insolence. Her refusal to respond to my movements, even in character, seemed brutally personal. As the orchestra built, I suddenly felt as if I had broken through a wall, and was able to command the stage. I realised I had already been crushed, a long time ago, and for that I was now unbeatable. I had nothing to fear. I simply had to persevere with it, endure the pressure of the moment and see it through. I thought I could hear Bruna laughing, but in the moment I supressed that sound I felt myself begin to triumph.

My movements stopped being emotional and became poised, precise, as if I was resolute in my convictions. For much of the second act Giselle has to stay *en pointe*, and summoning all my strength I was able to do this as if it was now the only way I knew how to move. My spins were quick, sharp. I felt no pain; it was as if bodily concerns were now beneath me. I had wanted to play this role for so long that I suddenly embodied it with ease. It was a relief to be Giselle, to be beyond even the reach of death. I looked over to Alina, as the sheer force of my presence rescued Albrecht, and I saw for the first time that she was merely a woman playing a role. She hadn't found a blueprint of herself as Myrtha, she wasn't tracing the path of her destiny through playing that character. Aware of what this moment meant to me, I was finally able to see and overcome what she represented. And with that realisation, I had finally vanquished her.

As the orchestra faded, the audience detonated with applause. In that glorious second I found that it was suddenly all over. I had just danced as Giselle. I remember how the applause roared in our ears, and Alina looked over at me with an expression I had not seen her have before. Albrecht and I took to the stage as flowers rained down upon us. The audience rose from their seats, the lights illuminated us, and we both basked in the moment. I couldn't help but smile.

The audience's fervour was such that we came back for eight curtain calls. And you may be surprised to hear this, Noah, but for once I did not shy away from enjoying it. I had been so immersed in getting it right that I had never thought of the sheer elation I would feel if I managed it. I had considered, in intricate detail, what it would be like to fail – but never this. I felt every part of my soul sing with delight, because deep down I knew that nothing could affect this moment of triumph. I had faced my own legion of personal demons, and beaten them. When it had seemed that I could no longer resist the forces of darkness, I had just continued to dance until they were finally overcome. As I retreated from the stage, I knew that I had guaranteed myself a second night in the role, when you would be there to see me. A second night that would be mine to enjoy.

When I stepped into the wings, Michael seized my arm. He held my left cheek in the cup of his hand.

'Astounding,' he said. 'Simply astounding.' I looked around to see the *corps de ballet* beside him, all still slightly breathless, jumping up to applaud me. In my dressing room as I sat amongst the huge bed of flowers, I didn't recognise the slim woman in the mirror with the huge smile on her face. I picked through the lush array of flowers and couldn't help looking for one signed with your name. I found a bunch of snow-white lilies, with 'See you tomorrow, N' scrawled on the attached card. I felt ecstatic. Ecstatic and tired.

My last night as Giselle was an entirely different proposition. Having got it right once, I'd alleviated most of the pressure. I even enjoyed the brief rehearsal that morning. Alina was far less competitive, having seemingly acknowledged that she had had her moment. In practice, Michael was softer, as if not wanting to upset whatever alchemy had induced the last performance. After Alina, Erin and Eve had gone home, Michael and I stayed on to fine tune a couple of moves. And then it was time to sleep, in a home that felt more comfortable than ever.

By the closing night, my body was starting to rebel. It had grown intemperate during the sustained rigours I had put it through on tour, and I took a couple of painkillers before the performance. There were queues around the block to see my final show, and even with the spirited ticket bartering, many were left disappointed.

Hearing the clamour outside my dressing room, I felt like a true ballerina for the first time. Dabbing on makeup, I now fully understood the aesthetics and demands of the job. I knew that I could draw from something personal to make the role dramatic, and I knew I had trained so hard technically that I could fulfil those requirements too. That night, charged with success perhaps, I felt ready for the life of a dancer. Alina, once so aggressive and attention-seeking in her dancing, was calmer, more generous, and my Albrecht was devoted and loving to the end. I decided to be more sensuous, more assured. My heartbreak was perhaps slightly more aesthetic at the end of the first act, and I kept something back for myself. I simply could not go through that torrid heartbreak in quite the same way again. But wanting to imbue the second night with something special, in the second act I imagined Noah that you were Albrecht. It was at the close of the first act, just before the spiral into madness that I saw you, sat just on the edge of the orchestra pit. The idea came to me then. And when the curtain rose for the second time, I imagined that you and I were Giselle and Albrecht dancing. Of course, I did not know at the time how much that dance would represent what would happen between us. I had only just overcome the intoxicating challenges of the role, and at that moment I would not have had the strength to even begin to fight the spectres that were about to encroach on me. But I had seen in you someone like me, fighting for something that they suspected was a lost cause. As Albrecht grieved over the death of someone he lost through his own betrayal, I too felt that you would grieve over something you'd lost – the hope of a nourishing love perhaps. The piece seemed to predict not only my future sufferings but yours as well. As Giselle danced to save him from death I felt I too was dancing to give you hope. I felt as if I had risen from the grave, the grave of silence that I had long buried myself in. And when my dancing had finally fought off the spirits, and saved you from death, I shot you a glance. How, through the dance, I became able to map out our lives, is beyond me. I had searched out this medium as a way to create something that resonated in time, and somehow I had succeeded. When, at the finale, I felt I had overcome those obstacles I wanted you to see that it was possible. The look you returned seemed to acknowledge that it was. And yet we could never have spoken of this strange and secret dialogue. How could we ever have possessed the tools by which to do so?

I wondered if you had seen what I was privately doing up there in front of all those people. The strange and mysterious dialogue I was undertaking with my past and my future. Only art can allow us such vague and resonant interactions. That night I didn't dance to seduce you, I danced to save you. And I did not yet know it, but the act of saving you would herald the moment the season ended, thereby bringing to a close a difficult but triumphant chapter in my life.

Love,

Yelena

Dear Noah,

How could you worry that I might have felt overwhelmed by your last letter? You needn't ever think that your interest in my life could seem excessive. I had never been able to thaw out the frozen river inside me for anyone before I met you, but now that I have it is all there for your consumption, Noah. And besides, you know how the details of your life fascinate me.

I remember that when *Giselle* finished you went out of your way to collect all the press cuttings you could find from my two nights. Every time we met you seemed to have another one. I didn't recognise the pale woman in the photos, she looked like a frightened fawn from a fairy tale, her body barely covered by a white tutu. I was keen to put that chapter of my life behind me, as a triumph I could recall if I wanted to. I couldn't help but be reminded of it intermittently though. After all, you insisted on quoting the articles whenever you could. A favourite of yours was *The Observer: Yelena Brodvich was born to play Giselle. Her performance was a triumph.* And you'd always follow the quote by saying, 'He's never given *me* notices like that. Or even at all.'

I remember my last morning at the studio, yes. It brought to an end one era and heralded the start of another, one that would offer challenges that I could not have foreseen. *Giselle* had just ended and that morning, for the first time, the studio seemed like a playground to me. It always surprised me that you found that studio such an evocative place. To me that glass panelled building simply represented work. That building represented the ultimate challenge to me because not only was it where I had honed Giselle, but it was also where I first struggled to connect with the dancers in my company. At first it felt as if a desert stretched out between them and me, a desert where language, culture, idealism and temperament floundered. And yet the desert did not only exist on that plane, it existed too on the endless expanse of the dance floor.

When I first began training there the sheer vacancy of the dance floor overwhelmed me, but it is only with fire, passion and a loss of the ego that one can emerge from them with dignity. Self-consciousness is no longer important when you are on the dance floor. Do you feel self-conscious when you write? It occurs to me how similar an empty dance floor is to a blank page, both wait lethargically for someone to come and ignite them. They are often brutal with their demands; although when those demands are dropped how wonderful it is to use that space as you wish. To write and to dance without purpose, simply because you enjoy being in the act. That was how I felt the day after Giselle ended.

The light from the high windows of that dancehall usually made the unblemished floor appear intimidating, but that day the luminescence excited me. The light now marked out parameters of possibility; how exhilaratingly wide they seemed. That day, for the first time in my life, I danced out of sheer pleasure. I'm glad you were there to be a part of this new chapter of my life.

I see now how accustomed you already were to that world, even without having visited it. There is an imperceptible gulf that dancers and writers traverse when they begin to work. With their head down, mute to the indifference of the world, throwing themselves into a task without a thought for themselves. They often fail, and they often fall down. They smear their sheets and kick at the air in protest. And then they stand on the precipice again and wait to leap across a divide that many don't know exists. The last we see of them, as they brace themselves for the fall, is the final moment when they gather themselves before diving once again. Every time, blindly trusting they can make something beautiful out of their next descent.

It was Erin's birthday, and the studio was empty except for her, Michael and me. The July heat made the air outside the studio shimmer, and the surrounding city became beguiling and enticing. The vast, metal doors to the studio were open and you were stood outside, leafing through your red notebook, and as I approached, I could hear the strains of OutKast's *Miss Jackson*. I greeted you with a kiss. You and Michael conferred, his hand on your shoulder as Erin turned the music up. I stripped down and began to dance.

That was the summer Erin introduced me to R&B. I instantly loved that sensual, glacial music, perfect for nights of cocktails and flirtation. That morning Erin taught me how to bump and grind to Justin Timberlake, and Michael laughed at the sight of two Principal ballerinas dancing like that. Erin taught me how to grind my hips, the two of us dancing to the rolling, melodic music until our bodies were covered in a sheen of sweat. We had the whole summer ahead of us, and we couldn't stop giggling.

'If you like this sort of music,' she said, 'then there's a club you must come to tonight.'

'I'd love to,' I said.

Afterwards I came over to embrace you, surprised that you didn't blanch at my shining, panting body. My hair was pinned above my head, and one leg of my tracksuit was rolled up around my thigh. 'She's not bad, your girl,' Erin said. 'Are you coming out tonight for my birthday too?'

'Of course,' you answered.

That night, I was able to enjoy the city for the first time. I had seen how, as the weekend approached, the city built a unique melody. By Friday the girls were in their finest dresses, and the streets were throbbing in one lilting song. It swam around the city walls, and I so badly wanted to discover the source of that sound.

We all met at a faux-exotic bar, on a roof garden high above the city. It seemed full of painted mouths, lustrous plants and elegant limbs. As I arrived, it occurred to me that some people lived their whole lives in places like this. My life had so far demanded I move from one precise venture to the next, never pausing to enjoy an atmosphere.

Erin, Eva and I were in our best summer dresses, and we headed out to toast the end of the season. We'd knocked back a few shots by the time I saw you moving towards the bar. Your friend Nick was at your side, and you were laughing as you met my eye. This would be the first time I would see you in your element, as a creature of the night. I saw the way you gripped Nick's arm as you laughed with him, just like you were brothers. I saw the way you effortlessly moved amongst all the women greeting you at the bar. How keen they were to be draped over you, photographed with you. How readily they laughed at any humorous intonation in what you said. Erin nudged me as Nick made his way over to us, with you just behind him.

'My friend Noah claims that he knows you girls,' he said. 'And that it would be alright if we sat with you. But if he's lying we can easily go somewhere else.'

'Well, there isn't much room here,' I said, trying not to smile.

Nick turned round. 'Noah, she says she doesn't know who you are.' He turned back to me. 'I'm sorry, he does this all the time.'

You came past him, laughing as you kissed me on the cheek. 'Yelena, this is my friend Nick. Nick, Yelena is a ballerina from the Ukraine. Yelena, Nick is an idiot. And a film maker.'

'You're a ballerina? How interesting,' Nick said. 'How long have you been in England?'

I remember that you and I kept our eyes locked on each other as I answered. Soon he had caught Erin's attention, and he started to untie balloons from nearby moorings, to offer her as birthday presents.

I felt your arm curl through mine. 'Are you relieved now that it's all over?'

'I am. It's kind of strange,' I said. 'For the first time in my life I feel I can really let my hair down.'

'Starting from tonight,' you said, with a smile.

As the people swirled around us, you kept your attention focused on me. You asked where I had found the distinctive silver ring I wore on my right hand, and I told you that Inessa had bought it for me just before I left home, and I hoped it was the first step in us growing closer again after our childhood, how we had grown more comfortable with each other once she started working with my Uncle Leo. I told you my plans, of where I wanted to travel, of how I wanted to be a choreographer one day when all this physical work was no longer required of me. I remembered wishing all my intentions were like yours, sharp as arrows, apparent to anyone present. As we talked, I finally felt like the woman people had always described me as. I had never recognised her in my own self-image before, but your attention made it all fit.

'Where are we going tonight then?' Erin asked, over the music. 'The club won't get going until half eleven at the earliest.'

'I'm having a few friends over for a party at mine,' Nick said. 'We've just finished wrapping a film I was working on so we thought we'd have a few celebratory drinks. And with you three also having a cause for celebration as well I'm thinking…' He weaved his fingers together, biting his bottom lip.

'Sounds lovely,' I said.

'Are you sure your housemates won't object to you inviting

a group of ballerinas along?' Eva asked.

'I mean it's not something we'd usually tolerate, but it's an important night for you three so I'm sure we can make concessions,' Nick said with a smile.

'You're so kind,' Erin said.

A few cocktails later, our strange group raucously wound its way down to Nick's house. Erin already had her arm around Nick, who had tied a balloon onto each of her tiny wrists. I remember her trying to stop him from doing the same to her ankles.

'I really think you should let me,' he continued, as she tried to stop laughing for long enough to fend him off her feet. 'Wouldn't it be great to just float into the party? Then my housemates really won't mind you being there.'

'She only weighs about four stone,' I called. 'Any more balloons and she'll float away.'

'Then she can go ahead of us, and tell everyone we're on our way,' Nick called back. Erin slapped him as he pretended to write out a note to tuck into her ankle bracelet, as if she was some sort of balletic carrier pigeon.

As we ascended a small flight of stone steps I saw that Nick's home was not the bohemian out-house I had assumed it would be. I looked up to see an elegant townhouse, its large windows filled with vague silhouettes. The sound of laughter and chinked wine glasses filtered down as your arm linked through mine. I could hear New Order's *Temptation* playing above us. When Nick opened the door he was greeted with a welcoming roar as we sidled in behind him. 'You go out for a pint and then you come back with a group of supermodels,' someone commented, as we removed our coats. 'We should have known.'

Upstairs, the chic furniture had been pushed against the walls, and the place seemed filled with the city's wildlife. They sprawled over couches, blew smoke through opened windows and flirted self-consciously with each another. The girls all seemed curiously doll-like, dressed in printed dresses; their dark hair held back with silver clips. The boys wore checked shirts, their high quiffs bobbed as they laughed and their lips were constantly pursed, ready to roll the next cigarette.

You moved into them with such ease. 'This is Yelena,' you said, to everyone who smiled at you. As people welcomed me with open arms and sloshed wine into my glass I felt myself open. I quickly learnt how to sip at wine while my eyes vaguely scanned the room, just as they all did when they weren't speaking. I learnt how to draw decadently from a proffered cigarette, how to touch up my lipstick while simultaneously talking, how to look up with cherubic eyes at any man who spoke to me. I saw the way people responded to me, and to fit the implicit expectations of their treatment I became more elegant and more composed. I learnt to take compliments, to smile benignly, to detach at will. I did not stop to think how a new, seductive persona might invite complications. Cameras flashed, their owners each time imploring us to bunch together. As each photo captured us I felt more startled, yet somehow calmer. My presence was in demand for the first time, and it felt good.

'So, how do you two know one another?' Nick asked, refilling my lipstick-tinged glass.

'Noah started coming to watch us practice while he was researching his next book, and then at the opening party we got chatting.'

'And has he told you that he's a famous writer? That he's kind of a big deal?'

You looked frustrated, and shook your head.

I laughed. 'I worked it out for myself. He was no help.'

'Have you read his book?'

'I haven't read his book, no,' I said, directing the remark to you. 'Is it any good?'

You cocked your head, and looked blank.

'It's hard for me to say exactly, because I still don't really understand it. Well, I don't understand how a book about a modern messiah living on a council estate in Holloway could get published when it was written by an author who's clearly never been anywhere near a council estate.'

'I have been near a council estate,' you insisted.

'Russian ones don't count,' he answered.

'I didn't think it'd get published,' you said.

'Neither did I,' Nick answered. 'It's pretty depressing, but then all half-decent books probably are. I liked the bit when the messiah called people to his house via a link on Youtube. What did he say again?' Nick adopted a grand pose and a haughty tone. 'Guttersnipes, underdogs, dreamers of the nation. Boys in satellite towns, girls waylaid at minor train stations. Flock to me and I'll shield you all, under my damaged wing.'

I laughed. You were still looking down.

'I liked that bit. Shall we turn the music up?' he asked, registering your embarrassment.

The room swelled until it was so humid, so fleshy, that it could not incorporate another body. At that moment the music was cut and Nick made an announcement. 'Edna and Rupert next door have asked that we cease and desist. I think that's reasonable. So we're going to The End.'

As one straggling procession, the party made its way up to the nightclub. From the outside it looked like nothing more than a black door amongst a row of indie shops. But as we walked up those stairs the vibrant music from within reached our ears, and I felt adrenalin course through me. At the top, a woman with pink and green hair greeted you with a kiss and ushered us to the front of the twitching queue. It gave me a guilty thrill to pass the assembled throng, and as the inner doors opened the music instantly ensnared our bodies, making us part of a single mass. The club was one long rectangle full of nylon dresses, coiffed hair and shining stilettos. You placed a hand at the small of my back as we started dancing.

The noise and the proximity forcefully encouraged physical expression. All around us people moved from being strangers to being confidantes in one quick, physical negotiation.

Every few seconds another woman – usually flamboyantly dressed – greeted you with a cry of delight and kissed both of your cheeks. They were all quirky and beautiful, and as you cupped hands over each other's ears I wondered how intimately you knew each of them. Their sticky goodbyes, with their fingertips clinging to yours, suggested that you'd been close to all of them. That and the way they only looked at me for a millisecond, with a flash of a smile, as you introduced me. I told myself to keep drinking and not question how you knew every woman in here. I gradually grew familiar with the dull pain I felt every time you spoke and their mouths erupted with laughter. I thought of their faces twisting in pleasure as you found yourself inside their long, shining bodies. But then the thought would be crushed by a huge whoop from the crowd as a beloved song began, causing every hand to push instantly into the air. And you'd take my hand, spin me in a pirouette, and kiss my cheek.

After many clammy dances and cigarettes on the fire escape, you finally led me back down those stairs. It must have been about four in the morning, and only then did I wonder where Erin and Nick had gone. I didn't recognise the voice that came out of my mouth as we staggered outside. I sounded like one of your women: vulgar, confident, only interested in the next buzz. For a moment I wondered if I was being moulded into someone, and if so where that might take me. But as we left the alleyway you held me still and kissed me, and I felt myself calm. I was glad to leave the urgent desperation of the dance floor. It seemed to cover everyone in a sheen of denial, which I knew would stay on them long after they left.

You took me down to the quayside. Now devoid of people, it seemed to persist in a state of shock. The lights from the city, yellow and red, quivered on the water. Silence emanated from the houses around us, settling our insides. We sat on the small artificial beach, enclosed by rope, above the water. It was almost too dark to see one another, and until the first light of morning we built castles out of the damp, soft sand. Once they were made I placed my head on your shoulder I closed my eyes, only opening them when the sun began to rise.

We sat for a few moments in silence, watching the city return to us. Then you led me back along the road, before raising your hand at a lone taxi.

Love,

Yelena

Dear Noah,

In the weeks that followed I enjoyed complete freedom for the first time in my life. The day always began when morning light fell against the blinds in your room. It started as a shaft of white that lit up my side of the bed, before gradually crawling over the rest of the room, lighting up the piles of books and all the discarded clothes. Having clung to one another all night we'd reluctantly separate, and you'd stagger off to the university to give your morning lecture.

Do you remember how you used to always hurry back for me? I'd be awoken by the clatter of your keys on the table and the sound of your coat falling to the floor. As you bustled into the room I'd sleepily pull my hair from my eyes. The sound of your belt unbuckling would always fill me with excitement as you slipped into the sheets beside me. I'd help you ease off your trousers, conscious of my creased appearance but excited by the intimacy that would follow. You'd let out a small sigh of relief as you pressed against me, kissing me as if you hadn't seen me in days. I'd prise myself from the sheets and lay on my back, wriggling as you rolled my panties from my hips. And then I'd sigh loudly at your audacity, as you first kissed my neck and then eased yourself carefully inside me. Our hands would clamour over each other's backs, our eyes would widen, and your hand would gently press over my mouth so the neighbours didn't hear us. We'd grasp each other joyously in our moment of release, before curling our arms around each other through the few minutes of calm.

I saw what a fine instrument my body had become, honed by years of discipline. Slowly I learnt to see it as more than a medium of expression. You showed me that my body was mine, and therefore ready to issue pleasure at any moment. Every second of pain it had experienced had refined it for every second of pleasure now. I gradually learnt to use the skills I had gained to give us both pleasure, and by enjoying my body for the first time with you an unassailable bond was forged between us. I feared the consequences of entering this bind – would it only resonate on a physical level with you?

It shocked me to learn that I had unwittingly possessed such abilities for so long. In those secretive, rapturous mornings we created an atmosphere of intimacy and decadence so potent that I knew we could step in and out of it at will. We started to map out with one another all the desires that we had long kept within ourselves. I realised that within us all there exists a crystalline, half-buried world of desire that can only be completely excavated if we meet the right person. It had been buried so deeply in me that it was almost irretrievable. I grew to love the decadent thrill of absenting yourself from the world and taking desire to its very extremes. On those excitable, urgent mornings we fully excavated those half-buried worlds. We learnt how to kiss and goad one another, how to delay and how to enthral. I learnt how satisfying it felt to allow another to find the root of their desire in you, expressed through the simple undulations of your body. I learnt how it felt to be so urgently desired that your mere presence became all that another could experience until they had finally found satisfaction.

It was not only physical intimacy that I came to enjoy. When we would lie in the sheets afterwards we slowly began to open up to each other, revealing the many zones we had kept hidden inside. In the past I had wondered how much one can endure before they're no longer able to speak openly again. At what point the cynicism and caution, cultivated by pain, becomes too stifling. I thought I had long passed that point. I didn't know that the shadow of caution could always be dispelled. It simply required the right person.

The closer we grew, the more I sensed that there was something important that you were holding back from me. It was apparent in the way that you always cradled your head on your fist and focused the conversation on me. And one morning, when you had been particularly evasive, I decided this needed to be addressed.

You had mentioned Elizabeth before, as the last woman you had called your girlfriend. I'd also heard the name Hannah mentioned a couple of times, but I had never enquired about her further. That morning I felt we were at the point where such names could become uncharted territory, but I also feared the impact of finding out something I did not want to know.

You were half out of the bed, perhaps trying to escape my apparent resolve, when I asked the question.

'Who's Hannah?'

You dropped your shirt and turned to face me. 'Have I not told you?' you replied, reclining on the pillow beside me. 'Hannah is my daughter.'

'Your daughter?'

'Yes.' You looked apologetic, suddenly vulnerable. 'She's five years old. I had her with Elizabeth.'

'You had her with Elizabeth?'

You lay flat on the bed, looked squarely at me. 'Somehow, I thought you knew. I'm sorry. We should have talked about it before.'

'I know,' I said.

'I was… I don't know.'

'I know,' I said.

You smiled, awkwardly. Then I smiled back, as if that could restrain the huge tension I'd felt suddenly arise in me. I feared that if this revelation did not knock me over now then it might do at a later date. I remember that for some reason I couldn't even look at you. I started fiddling with the blinds, all the time feeling your eyes on the side of my face, narrow with concern. As if you knew exactly how painful this conversation was for me.

'I'm still good friends with Elizabeth,' you said. 'Just friends though. I see Hannah every weekend – well every weekend that I'm in the country.'

You moved closer, and placed your hand on my cheek. My face must have grown cold, because your hand felt hot and heavy.

'How do I not know this?' I said, struggling to meet your eye.

'I know. You should know it all by now. Elizabeth and I dated for a couple of years after university. I met her as a student. In retrospect we were not as careful as we should have been. By the time she learnt she was pregnant we had broken up. To be frank, I didn't handle the whole situation well at all. In fact I was a coward. But I've gradually adjusted to being a father, and Elizabeth's been very patient with me.'

I tried to look composed. I knew that you could see this struggle – the slight withdrawal of something in my flesh when you reached out to me.

'I've been waiting for the right time to properly explain,' you finally said.

'You kept it from me,' I answered.

'It's not that. But – I should have told you sooner.'

'Yes.'

I forced myself to keep it together. This doesn't have to be a problem, I thought. You don't own him; he's only been with you for a matter of weeks. I looked up at you and smiled. But you couldn't quite smile back.

The truth is, part of me was devastated, and I knew you could see that. This felt like a sudden, deep wound that could easily become infected. I knew I had much to be grateful for in having met you, and I decided instead to try and dwell on that.

A few days later you asked if I would like to meet them, and when I said yes some of my excitement was genuine. I wish that I had been more aware of my state of mind when I agreed to that so soon. Dancing Giselle had taken a huge amount of endurance and discipline, and all that pressure had suddenly released the moment the final curtain fell.

I didn't know then that when a vat of pressure is released from one chamber in the brain then it must be replaced by something else; it cannot remain a vacuum. Now that part of my mind had been relieved of a certain presence it needed to replace it with something. It was happening as inevitably as autumn slides into winter.

Just as we had opened onto one another, we similarly began to open onto the city. We had found out how to live intimately with another, and then through the city we found out how we wanted to live. Although you always had an extroverted side, it was only with my accompaniment that you were able to finally live there as you had always wanted to.

Both of us, suddenly emboldened, took to the city with a ravenous hunger. I saw that you were now able to hone your appearance so you could dress how you had always wanted to. It was as if with me at your side, you were confident enough to step out of your shadows. In the past I had always rejected outfits that clung to my figure. But now for the first time I felt able to embrace my attributes. A dress was no longer something I had to live up to, if anything it became a container for my exuberance. I fashioned my hair into a modern style that I had seen in magazines. I began to never leave the house without a flash of red lipstick and a sharp pair of heels. I even allowed you to occasionally buy me jewellery, when we saw something in a shop window that I took a fancy to. You encouraged this development, but for some reason I felt sure that it had emanated from me.

I learnt that I had fully emerged from my cocoon one night when we entered a bar together. I had on a chocolate coloured fur coat, to go with my new hairstyle. Nick was sat in the bar with some friends, and I saw the way they all turned to look at me as we drew near. That had never happened before.

'Noah,' Nick said, rising to greet you. 'You haven't even ironed your shirt. You simply do not deserve to have this beautiful woman all to yourself.' I laughed as his friends all roared in agreement. You dismissed them with a gesture, but I could see that you also looked a little proud. I got the slightest feeling that you wanted us to stay longer with them because of how well my presence reflected on you. It was not a feeling I had ever experienced before.

During the evenings we started going to concerts in the great hall that overlooked the river. I remember how precious I felt every time you proudly introduced me to some famous writer or journalist after the show. I felt ornate and exotic, because for the first time that was how I looked. At drinks parties, held in apartments high above the city, I finally started to carry myself as if I was something to be revered. When introduced to me, men stooped as they delicately kissed my hand. The other guests were inevitably decked in evening wear, their laughter laced with the inflections of the privileged. Yet I felt comfortable around them, and able to act aloof and bored like they did. But I was never bored, never for a second. I was enchanted by everything the city had to offer us. My new pose was seemingly not simply an act, but an elongation of my personality. At the parties and concerts, and as we flitted between the bars, it felt as if the two of us had been given the keys to the city. The famous writer and the accomplished ballerina, side by side, two sparkling new features on the skyline of the city.

Love from,

Yelena

Dear Noah,

I never told you that on the nights leading up to that dinner I repeatedly dreamt of Elizabeth. It happened the first time after I had returned to my flat to take a call about our next season. After all the rich experiences with you I felt cooled by the many pale planes of my room. But the phone call left me feeling very uncertain about many aspects of my life. As I lay in bed alone that night I tried to not let the questions engulf me. It was then that I had my first dream of Elizabeth.

My mind was moving at a lumbering pace; it felt intoxicated and nauseous. An image arose out of this fog – one of a singular eyelid, painted dark purple, which extended out to a long, curved eyelash. Panning back from this image I saw a woman, small and contained, who even in stasis possessed a distinct liveliness. She had long dark hair and an open, unguarded expression. There was a slight hint of mischief in her smile. She was sat at a small trestle table, upon which were placed several tumblers of whisky. They sparkled in the ochre light of the rather cluttered drawing room she was seated in. Panning back further, I saw that she was surrounded by five men, all of them gazing at her as they chatted amongst themselves. The smile that teased at her lips betrayed her pleasure at this usual turn of events. Considering her more carefully, I decided that she had a cultured, European air about her. Even without speaking she conveyed an aura of exoticism. She was wearing a caramel brown dress, and despite being only faintly made up she seemed very comfortable in her skin. As the dream continued the men drew in closer around her and she lay back on the chair. The chattering grew louder, with all the men turning to one another and loudly agreeing how desirable she was. The dream ended with the image of her smile, broadening slightly as the men drew in closer. The name Elizabeth was never mentioned, but I knew it was her.

When I met her in the Italian restaurant, she was exactly how I had imagined her. Perhaps a little less refined, a little less hidden. You and I were sat at the table by the window and when she came in she was holding Hannah's hand. As she smiled at us I remembered the fragment of a dream that had followed the scene of her with the five men. In it, I had seen her step onto the back of a motorcycle, still in the caramel dress, clasping her body against a handsome man as the bike roared to life. As the motorcycle had streaked past me, I had seen that the man driving it was you.

As they rounded the tables I saw Hannah properly for the first time. At that instant I realised that however close the two of us became, Elizabeth had still given you something more beautiful than I ever could. As they moved to the table I felt ridiculous and insignificant.

Before leaving your house I had fretted over my outfit, before eventually choosing a white dress with cream flowers faintly sewn into it. As she came to the table I saw that Elizabeth was also wearing a floral dress, but one bustling with rich red roses. Next to her I feared I would look drawn and lifeless, but your evident sudden happiness dispelled my negativity. As she greeted you, orange and yellow flames from the open kitchen torched the ceiling. Hannah turned and laughed at the spectacle as you kissed the side of her head. Then I kissed Elizabeth's cheek, her hand clasping momentarily on my shoulder. It gripped me, a little too tight. Over the years I had grown convinced that my aloofness protected me. But Elizabeth's air of instant intimacy made me question if that approach had been unnecessary.

Hannah wanted to look at the open kitchen, with all its bright and dancing flames.

'Darling, come and sit down,' Elizabeth said, taking her by the hand. 'We'll go and say hello to the chefs later.'

'You've promised now,' Hannah said, clambering onto her seat. She took a big sip from the glass of water you had waiting for her, before she gave in to your smile and scrambled over to hug you. You kissed her on the head again, and then placed her squarely onto your lap.

'Hannah, say hello to Yelena,' Elizabeth said, looking over the menu. 'Yelena is Noah's new girlfriend.'

'Are you an actress?' Hannah asked.

'She's a ballerina,' Elizabeth said.

'A ballerina,' Hannah repeated, chewing on her thumb.

'She'll worship you now,' Elizabeth said, flashing her eyes at me. 'She loves ballerinas.'

I smiled.

'Are you the Swan Queen?' Hannah asked.

'I was once,' I said.

'That's good,' she answered, vaguely.

'What was it this season?' Elizabeth asked. 'I'm sure I saw you in the papers.'

'She was Giselle,' Noah said.

'Giselle,' Elizabeth said, pronouncing it incorrectly. Noah smiled apologetically.

'I always wanted to be a ballerina,' she continued. 'It's one of those many things that I always felt was unachievable though.' She laughed, raised her eyebrows and began to flick through the menu.

'What do you do?' The nerves exaggerated my accent, and I felt Noah look at me from the side of his eyes.

'I mainly direct small, and very temporary arts festivals. Which basically means I pamper the egos of artists and pretend that I understand their work, even when it's just lots of photos of apples sat on cushions like it was today.'

'Is it paintings?' I asked.

'Often it is,' she replied, tearing off a strip of bread. 'And to be honest, I prefer it when it is because despite the… hokum I often have to sell, my love of paintings hasn't diminished. Which unfortunately means my flat is full of discarded paintings that are pretty much worthless. Noah will tell you.'

This reference to your shared past made me recall the second dream I'd had of Elizabeth, the night after. With you on top of her, pushing her onto the floor and tearing off her shirt, surrounded by paintings that were yet to be hung. After a few glasses of wine you'd spontaneously decided to try and to conceive a child that night, and as a result you were tearing into her with a ferocity that you'd never had for me.

In the dream I wanted to pull the two of you apart but I was unable to, it was as if I was watching this happen in a film. I couldn't stop the scene from playing out until the horror of it became so vivid that I suddenly woke up.

Hannah took my hand. 'Do you have to be so pretty to be a dancer?'

I laughed, and felt myself blush. 'It's not the most important thing.' I looked at Elizabeth. 'Not that I think I'm pretty.'

Elizabeth's features didn't move an inch.

'But you are pretty,' Hannah said. 'I want to be a ballerina when I'm tall enough, and if I can I want to dance as the Swan Queen.'

Elizabeth laughed. 'Then you will,' Noah said. 'Perhaps after dinner you can show Yelena your dancing, and she can see how good you are.'

Hannah's eyes widened.

'She'd like that,' Elizabeth said. I looked down at Hannah, and just couldn't help wishing she was mine. I sensed Elizabeth saw that look, and pitied me for it. I wondered if it was a look she had seen people have many times. Her eyes moved on to you.

'How's the book going?'

'Very slowly. I sometimes wish I hadn't chosen a ballerina for my main character.'

Elizabeth looked at me. She seemed poised to say something, then seemingly resisted it.

'Still, more enjoyable to write about than infanticide, I expect? It was particularly sensitive of Noah to write about that subject just after he'd become a father, Yelena.'

'The book really wasn't meant to be taken very seriously,' you responded.

'Well I can see why it was. It was very powerful.' She turned to address me. 'Noah is unnecessarily critical of his own talents,' she said, in a stage whisper. I noticed her long, navy-blue fingernails that were carefully varnished. They trailed gently down the side of the menu. 'You'll notice that yourself, I'm sure, when you give him your verdict on his new piece,' she said, not looking up.

I looked quizzically at you.

'Noah hasn't shown me any of his current work yet,' I said, very quietly. 'I would like him to though.'

For a second she looked at me coldly, but then the expression seemed to soften into one of pity again. I felt weak, but then reminded myself that I was a Principal ballerina now, and had not become one by being pitiful. I smiled faintly back at her.

'I think I might know why Noah hasn't shown you his current piece yet,' she said, with a small smile.

'Elizabeth – don't,' you responded.

'What do you mean?' I said.

'It's just a little joke.'

I looked at you. 'I haven't really had the chance to yet. What with you dancing Giselle,' you replied.

Elizabeth raised an eyebrow.

'What am I missing here?' I asked.

'It's nothing,' she continued. 'Something silly. It's just – I always agreed that I would only ever marry Noah if a book of his became a great success. And a few weeks ago he told me he was sure this one was going to be, and so he proposed.'

The air in the restaurant suddenly plunged to below zero. I'd suddenly lost the ability to speak. You dropped your glass of water, which hit the table with a muffled clatter. You closed your eyes, your head dropped. Hannah's became still, her eyes passing between Elizabeth and me.

'As a joke?' I asked.

Elizabeth looked momentarily at you, a little something playing on her lips. You looked at your glass, my eyes following yours as it slowly settled.

'A few weeks ago?' I continued.

Moving to assure me, you slowly placed your hand on top mine. But when I looked down, an icy shock passed through me as I saw that my fingernails were suddenly painted navy blue. I never painted my nails.

I gasped, and suddenly recalled my hand. A glass tinkled in the distance, and it felt deafening. 'Are you okay?' Elizabeth asked. And then, I suddenly remembered my third dream. From the previous night.

I had dreamt that you and Elizabeth were topless in bed, her head on your lap as you read your work to her. In one hand you held a sheaf of papers and with the other you were stroking the side of her face. The sudden recollection scalded me so viciously that I felt sure I would faint.

'Yelena?' you asked. 'It was just after you and I had met. We weren't dating yet. I – I got carried away, I felt so happy that it was going well.'

'You got carried away?' Elizabeth said, mimicking the fragile tone of your voice. 'Charming.' She looked at me. 'Knowing Noah, I wouldn't read too much into it.'

'I'm not allowed to read his work either,' Hannah said. Her voice came from a cavern miles away. Finally, my vision settled on Hannah. On her small, dark bob of hair and her wide, worried eyes.

'That's because Daddy's writing is for grown ups,' you said.

'Because it's filth,' Elizabeth whispered, before laughing brightly, and in that brief interval I regained myself.

'What's filth?' Hannah asked.

'It's what you have around your mouth, young lady. Now we're going to wipe your mouth, and then you're going to order your meal.'

I felt your eyes on me. I had no idea how obvious my flutter had been, but it was apparent that you at least had seen all of it. 'It is hot in here,' you said, as Elizabeth looked down at her menu.

'That's true,' I replied.

Elizabeth eyes stayed on the menu. Hannah's stayed on me. Your fingers clasped mine.

My fingernails were still painted blue.

I wished I had not chosen that dress to wear.

I wished that the room would settle.

I wished Elizabeth's eyes would move off my features, raking over them for every inch of a reaction. Suddenly I couldn't fight it a second longer.

With a loud clattering, which seemed to draw the attention of the entire restaurant, I found my feet. 'Excuse me for a moment,' I said.

You looked blank. Elizabeth smiled, wanly. But her eyes stayed fixed on the menu.

I made my way to the ladies toilet, and thanked fate that it was empty. Once inside, I lay my palms flat against the surface either side of the sink and looked at my reflection. I could see the small islands of makeup that I had dabbed onto my face in the half-light of your room. The skin above my cleavage was wet, with what seemed to be cold sweat. My expression was familiar, one of suppressed panic. I had last seen it on the night that Alina had taken the role of Giselle. The last time I had felt this inadequate, this haunted. The two feelings seemed to be lashing together with a disquieting regularity, striking me with a powerful blow whenever they combined. Suddenly, I recalled the memory of Bruna's twisted laugh. Years had passed and yet there it was and the sound was enough to make my hand tremble.

I straightened up, and looked in the mirror. I had a famished look in my eyes. A sinking feeling told me that all this was due to my incapacity to handle the world. I looked as if I was silently begging for a reprieve from all of the conflicting demands that I could not understand. You had made me feel happy and liberated; you had seemed pure and untainted. Emotionally, I had invested so much in you the moment you first laid eyes upon me. I had felt saved, merely by your attention, however stupid that was. But now I knew that weeks after that point you had been asking your former girlfriend to marry you, and now she'd brought it up you hadn't even denied it. It had been her who had minimised it. There were so many questions I could not answer, and it was unusual that I was asking them of myself with such urgency.

I sluiced water around my face. My chest now felt hot and fiery but I did not dare dab it, for fear that I would come out covered in water stains. I could feel damp patches building around my armpits, and so I told myself to keep my arms at my sides. As I prepared to leave I suddenly felt that swinging sensation at the back of my head again. I gripped the sink with both hands until it faded, and then told myself I had to go back.

I stepped behind a row of potted plants, through which our table was just about visible. Peering through the leaves I saw Elizabeth smile, curling her hair behind her ears. You were leaning into her, cradling your fingers together. It looked as if you could take her hand at any moment. With Hannah completing the soft triangle of bodies I felt that by merely approaching the table I would be tearing a family apart. I silently cursed myself for having used my barren body for archaic dances rather than for nurturing another life.

I heard Elizabeth say, 'She did look a little… gaunt.'

You nodded, slowly. Elizabeth looked up and said, 'She is very beautiful. They always are.'

You laughed nervously, just as I passed the plants and came into her eye line.

I was not able to properly engage for the rest of the meal. I asked questions, I tried to expand upon my answers, but it all felt forced. After a while I focused my attention on Hannah, who asked me to take her over to look at the cooking.

'You don't have to,' Elizabeth said.

'I'd like to,' I answered.

Over by the open kitchen I held Hannah's little hand as she looked up at the orange flames. Some of them reached up to the ceiling when they threw meat into a pan and every time that happened Hannah squealed and held my hand tighter. I picked her up for a brief moment so she could see better, and I felt you watching us.

The cooks fried steaks, chopped herbs and kneaded dough. The sound and colour of the kitchen was almost too much for me. I closed my eyes and tried to shut everything out except the warmth of Hannah's hand in my mine. I was eventually able to shut out all the noise and clatter until all I could feel was her hand. It soothed me, made me feel human again. I felt a powerful love for Hannah. And then I opened my eyes, and looked down at her just as she said, 'Are you sure you're alright?'

With love from,

Yelena

Dear Noah,

I suppose I didn't think how worrying it would have been to read my last letter. The first time I read your reply I merely skimmed over it, as I didn't want to be dissuaded from ever giving you an honest account. In your endless quest for objectivity I know you seek absolute truth, but you fear it as well. You wrote that in trying to understand what happened between us the truth 'has to be built, brick by brick'. You said that you had built a wall, of sorts, by yourself, but time had filled it with fissures and indentations, which my letters served to treat. This makes the truth sound domestic and rigorous, but I don't feel it ever is. I feel that we can capture the whole truth when it comes to one aspect of us – desire perhaps. But we can never capture it absolutely, from every perspective, as I know you wish we could. We are still flailing at petals, Noah, but that doesn't mean it isn't an honourable intention to try.

Therefore please forgive me if I forge ahead with telling you what happened next, however difficult it may be to read. We can only treat the lacerations of the past once we have seen them all, because ultimately, these letters concern the need we both have to find a way back towards one another.

You were kind to me after that dinner. You already knew me well enough to not enquire too deeply as to the cause of my little flutter. I felt crazy for having ever seen you as something pure, in a damaged world that constantly felt dirty.

By the time we were back at yours it was starting to grow

dark and leaves were flitting over the pavement, as if hurrying secretly to some unknown destination. You made a pot of dark, sweet coffee and I looked out at the park from the top floor of your house. You placed your arm around me, and asked if I was alright. I knew it was too soon to give you the whole truth, but I did hope that you could perhaps work it out for yourself.

'What did you think of Elizabeth?' you asked. 'She seems to like you.'

'I like her too. And little Hannah is just adorable.'

You moved to sit in the corner of the room. From there my shadows fell over you.

'You seemed a little shaky tonight,' you said.

I remember pausing, and then pacing slowly around the room. I didn't want you to think that I was crazy, so I knew I had to carefully word my response. As I walked, I suddenly went *en pointe*, and you laughed. I rushed over to you and held your hand. I suddenly felt a wave of love for you, which broke into small splashes of honesty.

'She is so beautiful, Noah. And she has given you Hannah. I know it's stupid, but I couldn't help wondering what exactly *I* give to you. I can understand why you asked her to marry you.' It took quite an effort to sound like I believed what I was saying, and I felt something drag through my heart as I said it.

'I did it because for a brief time it felt like the right thing to do. Elizabeth is wonderful and I am blessed to have been given Hannah, but what you and I have is so rare. It's what everyone goes on endless, horrific dates trying to find: a genuine, mutual fascination. An unshakeable empathy not just for each other's lives now, but for the lives we had before we met. And perhaps most importantly – an unquenchable desire.'

I laughed as you squeezed my waist. I gave you a look of relieved suspicion, yet inside me nothing had changed.

'Elizabeth and I are good friends, but it was right that she turned me down. She only ever offered me stability, comfort, and that's not what I really wanted. I adore your complexity; it's what makes you so intriguing. It places me on a journey, Yelena, don't you see? With you there is something to find. There is a map to follow. That exhilarates me. This evening, when I saw how troubled you were, it just made me like you even more. Do you know what I mean?'

I did. I placed one of your jazz records on the gramophone, and we didn't say another word about it. We listened to the music, and I lay my head on your shoulder. The scent of recently brewed coffee lingered in the air, and the leaves stirred outside.

It was the following day when I made a mistake. I suppose it was to do with the fact that since *Giselle* ended I had created a space that I needed to fill, and I began to fill it with worry for us. Although I had feigned nonchalance when learning about the marriage proposal, the truth is that it had completely blemished my vision of you. I needed to distance myself from these encroaching thoughts. It was in an effort to find another way to cull that frenetic movement of my mind that I started to dance to the music of *Sleeping Beauty* when you went into town to meet your agent.

I danced slowly at first, but then my body felt driven by the thought of releasing all its tensions. I loved the sense of mastery I had over the music, a sense I had never experienced with any other aspect of my life. I began to speed up, and reproach myself for not having danced for a couple of weeks, until I suddenly felt a tearing sensation at my ankle. I cried out, and fell to the floor like a lotus. I stayed there for a good half hour, rubbing and kneading my ankle and waiting for the sharp, knife-like pain to recede. By the time you were home I was hobbling around the house, and you were rushing to call the physiotherapist. I found it in me to laugh. Fate, it seemed, was telling me to stop.

The next day the doctor advised that, as a consequence

of the twist, I would be pretty much housebound for a week. You were never very good at taking care of yourself, but you did all you could to take care of me, and seeing how much the twist impacted upon my sudden sense of freedom you said that in a few days you were going to whisk me away for our first romantic break together. While I was incapacitated you charged me with the duty of choosing our destination. And so, while you pummelled away on your typewriter downstairs, I scoured the internet for the perfect excursion. For now, the void was filled. Eventually, I chose a beautiful country house in Scotland. I imagined long mornings spent in four-poster beds where we lazily ate breakfast before making love. I'd at last get to see the inner workings of your mind, reading your next manuscript as you showered. We'd then spend the afternoons out in the country, talking endlessly until we found a country pub to settle down in. There wouldn't be a lot of walking, but a few sedentary days would do us no harm.

It was the following afternoon when your agent called and requested that you meet her urgently. You rushed out of the house, only to return many hours later. Shamefaced, you told me that we would have to postpone our holiday. Your agent had recently managed to arrange a meeting with the publisher you had always wanted, one who could help you break through internationally. She had recently persuaded them to read your work, and they were apparently about to make you an offer on your next book. You were sorry, you said, but you couldn't miss this opportunity. You were going to have to go straight down to London to hear what they had to say.

Although I was pleased for you, I was devastated as well. I knew that you would probably now become very busy and that our time away together would be indefinitely postponed. It sounded as though you would need to be in London for the best part of a week, and so I insisted that you leave me with your work in progress. You agreed, and after many apologies and kisses you left the next day, excited and distracted. I was alone in your house, and still struggling to cross the room without tripping over.

I don't say this to blame you; but that was how it was. I would never have held you back when you were on the cusp of great success. But the truth is that, without something to fill my mind, it was suddenly left to its own devices.

I have to take a deep breath now, to prepare myself to relive what happened next. I know that it will be difficult for me to try and commit the madness that followed onto the page. Out of all my letters to you, my next one will be the hardest to read. Please forgive me for what I am about to confess. Some aspects of the story you will be familiar with, but other parts will have been too painful for you to dwell on. But I truly believe that the full story must now be told, otherwise these letters will have been a futile exercise; and we have by now revealed too much to allow that to be the case.

With love,

Yelena

Dear Noah,

By then your world had already become a deeply intriguing place to me. I had glimpsed at its real workings only sporadically, and in your home I could not help but look for traces of the real you. It was a quirk of fate that I was left alone in your house for those four days. My landlady had informed me that renovations were being undertaken on our block for that month, and along with the twisted ankle and your agent's meeting, events had conspired to leave me alone in a maze of your making. I could not help hoping that I would find you at the centre of it, even in your absence.

Your home did not disappoint. Even the most casual visitor would have seen that it served as a rich exhibition of you. Your different sides were on show amongst the sculptures, the paintings, the records and the books. Each one seemed to hold a story about you. Who had painted the portrait of you, using just red and orange, that hung in the hallway? Why did you have so many Bowie records? Who had made the sculpture that was so unnecessarily prominent in the kitchen? With each hour that passed I could not help delving deeper into your world.

Staying in your house offered a way to stave off the feeling of abandonment. Remember, Noah, I was alone in a country I knew little about, unable to work and pretty much immobile. As a result of what Elizabeth had told me, the feeling of worthlessness still lingered and I was plagued by questions. I do not illuminate my frame of mind to then try and excuse my actions, merely to draw a backdrop for them.

I decided to fill my attention with your writing. At first it worked too, because it was so obvious that your new protagonist was based on me. She was a dancer, trying to escape her dark past by creating a new identity for herself. She was successful at it too, and as the story progressed her ghosts progressively vanished, as she became the person she wanted to be. I was struck by the lavish way you described her, she did not appear haunted by the past at all, merely determined to leave it behind her. She had always known that she had her charms, but she had only recently been in situations where it could work to her advantage. I found myself in the strange position of envying a character that was based on me. She was more fanciful and inspirational than me. Of her, you said, 'She didn't think that by hanging a chandelier from the ceiling you made a room with a chandelier. She felt you'd made another world which you could slip in and out of by some vague process of application.' Although I did not recognise myself in that description, I hoped that one day I might.

At that stage you did not know what exactly I had run from, and I wondered how differently your novel might have developed had you known about Bruna. But your depiction of me was not rendered obsolete by any understandable ignorance. You offered me some compelling insights into the way I present myself. You described real situations I'd been in, in which you made me sound more articulate, more persuasive, than I had ever thought I was. I found myself invigorated, as well as slightly unnerved by your depiction of me. I wondered though, had you been sticking so close to me so that you could better describe your character? Had you been encouraging my personal development so that it fitted with that of your protagonist? The Yelena in your pages was more focused, more successful than I had ever been.

I consumed your whole book in one sitting, and was enchanted by your use of language. I read your story while slowly pacing around your home, and as I finished the final pages I found myself again distracted by the objects there on display. I was fascinated by the thought that a home could reflect the inner architecture of its owner. Wanting nothing more than to hold onto you, I felt that by understanding the parameters of your world I could ensure my presence in it. At times, the feelings of doubt and fragility in my mind were forming into sneers from a familiar, husky voice. Bruna was there, ever present in my moments of weakness. Her presence had developed from the sound of her evil laugh to her instantly recognisable taunts. *You'll never keep him,* it seemed to say. *Your only hope of holding onto him is to find out everything you can while you have the chance, and then using that to bond him to you.*

I began to see your home as though it were something different. I paced each room, looking for the smallest clue as to the real you. I had to know you completely. I had to know you better than any woman ever did. I noticed a drawer embedded in the side of your couch. Slowly, I opened it, and a raft of letters and photos poured out onto the floor beneath me.

I never went looking for them. Not really. They found me. But I could have bent down, put them away and closed the drawer. My conscience will not allow me to deny that having seen them I couldn't resist exploring them. As I picked the documents up, a black and white photo of a dark-haired girl caught my eye. She was lying topless on your bed, laughingly shielding herself from the gaze of the camera. I could not make out her face, and before I knew it I was searching through the letters to find other photos from the set.

I found that there were many of them. And that furthermore, you had charted her body the way a mariner might chart an ocean. There were the stills of her, laughing as you photographed. Many, many photos of this girl in exactly the same pose, her chin perhaps propped up by her fist so the lens could languish on the sensuous curl of her back. Other photos, captured with the accuracy of a fetishist, which focused upon the accentuated muscles of her chest, your fingers sometimes trailing upon them. You seemed enraptured by the way she twisted her hair into one thick lock, allowing it to fall over her left shoulder. The camera also adored the sharp slash of paint around her eye, the slight digress of eyeliner in its corner. At the foot of one photo I saw that your muse had signed her name. In thick, smeared marker pen there was the single word 'Catherine', and the date.

I couldn't help it. I started to delve deeper into the documents, looking for that distinctive signature again. 'Keep going,' the voice seemed to say. 'It would be utterly pointless, cowardly even, to stop now.'

I found a couple of shoeboxes filled with letters – all signed by various different women. In one box I saw that every letter ended with her distinctive, lazy scrawl. As I read her words I experienced an exhilarating, singular thrill, knowing that I was trespassing into a realm that could be very dangerous. I started to think it was worth the risk, it was possible that by doing this I could soothe my own anxieties and also gain enough knowledge to work out how to keep you. I want you to know, Noah, I read those letters like an archaeologist searching for a mysterious subject through miles of sand. I was looking for you. It was never mere nosiness or abandon that drove me. I don't know if it makes my intrusion better or worse, but the mutual fascination between us fuelled the search. A symptom of love, you might argue.

The letters suggested that you and Catherine met just after you'd broken up with Elizabeth. Catherine, it seemed, was a sculptor who you had met at an exhibition. There were various references to 'the night of the exhibition', where you had first been introduced. You'd started to argue about a certain painter. Bickering inevitably turned into flirtation, leading to a meeting that began a passionate affair.

Catherine's first letters were waspish, dismissive, but the

writing suddenly became sexualised and even aggressive. Letter after letter detailed the two of you at your most intimate. How she loved to be scratched in the act of lovemaking, and how you in turned loved the way she reacted. The precise sound of the scream she made when you bit her neck, which you described in indulgent and onomatopoeic terms. You described the way the tone of her voice lowered after you had brought her to climax, and the effect that had on you.

My eyes struggled at first to linger for long enough on the details. Gold heels with long stilettos were mentioned, a perfect black dress that she wore on a certain night out, when the two of you took a taxi to nightclubs on the edge of the city. Clasping yourself together for hours to the sound of dirty electro music before going home to inevitably act out your fantasies on one another. Corsets were mentioned, black ribbons that tied together wrists, stockings worn with a great sense of erotic occasion and then ripped to shreds in the act of lovemaking. The images searing past me, some lodging in my consciousness, some just glancing past me – too painful for me to yet absorb.

Having ensnared her, it seemed that she now suddenly expected a great deal of you. You had to live up to some agreement that was never specified. It seemed evident that whatever the agreement was, it was asking a lot of you, as she only ever seemed to reference it using critical terms. I remember reading the sentence, 'If you want really me, then you must prove you are what you say you are.' It seemed that you had perhaps captured every inch of Catherine's body in the photographs because you had quickly learnt that she would only briefly be in your life. Whatever she was asking of you, you evidently didn't feel able to give it. In the end I read every letter of hers in that box – but this mysterious agreement was never specified. What was apparent though, was that your relationship was more physical than emotional, and that you were both giving one another something that no-one else had offered before.

I was slightly relieved to see those photos covered in dust as if you hadn't needed them lately, and yet I wondered why you had not photographed me in that way. The letters betrayed that she was of Italian origin, but that she had lived in England for the duration of your affair. You had once mentioned that your last serious lover had suddenly vanished from your life, and I did notice how suddenly the letters ended. You had never explained to me why she disappeared, and I found myself scouring the final letters for traces of an explanation. The only possible explanation seemed to lie in her repeated declarations that you prove yourself to her; and these requests became more and more pronounced in the final few letters. I could only conclude she then vanished, and must have left much unresolved in you.

It shames me to admit that I became so consumed with the thought of this elusive woman that at one point I spread out all of Catherine's letters and photos on the floor. I hoped this would allow me to learn and then mimic what it was about her that had appealed to you, so that I could come to replace her completely. But all I did was intoxicate myself with the impressions left by a ghost. I knew all about the urgent way you made love, the way she liked you to rub her hands, the afternoons you spent hunting for antiques along the coast. But of course, the real Catherine remained undefined, embedded somewhere amongst that distinctive, looping handwriting. Eluding both you and me.

The thirst for knowledge consumed me. I needed to know more about the woman I so desperately wanted to replace. It didn't even help to recall the assuring words you had left me with. I was now so panicked that I was unable to use them, and so they couldn't calm me. Despite my best attempts to reason with myself, when I visited the pharmacy for painkillers I found myself cautiously browsing the hair dyes, eventually fixing on a brown tint that promised the exact sheen your camera had evidently striven to capture. Back at your house, I washed it through my hair whilst singing; to try and convince myself that this was just something I was doing for fun rather than trying to mimic and transcend the elusive charms of a ghost. Afterwards, focused on the mirror, I bunched my hair into one single lock and place it over my shoulder, and found myself perfecting the pout that had come so naturally to her.

I was suddenly overcome by tiredness. I left the letters on the floor and went up to your bed. I had the sense of a knot tightening in my head, a feeling I had not had since the days before the Vaganova. A feeling which then I had only ever been able to relieve with the guilty, sterile comfort of a razor blade. I found myself in your bathroom, looking for something sharp. 'No, don't,' I told myself. 'Don't give in to it.'

Without the relief of release, sleep did not come quickly. I was left to fight with those thoughts in the darkness; vulnerable to being carried wherever they wanted me to go. I knew there was no escaping the fact that I had just crossed a boundary, and entered a place that it would not be easy to return from.

Yelena

Noah,

This isn't a letter so much as a confession, and I know you are aware of that. That night, there was tension inside me that was building and building. It felt impossible to relax in a place that I now knew contained so many secrets. I found myself curling up in a small corner of the bed, trying to tell myself that this would all be resolved as soon as you came back.

Part of the tension came from guilt, and another part from fear. A kind of skewed logic had begun to take hold of my brain. I had damaged our relationship by betraying your trust and yet I hadn't achieved anything in doing so. After all, I didn't have enough information to feel that I could keep you. So I decided that I might as well go further.

I got up, walked over to your computer and switched it on. As it whirred to life I told myself that I would only look for your writing on it, which would allow me to understand you more. I felt I was only addressing the concern that Elizabeth had raised; that I should be reading your work. Just as the computer started up, a small envelope shaped symbol appeared in the corner of the screen. Above it, the caption read: 'You have 1 New Message – from C'.

I clicked on it. I can't justify each decision from now on, I was caught in the momentum. As I opened the email there was a small portrait of its sender in its top left corner. A shiver went through me as I saw that she had a thick crop of dark hair, but the photo was too small to distinguish her features. The email had only been sent a few hours ago, at 6.13pm. It read:

Dear Noah

It was lovely to see you at the talk last week. It's such a shame we weren't able to speak for longer, but I understand that you have many commitments to keep. Nonetheless, our brief conversation was just as illuminating as I had expected it to be. I do hope you get the chance to look up my most recent work, as you mentioned you might. It would be thrilling to hear your thoughts on it.

Xxx

C

I read the message once, with an encroaching sense of horror, and then again and again. I feel feverish now, just recalling that moment.

The email seemed to demonstrate just how cursed I was by fate. Here I was, immersed in your home, pining for your return, and yet here was proof that you were flirting with other women. The email instantly called into question the validity of all the hopes and expectations I had for us. During the dizzying hours that followed I urged myself to find it in me to trust. But then I had no experience of rightfully trusting anyone. What I did have was the sense that I was missing something if all seemed well, and there, in tedious black and white, was the proof that my suspicions were reasonable. Suddenly all my guilt about reading your letters evaporated.

After a few tense hours between the sheets, my mind told me not to simply give in, but to fight. I quickly decided that I must respond to this 'C'. I had to message her back, to neuter this threat. I was going to masquerade as you, to subtly investigate just what was going on. And then I was going to cover my tracks.

I carefully typed my reply, anxious to use exactly the right tone. It had to be both subtle and flirtatious, a careful approximation of the manner in which you'd have spoken to her. I felt strangely comfortable adopting your tone – inquisitive, calm, and yet quietly attentive. I enquired about where I might find her new work, mentioned it was a shame we'd not spoken for longer. I knew that my reply needed to be ambiguous enough to accommodate if you had just met her, or if you'd known her for a very long time. At the end of it I mentioned that I was no longer using this email account, and I diverted her to a new email address, which I quickly registered and activated. I remember that it contained some variation of your surname. It pains me to think it probably still exists, somewhere in the digital wilderness. And before I had even checked it, it was sent. I then deleted my reply, along with her original email so you would never know she had been in touch.

I kept the new account open on the screen. A few minutes later a response appeared in it:

Dear Noah,

What a pleasant surprise to have such a quick reply! As a famous writer I didn't think you would get the chance to reply to such vague requests by admirers, especially at night! It would be an honour to show you my new work. So many of the people at those events are old and boring, you were the first vaguely interesting person I had spoken to all day! Perhaps one day we can meet again and finish that conversation?

Xxx

C

That was definitely where it should have ended – well, clearly I see now it should never even have gone that far. I needed to know if this 'C' was the elusive Catherine that had left so suddenly. I needed to know if she posed any real threat. I needed to meet her.

Dear C, (my reply read)

Why wait? Let's meet tomorrow at 12pm, under the statue in the town square. We can go for a bite to eat, and you can tell me more about your work.

x

Noah

The email felt like a clumsy, temporary solution, but I felt emboldened by the thought that I was tackling my anxieties head on. In a strange way, Noah, at that moment I felt proud that I was fighting so hard to protect our relationship. Only now do I see how flawed my logic was, how twisted my concept of normal behaviour had become that night. You would be away for a couple more days, and I told myself this would give me plenty of time to identify 'C', remove her from your life, cover my tracks and perhaps even prepare a fitting confession for when you returned home. That night I almost slept well, because I was able to convince myself that very soon this mental intensity would be over, and I would be able to go back to enjoying my new life.

The following morning the sky was overcast, and it looked as if it would rain at any moment. I dressed smartly, already formulating in my mind how I would handle this meeting once it was confirmed. My reflection in the mirror, with my hair now darkened, somewhat frightened me. I ran my fingers through it, and let it fall naturally down my back. To lighten the change in me I wore a slash of red lipstick, with my black raincoat and high heels. There was just enough time to check for a response from C before setting off. Sure enough, there was a new message:

Noah,

How exciting! I never thought you would want to meet. I will be there at 12, wearing the same red coat that I had on when I last saw you. I can't tell you what a thrill this will be

for me!
C

I didn't have time to consider all the allusions of her response. I grabbed an umbrella, and made a quick obsessive-compulsive sweep of the house, thinking what a burden and a treasure it had already become.

The square was well appointed for my purposes. It was overlooked by a small café from which the statue was clearly visible. Usually the square was a stamping ground for gothic teenagers and romantic liaisons, but today the bludgeoning sky had rendered it empty. From the café, I had a perfect view of anyone arriving. My internal rhythm had increased to an almost audible hum, and I felt slightly dizzy.

At 11:55 a very slender, dark haired woman in a red trench coat stepped into the square. She looked up to check that she was stood under the statue and then looked around. I leant against the window to get a better view of her and yet her features remained imperceptible to me. At that moment the sky rumbled, and I realised that through an additional sheet of rain, C would be completely impossible to identify. I scattered coins on the table and rose to meet her.

At that point I had no plan, Noah, no idea of what I would say to her. How on earth could I justify introducing myself when she was expecting to meet you at any moment? As I tied the cord of my coat around my waist my mind worked quickly, flicking through a series of reckless options. I could create any reality for us both; all it took was choosing the right words. For a moment I wondered if I could just pass her by; it might give me long enough to catch her face, and allow me to end this madness right now. As I left the café I honestly intended to do just that. God knows how differently my life might have turned out had I stuck with that resolve; it almost does not bear thinking about. But as I drew close, she looked up, and I realised that I was looking into the eyes of Catherine. Here at last was the proof that I was not good enough for you, Noah. I felt sick to my stomach. All the fears that I had struggled to keep tied down were suddenly torn free from their moorings. They crashed around my head, smashing up all the furniture of my mind. But still I kept walking towards her.

My eyes widened, and my gaze locked into hers. It was inevitable then that we would speak; it was inevitable what would happen next. I would always react the way that I was about to, and the consequences would therefore always be the same. My window of sanity had passed. She looked at me, baffled.

'C?' I asked. She looked at me, her eyes already slightly accusatory. It certainly looked like Catherine, and yet I didn't feel angry at her, for worming her way back into your life. I felt intimidated.

Of course, in this setting, she was not the Catherine that I had seen in your photos. She had been captured only in snapshots, the profile of her face, the sweep of her hair. Assembling all those images into one expectation was never going to be easy. But I did know that familiar dread inside me when looking at her, the same dread I had had when rifling through those photos. Even if her face was thinner, slightly harder than I had expected, it was still Catherine.

'Yes?' she said. I faltered, and the rain started to come down.

'I'm Anna, Noah's secretary. I'm afraid he's been detained.' The words flooded out, and I settled readily into this new role. It fit me much better than the queasy persona of a jilted lover. She looked back at me, and I felt assured by her acceptance. Her expression was not one of subdued anger, as I had expected it to be.

'His car was scraped by a lorry when he was on his way here, and it was quite badly damaged. He's okay, but his phone was broken and he has to go and get his car fixed as he needs it to travel to London tomorrow. He asked me to call by to send his apologies.'

'Oh. Oh right. I'm sorry – are you sure he's okay?' She looked deflated, concerned. The rain was coming down, and the thick droplets were suddenly soaking both of us.

'Shall we – shall we go inside for a coffee?' I asked. 'And get out of the rain? Then I can explain it all.' I was already eagerly awaiting the ten or so steps it would take to the café, during which time I could try and determine for sure if this was Catherine, and if so what she was doing back in touch with you.

'Er – okay,' she said, looking disappointed for the first time.

We stepped into the café, but those few steps were spent shielding ourselves from the onslaught. The sound was suddenly muted by the closed door. 'Coffee?' I asked.

'Yeah sure.' She looked ready to stand up. 'To be honest, I'm just glad that Noah's okay. I can meet him another time. That's not a problem.' She looked slightly confused.

'The rain is really coming down,' I said, and looking past her I was relieved to see that this was true.

The waitress served me two coffees, and I carefully put them onto a tray. As I moved over to the window, she stayed silent. 'I think we should probably stay inside until it passes, it'll hopefully only be a quick shower.'

'Did you say your name was Anna?' she asked. I wondered if she had somehow worked out exactly who I was. 'Yes, I am,' I said, clumsily. 'Are you a friend of Noah's then?'

'No,' she laughed, and she shook her hair free of raindrops. I saw then that she had dyed her hair into a slightly darker shade, and that she had lost weight since those photos had been taken. She looked younger, somehow, and she seemed to have less presence in the flesh than she did on Polaroid.

I wondered if, having lost weight and changed her hair she had seen your name on a literary listing and come to make your acquaintance as a new fan of yours. After all, it had been a good five years since you had been in touch and it was possible that she could have presented herself to you as a different person, having perhaps felt deeply embarrassed by the manner in which she had left your life before. Telling you that her name was C might have allowed her to have another chance with you. And you, aware of her striking resemblance to someone significant who had vanished from your life, might have been intrigued enough to take her number, perhaps without as yet telling her that she closely resembled a former lover of yours. And perhaps consequently only I was aware of what was really going on. Catherine was trying to worm her way back into your life by posing as another woman, and you, not knowing this, were allowing her. But why were you doing this? Maybe you felt that her resemblance to Catherine would allow you to exorcise your demons for her through another woman. But this was Catherine, I told myself, nodding slightly as I thought it and as my eyes met hers. In writing this down, I can see now how far the vague concept of logic had slipped.

I instantly decided that I should try and ingratiate myself with her, to find out exactly what it was about this woman that had made her so significant to you. Only then, I thought, by understanding her charms, could I usurp her in your affections and remove her permanently from your life.

'I met him at a literary convention the other week,' she said. 'I was overwhelmed by his last book and had written to him about it months ago, but didn't receive a reply. At the convention we got chatting and – I'm sure just out of politeness – he asked for my email address. A few days later I wrote to him, and to my great surprise he asked me to meet him here. But now that he wasn't able to come, I wonder if I've lost my chance to ever see him again.'

'Not at all,' I said. I must have looked at her admiringly, marvelling at her manipulations. To think that she was so determined that she hid the truth even from me, a perfect stranger. Thank goodness, I remember thinking, that I *had* studied those photos. Otherwise she might have succeeded in her intentions. But now I had an opportunity to prevent her clawing her way back into your life.

'Not at all. Noah very rarely agrees to meet any of his fans. He must have felt a connection with you, to offer to do that.'

'Do you really think so?'

I thought that she played the role of the naïve, star-struck fan, who happened to be beautiful, with great conviction.

'Oh yes. I know from working with him that he very rarely spends time with other people at all. If he has invited you to meet, it must be because the two of you really hit it off. He wouldn't have done it for any other reason.'

She suddenly looked suspicious. 'I am a little surprised that a writer his age has a secretary. Are you a big fan of his work then as well?'

'Very much so, however much other people love his work, I feel it cannot compare to how important it is to me.'

Suddenly, I was speaking as Yelena. Almost pleading that she understood how essential you were to me, begging with her not to steal you from me. 'It cuts both ways though,' I continued. 'He asks me to read his work while it is still in the early stages and then give my opinion on it. I'm lucky, because I don't believe that he does that with anyone else.'

'You are lucky,' she replied. 'And I understand how you feel about him too.'

Her eyes levelled into mine, with a glint that I suddenly found compelling.

'I can see why Noah wanted to meet with you though,' I said. 'I can already see that you share the same empathic perspective that he has, that you too have that sensitivity. He is obviously susceptible to the charms of young and beautiful women. But what man in his position wouldn't be?'

She quickly looked up at me, surprised by this sudden change in tack. I felt a sense of triumph, and wondered if I had just outmanoeuvred her. But then her expression brightened, and she seemed to feign a blush.

She smiled. 'You're very kind, and I think that you might be right. Why else would he choose you for a secretary? He clearly has a taste for women like us.'

The rain outside had ceased. A slight sheen was rising from the concrete. The café, though still half empty, now felt a little humid.

'And who can blame him?' I asked. Her eyes met mine. I sensed that something in her manner had shifted. She was suddenly no longer practical, concerned. Her body was responding to me in a different way.

It was then that I remembered the details of the photos I had so rabidly consumed. I realised that if I had been able to draw Catherine to this point, why wouldn't *I* be able to seduce her too? The logic of this decision seems mad now – she had gone there to meet you – but at that moment my reasoning seemed strong and clear. If I were to seduce Catherine, I would finally get to see exactly what it was about her that you had found so attractive. And then, and only then, could I fully replace her.

'The rain has stopped,' I said. 'But shall we get another coffee?' Her lips parted, and I remembered that in the photos they had been plump, red, eager to ease into a smile.

'Why not?' she said.

I waved the waitress over to our table. As she poured out the dark, thick coffee, I felt C's eyes analyse me.

The next time I was consciously aware of what I was doing, was when we arrived at C's flat. It was late afternoon by then, and the world seemed to be giving off a porous fragrance.

Her flat was small and artfully cluttered. I remember looking for sculptures, and feeling relieved after observing a couple, but I felt unsettled by the red and black Francis Bacon prints on the wall, the facial features on each clouded and indistinct, lacking any clarity. They seemed to surge towards me and taunt me. I remember the precise way she placed a glass of white wine beside me as we sat in her drawing room.

The way that, after many searching and purely cosmetic conversations, she stopped perching on the edge of the couch and moved to sit next to me, placing her hand around my neck. I had never seen a woman up close like this before, never seen a painted mouth open for me in such a sensuous manner, and yet I was aware I had constructed this situation myself.

I suddenly found her presence powerfully involving and I kissed her with real tenderness. I felt a wave of passion pass over me. Closing my eyes I could see your body, clasped against hers as mine now was. I unbuttoned her shirt, which revealed a shaft of her ivory white chest. As she leant back on the couch I could see your mouth closing on the swell of her breast, which rose to a tight peak. I kissed her, searching for your essence within her. Somehow I was able to sense it, distant and elusive. It existed in the root of her passion, suddenly awakened as I circled her waist with gentle and yet insistent fingers, before eventually finding the source of her pleasure. I could almost feel your presence when her body broke open, when her shirt fell from her slim shoulders. I wondered if I was touching her in the exact same way that she had touched you, but that wondering soon turned into an urgent need to make sure I was. I imagined that it was your hands that passed around her neck, that gathered her from the shoulder blades. Your hands that implored her to turn over, and your eyes that took in the pinched quality of her flesh, the smooth S shape of her back. In imagining it was your lips that explored the texture of her neck, it seemed to become so.

The hands that unbuttoned my blouse were gentle, and yet accommodating too. When our bodies finally merged, it was your name preying upon my lips, the thought of your back and body that consumed me as we pressed against each other. I sought you in her tender and shivering flesh, chased you, with fingers and lips, across the plane of her navel. Though it was C and I having sex, I was acutely aware it was not only the two of us that were present. Your ghost encircled us, eased our fluttering bodies together. Her thighs opened, wanting you to ease inside her, and yet I met that welcome with a tender embrace. She came in my arms, overwhelmed by my insistence to find you within her. As she caught her breath we held each other gently, and I found you again in the nape of her neck, the scent in her hair. You embodied me, your words scrolling across my consciousness as I kissed her neck, my teeth drawing from her lips the exact reaction you had strived so hard to capture in your letters. As I searched for those precise sounds her body responded – questioning and yet plaintive. I could sense her wondering what was driving this fervent exploration, but then the sound of her pleasure turned to a plea for mercy as I bit her neck. Suddenly your description seemed to exist in another world, as here there was only the remonstrating expression of a beguiling woman. 'You drew blood,' she whispered, her hand clasping against her neck. Gathering her thick, dark hair in my hands I moved to soften her anger, kissing her mouth, my fingers urging the tensed muscles in her back to relax. Her reaction was wordless, a brief bodily rearrangement. We began to move in rhythm again, and I felt your presence knife down my arms and into my fingers as I began to scratch her flesh. How exactly had you done it again? For a moment her body broke upon, her pleasure rising to another crescendo. I felt so exhilarated by the thought of her responding to my scratches just as she had done to yours. I was capturing it all. My eyes, I knew, held no tenderness now. They studied her for the times I would replicate these exact sounds, the exact myriad collapses of flesh. Her eyes met mine, retracted at the studious expression glazing my face. 'Don't scratch me,' she ordered, the end of the sentence breaking the erotic clamour of her insistence into something more suspicious. 'You're hurting me.'

But your presence was overwhelming me, so much so that I had no choice but to chase it through this woman's retreating flesh. I had to make her come again. I had to hear the alteration in the tone of her voice, the one you had rhapsodised over in potent cascades of letters. But her eyes were tightening now, ready to condemn. Whatever game she was playing with me now seemed to be rapidly losing its charm. I was possessed, consumed by my craving to find you, and with it the physical relief I desperately craved. I knew my body would only be satisfied when my mind was. But our bodies had lost our connection, her arms tightening to keep me apart from her rather than close. I needed to bring her to a climax again but she was preoccupied only with my pleasure – with finishing it. I tried to throw her onto the bed but she slipped off me, her arm pinning me against the sheets. 'Stop it. Let me kiss you.'

'Lie down,' I replied, soft and yet firm.

'You're hurting me,' she whispered, clutching her hair in her fist and bunching her thighs against her chest. 'Give me a moment.'

I had been so close to the final prize that I felt my body revolt in anger. It desperately wanted release, and yet I knew I had pushed this woman too far. 'Lie down,' she said. 'Let me.'

But my hand swept hers from my breasts. 'What's wrong?' she hissed.

'You're stopping me,' I said. 'You know what I'm trying to do and you won't let me.'

She sat bolt upright, the colour suddenly vanishing from her cheeks. 'What are you talking about? You're scaring me now.' She whipped the sheet around her breasts. 'Perhaps you should leave, Anna.'

'So it's not a game any more, when I come close to the prize? Is that how it works?' The combative tone felt so jarring, given the recent tumult our bodies had both been in.

'The prize? I don't know what you're talking about.' The tone became authoritative. 'There's something very wrong going on here.'

'Wrong? I'll tell you what's wrong Catherine. You pretending to be someone else to try and get Noah back. Pretending to be this innocent C woman just to ensnare him again. Isn't that sick? Well you had your chance, and you disappeared from his life. He's mine now, and I know how to keep him.'

'I want you to leave,' she said, grabbing her shirt and pushing her arms through it. 'Right now.'

'So you don't deny it Catherine? You don't deny that I'm right?' My thighs were bunched against my body now but I felt coiled, ready for the confrontation.

Her voice dropped. 'My name isn't Catherine, Anna. It's Cecilia. And I think this was a mistake. You need to leave.'

'I'm not Anna, and you know it. And you're not Cecilia either.'

'You made it all up,' she said, pushing her fingers through her hair. 'Noah, the accident, you're just some perverted... what are you?'

'I'm his girlfriend, Catherine!'

She didn't respond immediately. She moved over to the dresser and grabbed the purse that was sitting on it. Snapping it open she flashed me the ID card, housed in its transparent slip. 'I'm Cecilia Marks,' she hissed, jabbing at it with her finger. 'And I have no idea what you're talking about. I want you out of my house. Right now.'

I grabbed the purse from her as she started to sweep up my clothes, her movements heavy with disgust. I looked at the ID card. There, below her scrubbed face, now so different from the Catherine in the photos were the words 'Cecilia Marks.' In desperation I flickered through the rest of the contents: store cards, credit cards, fluttering loyalty vouchers. All with the same name printed on them.

The blood drained from my face. 'I don't believe it.'

'I don't care what you believe, Anna, or whoever you are. Get out!' she screamed.

She threw my clothes at me. After a second's pause I started to flail at them, pulling them onto my body as I staggered to the door. Suddenly it all fell into place. The hair, the face.

The name. A knife-like pain tore through my head. What had I done?

My journey home is a blank; I can only recall that it contained the metallic whir of the tube, and the peculiar yet by now familiar ringing in my head. Back at your house, I felt relieved to have brought that confusing and exhilarating chapter to a close. Then I heard a noise – from your bedroom. I called out your name.

It was only when I had rounded the corner to your room that I saw you on your knees, beside your bed. Your arms were full of Catherine's letters. Their exposure felt somehow indecent; their sheer number overwhelming.

'You're back early,' I said, my voice quivering.

'Yelena. What's been going on? Why are my private letters everywhere? And why is my email account open on the screen? Yelena?'

'I – I didn't think you were going to be back for another three days.'

'Jesus, what have you done to your hair? Yelena, what's been going on?'

The pain in my head suddenly became too much to bear, and I collapsed onto you with a quiet sob. Finally I spoke. 'I slept with someone else, because I wanted to keep you,' I said, my voice gradually rising.

Your arms suddenly stiffened, and you eased me off you. I looked up at you.

'I came across your letters by accident, and I read them. All of them. Especially Catherine's. I'm sorry Noah, I became so jealous. And I ended up checking all your emails and I saw a flirtatious one from a woman called C, and I thought she was Catherine, trying to get you back.'

'What Cee? I don't remember any Cee,' you said, clawing your hand through your hair.

'And so pretending to be you I arranged to meet her. And then I turned up to confront her.'

'And… did something happen? Did you sleep with her?'

Dumbly, I nodded. I looked up, to see you looking scared and confused.

'Why?'

I loathed myself so much. I moved over to you, tried to hug you, tried to make sense of it all.

'Noah, I'm so sorry. I'm sick,' I said. You stepped away from me. Your eyes were not quite able to level at me.

'I need you to get out of my house right now.'

Tears overwhelmed me, and a second later I was clambering down the hallway. I heard your voice behind me, beckoning me back in, needing all this madness to be explained. But my anguish, and fear at what I had become propelled me out of the house. I tore open the front door and ran out into the street.

I had to get out of that house. Away from your voice, your presence, and all the awful implications that had now come with it. I ran to the end of the road and then left around the blind corner, still with no idea of where to go. I rounded the corner too fast to see the small, black car that was tearing down the street. The startled expression of the young man at the wheel was all that was visible to me as the car struck, and with a sickening jolt my body crumpled into it, my head striking the windscreen as I blacked out.

Yelena

Dear Noah,

Certain images from the crash scorched themselves on my memory. It took many months to piece them together and create a narrative.

I remember the rising, ugly pain at the back of my head as I lay on the tarmac. I remember the scent of burning in the air as I looked up and watched the driver writhe in his chair, desperate to escape his vehicle, which had smashed into the wall in front of me on the left. That sense of enclosed madness, unacknowledged by the world, that existed until strangers finally swarmed around us. Then the panicked interventions of people desperate to appear composed for me, though they must have had no idea what they were supposed to do.

Someone asked me where it hurt and I told them that I couldn't move my foot. The end of my leg felt watery and disconnected. I wanted to snap out of it, but the pain was so enormous that I couldn't compose myself. I remember the scent of wax from the coat of the man who held me up, asking me exactly how I wanted to lie, and the heady perfume of the woman who held me against her, telling me jokes until the ambulance arrived. I clung onto her tightly, trying to laugh out of politeness, and I occasionally sensed her mouthing instructions to other people standing over me. I remember the relief of seeing flashing lights, as the strangers parted from around me.

'My name's Carole,' the paramedic said. 'What's your name?' I remember for the first time wanting to cry as I heard my trousers being cut off, and how exposed and weak I felt in front of all these people. The endless wait for the paramedic to inject me with something that might dull that jagged, dizzying pain. Being strapped onto a stretcher as my neck was put in a brace. Being lifted into the ambulance, the paramedic telling the driver to go smoothly over the bumps as she carefully placed an oxygen mask over my face. Telling the paramedic to call you on my mobile, still somehow wedged in the pocket of my now shredded trousers. Then in A&E, the nurse who held my hand while the medics crowded around me. The moment I saw a flash of red at the end of my leg for the first time, and the way it made me convulse. The excruciating pain I felt as they pulled my foot back into position, but the way the nurse made it easier by holding my hand and trying to make me laugh.

It was then that you rushed into the room. Someone must have called you, and I remember the sudden exclamation that arose from the staff as they rushed to prevent you from overwhelming me. 'I'm her boyfriend,' you said. 'I need to see her.'

Amongst the chaos the expressions we gave one another were so complex, Noah, so conflicted. You stroked my cheeks and I laughed with the relief of now having you beside me. 'It's okay. You're going to be alright. Everything's going to be alright,' you said.

But you were quickly forced to leave, as they put me on a drip and took me away to the X-ray theatre. I remember seeing a doctor draw you into the corner of the room and question you about the events leading up to the crash. I overheard the word 'psychiatrist' being used, but at the time I didn't worry about it. As I was wheeled past you I simply assumed that we would be reunited in a few minutes.

In the X-ray theatre, the murmurings around me suggested I had got off relatively lightly. Although the focus of concern was my leg and foot, the rest of me was also scanned, and most of my body seemed to have escaped injury. I was taken up to the High Dependency Unit.

Although two days passed without me hearing from you, I didn't dwell too much on it. I assumed they were merely being careful, and through those static, restricted days I simply concentrated on sleeping and trying to get comfortable. That wasn't easy though, because during the night, every four hours I was awoken by the voice of a stranger. They pressed pads on my chest, strapped belts to my arm and pushed thermometers into my ear. After a couple of days of this I was moved into the general ward, and given the room to move a little more. The nurse who wheeled me downstairs told me that the insurance from the ballet company entitled me to private healthcare, and that I would soon be transferred to another hospital. I just closed my eyes and tried to push out the pain.

At the new hospital, I was given my own room. A small, pale cube on the top floor of a building, housed somewhere on the outskirts of the city. For the first time since the chaos of the crash there was room for solace and reflection, though my life was inevitably punctuated by the regular, urgent interventions of the nurses.

At the back of my mind, I had known that the activity of the last few days was all leading up to something; that it would probably end with something explosive. The pressure I had placed upon myself throughout *Giselle*, and then in my self-appointed role as your custodian, had been unsustainable. With you then having suddenly left me alone for a few days, I had had nothing to do with all of that frantic activity in my brain, and I knew it had manifested itself in the hysterical, skewed logic that had led me to contact Cecilia. During that time, I had been impermeable to reason, but being incapacitated now forced me to retread the path that had led me here.

Thinking about it, I realised that I had by now grown accustomed to living in goldfish bowls. Firstly in Donetsk, then at the Vaganova, the Mariinsky and finally during *Giselle*. Ever since my childhood I had always been focused on a single goal, thinking in a constricted way, and driving myself through some tunnel towards what I eventually hoped would be daylight. This had benefited me as a dancer, but it had also meant that my brain was so used to pressure that when it had no task to address, it had to find it elsewhere. I knew that there had never been any reason to suspect your integrity. I should have seen it all along, but somewhere along the way I had become lost.

The diagnosis from the doctors was that I had broken my foot as well as the largest bone in my calf. The calf would require a metal rod, and the foot would require screws and wiring to fix everything back into place. As I lay in bed after the operations I remember I felt simply glad to be alive. I felt grateful that my mind had suddenly been cleansed of that swarming red mist, which had led me to such dark places. The doctors had evidently been told I was a professional ballerina, and during the early days they skirted around the issue of whether I would be able to dance again. It was already clear to me that I would struggle to dance in a professional capacity. Perhaps it was the morphine, but I felt strangely relaxed about this, despite the great sacrifices I had made over many years.

Dancing had been a way of escaping my childhood, of making me feel worthy, and as such it had been a successful strategy. I had danced the role I had always dreamt of performing and in so doing I had explored, and to some degree broken out of the blueprint that I had believed that role offered for my life. But dancing had also come with great costs. Great physical pain, and great mental endurance. I could not help but feel that there must be easier ways to live.

I knew that I needed to address this tendency for faulty reasoning, in order to prevent it from ever harming me again. But I would have been surprised to learn that my appointed psychiatrist, a man with wisps of white hair burgeoning from the side of his head, could assist me with that.

I first encountered Dr Ibarra through his laugh, which

echoed down from the nurses' station during the early morning medicine distributions. It was a distinctive sound, a kind of earthy hee-haw, which replaced the sterile hospital air with a sense of reassuring liveliness. But once he'd poked his head around my door it was immediately apparent that he was no clown. In fact he looked like the kind of mature man you would see sat amongst the courtyards of Florence or Milan, playing cards with his friends as the sun came down. He smiled at me, with his head bowed and his fingers clasped together in an intricate arrangement. I felt an immediate urge to make him like me.

During our first meeting he sat by my bed and said very little, merely leafed through my medical notes with a kind of academic restlessness. From his notes I caught fragments of sentences. 'A history of anxiety attacks and dizzy spells' … 'Possible paranoid episodes' … 'The encounter ended with her meeting said woman and pursuing a sexual liaison.' It seemed pretty apparent that your conversation with the doctor, Noah, had led to my psychological profile being sketched out for the first time. While the doctors and nurses would be concentrating on helping me to walk again, Dr Ibarra would clearly be focused on the mental processes that had led to the accident in the first place.

'You're a ballerina,' he began. 'Of some repute. Is that right?'

The voice was gruffer than I had expected, but it had a warm edge to it. I caught a glimpse of what looked like a chess strategy marked in pencil on the back of one of the pages.

'Do you play chess?' I answered.

'Ah, well,' he removed a crescent moon pair of glasses from the end of his nose. 'I am interested in strategy. Both behavioural and psychological.' He gestured at me with the glasses as he spoke. 'Do you play chess?'

'My father taught me. I haven't for a while.'

'Perhaps we will begin to play soon. Everyone's lives, Miss Brodvich, are led by a strategy that they have decided to deploy. My job as a Psychiatrist is to untangle the strategy that you have been using to date. And to only release you back into the world when we feel we have adjusted that strategy, where necessary, so that it is more likely to result in victory.'

'I think I follow.'

My eyes were in fact following those softly sketched chess moves, clearly drawn by Ibarra during some quiet moment on the ward. As he turned back to the front page of my notes I caught the words at the top of the page. 'An episode of paranoid psychosis caused by acute stress'.

'That?' he asked, noticing what my eyes had been fixed upon. 'That is the working hypothesis as to why you have ended up here. But it is nothing more than a hypothesis. It might well be completely wrong.' He opened his arms out with a small smile. 'But don't worry about that. For now, you should rest. We can begin coordinating strategies once the time is right. For now, the priority is to keep you safe.'

'What does that mean?'

'You have endured a lot of stress in recent times, Miss Brodvich. When you have not been given stress, I wonder if you have sought it out. Therefore my job is to prevent your brain from doing so again, which is why I must recommend that Mr Stepanov refrains from visiting you until you are back on your feet.'

'You really think that will help?'

I felt my body grow cold. How long would you be kept from me? I wanted to protest and yet, as he placed his glasses back on his nose I could not help still wanting to please him. He tapped the chess strategy in his notes. 'You see, we have already begun playing.' He adjusted the glasses and glanced quickly at me. 'Rest yourself,' he said, before rising and leaving the room.

During his first few visits, Ibarra focused on understanding my childhood in Ukraine, my family background and the details of my medical history. As far as English medicine was concerned I had not previously existed, but such high quality care evidently required that they quickly gain a detailed understanding of me. I tried to avoid mentioning Bruna, but as time went on I could sense, from the tone of my voice, that I'd betrayed that she was significant. Not much later, at the conclusion of a session he said, 'I think next time we need to talk about this lady a little more.'

I didn't know how to respond. 'I'm not sure we do. In fact, I can't see how discussing her will help me now. I think walking is my biggest problem.'

He seemed to balance the words that he should use next very carefully. 'But perhaps walking isn't your biggest problem, Yelena.'

'I think it is,' I said, too tired to be as withering as I'd have liked.

He leant forward. When he replied it was with more precision than he'd ever used before. 'Whatever it is, Yelena. Whatever might have happened, we can find a way to start fixing it.'

I looked at him, wanting the expression in my eyes to overpower his offensive instincts and his constant confidence.

'We can find a way to start fixing it,' he repeated.

I looked back at him, and slowly became aware of what he wanted me to relive.

Suddenly, I felt something grip me and hold me tight. In a horrible instant all the air trickled out of my throat, and my body felt empty, winded. I had the powerful sense that Bruna was back in my life. Ready to begin tormenting me once more.

My body went still. As I gradually looked up, Ibarra was looking right at me. I swallowed.

He looked concerned, but as if it was perhaps for another day. 'Okay Yelena,' he said, resolutely,

'Don't go,' I said. 'Not now.'

The words sounded thin. As if they had been forced out without the power to shape them normally.

He exhaled. 'I'll come back tomorrow,' he said, reassuringly.

'And then I'd like us to focus on your stepmother a little more when we talk.'

I heard her laugh. The room felt cold.

'Please. Don't go,' I whispered, as quietly as I could. I didn't want her to hear.

I could hear Bruna breathing.

Slowly, he gathered his notes together. As he stood up, wrapping his coat around him, I felt my body stiffen even more. 'Wait,' I said, and I reached out and took his hand. With a gentle smile he stopped, and allowed me to hold it.

I could still hear her breathing. I closed my eyes. My head was bowed and I refused to let go of his hand. 'Yelena,' he said.

'Please just stay. Just for a minute.'

He exhaled, and in his eyes I could see something in him give way. He tussled with it for a moment, then said, 'I'll stay here for as long as you want me to.'

I sat there, my head down, gripping his hand until the breathing stopped.

I tried to avoid the next session, but the purpose with which Ibarra entered the room told me that he was only interested in Bruna. If I had known a way to open up to him I would have done, but where could I start? How could he possibly understand all that happened?

He sat down, bringing my thick medical folder onto his lap. Then he looked up at me and, as if thinking better of it, he turned and slipped the folder onto the trolley behind him.

Suddenly I felt it. Bruna was with me again.

'We only have to do this as much as you want to,' he said. For a moment I wondered if he was going to take my hand. 'It's important that we take the first step towards fixing this.' I tried to draw comfort from his eyes.

Bruna moved behind me. Instinctively, I clasped my body, but the room still went cold.

He was whispering now. 'I can see that whatever happened with your stepmother is very significant, Yelena. Talk to me, and then we can start to fix this.'

He can't fix anything, Bruna said. I closed my eyes, and bitterly wished I was anywhere else. I felt my body tighten, and the hairs on the back of my neck stand up.

Tell him, Yelena. Tell him whose fault it is that you are in this position.

'We can't fix anything,' I said.

'We can,' he insisted. He leant in. 'Are you okay?'

I took a deep breath. I wanted to tell him. I thought that would make her voice go away. But I was scared of provoking that horrible, sickening laughter.

And yet I also knew there was only one way to begin.

'My stepmother,' I started.

Don't you even dare, the voice said.

'My stepmother used to… '

'What?' His eyes met mine.

I felt very aware of the fact that I had never told anyone, and why I had never felt able to share it with anyone before. It was too big, too confusing. And I couldn't do it now, not with her here. I just had to get through the next few moments.

'Yelena, you must tell me. You can't keep it to yourself any longer.'

'My stepmother. She used to… she used to… '

Don't you even dare, she said, the voice growing louder.

I looked up. Ibarra's eyes, filled with a concern. 'She used to what?'

'She used to touch me.'

He bowed his head. 'Just you?' he asked, reaching for his pen.

You really are disgusting.

'My sister as well. My little sister.' I sounded defiant, even to me.

He started to write. Each scratch of the pen was deafening, yet seemed so futile.

'Have you ever told anyone about it before?'

You are sick, if you think that happened, she said.

'It did happen,' I snapped. Ibarra looked startled.

'I have no doubt that it did, Yelena,' he said.

'It happened for years.' I could hear her breathing. 'No, I've not – I've never told anyone before. She… she wouldn't let me.'

'She wouldn't let you?' He asked, his voice a kind mimic of mine.

'Sometimes… sometimes I can hear her voice. I can hear her laughing.'

He stopped, his eyes interacting with mine, but with a new intensity in them that I had never seen before. 'Yelena,' he said. 'Is she with you now?'

Slowly, trying to block out the breathing, I nodded.

'Yelena,' he continued. 'You must tell me. What has happened recently, this accident and what led up to it, I'm sure it's partly because you've never been able to deal with what happened to you as a little girl. Do you understand?'

I nodded.

'I suspect that she is at the root of all this. Now, I'm afraid, Yelena I need you to tell me everything you can remember. I think you've kept this to yourself for a very long time, and a secret like this can cause real damage. It can make you truly corrode from within. Now, you must allow me to help you. Do you understand?'

You are finished.

'I don't think I can,' I answered.

Of course you can't.

His eyes fixed on me, with that same intensity. 'Yelena… can you hear her now?'

Go on, she said. *Try and tell him.*

Slowly, I nodded.

Ibarra exhaled. 'Good. I think we're starting to get somewhere.'

'Please help me,' I whispered.

'I am going to help you.'

I felt my voice crack. 'You've got to help me.'

'She's not there' he said, leaning forward. 'Yelena, it's just you and me.'

I felt completely unable to move. 'Are you sure?'

'I'm absolutely sure.'

I was shivering. But then, as he placed his hand on mine, for a second I felt as though the breathing had stopped.

Through the course of those sessions, watching Ibarra's pencil dance over sheaves of paper, I gradually realised how much you had already told him about me. I knew that you had told him about the dinner with Hannah and Elizabeth, the recent changes in my manner, the circumstances leading up to my meeting with Cecilia. But it was my childhood that he kept coming back to, again and again – the abuse, the self-harming, the voices during *Giselle* and now. He said it would take time, but he was sure I could begin to move on from them.

When your name was mentioned, I became less able to hide how desperate I was to see you. When Ibarra mentioned that you were managing the treatment I was receiving, I felt delighted. Even when the caveat was that you were still being advised to refrain from visiting me.

'I understand that your accident occurred at a most difficult moment in your relationship,' Ibarra said, his eyes narrowing. 'Have you considered how it might be important for Mr Stepanov to have time to digest what has recently happened as well?'

I wanted to argue with him, to appeal to his sense of humanity. But somehow I sensed it would be futile; I knew he had already decided that for now, the two of us needed to be kept apart. He said it was in the interests of my welfare, in terms of triggers to psychological episodes. At times I wanted to tear those blessed papers from his hands and rip them into pieces, but over the course of our sessions together, I felt myself being gently moulded by his words. My worldview began to gradually adjust and something told me not to resist his advice, however counter-intuitive it might be.

Dr Ibarra gave me company in an intellectual sense, but the moment those sessions ended I inevitably felt very alone. I was gradually brought off the morphine, and that sense of quiet euphoria gradually disappeared. I was suddenly acutely aware of how uncertain my life had now become. How would I make a living? Would it be possible for us to rekindle our relationship? How would I handle life in a country that was so new to me? These questions gradually lowered onto me like a heavy curtain, which I began to feel pinned under. It was all too easy to focus upon the next concern – the pain in my ankle, or the need to make a certain phone call. At times of stress they were poised, ready to overwhelm me. I knew the time would come when I would have to face them.

Erin and Eva came to visit me in the hospital, and although I was glad for their company, I felt oddly unable to open up and share what I was going through. They now felt like characters from somebody else's life. It was a life that I knew well in theory; I was well acquainted with its details. But it felt like Erin and Eva were speaking to a Yelena who no longer existed. In her place was a broken, lost woman – a pale imitation. A person who had to pretend to be something she no longer was, in order to prevent making people feel socially awkward. I was starting to grieve for my former life.

Erin would concern herself with making sure I was lying comfortably, and then we would sit in a companionable silence, or play cards. Eva felt only able to talk about ballet, and she constantly reprimanded herself for sharing current experiences that I would perhaps no longer be able to have. Though I was grateful for their company, I felt that an invisible barrier had been created, and I didn't know how anyone could break through and reach me.

Sometimes, during the long hours I sat in the dayroom, I

would watch when a boyfriend came to visit another woman on the ward. Often I'd turn the music off in my headphones, and close my eyes and try to listen in on their conversations. Out of the corner of my eye I would try and take in the way the boyfriend reached out and touched her on the arm, or the precise way he leaned closer to whisper. I'd subtly watch them have a quiet game of cards, during which I knew a smile drawn from her lips represented a significant breakthrough for them both. When the boyfriend got up to leave, I'd close my eyes, and try to take in the final words he passed on as if they were for me. I imagined it was you craning over me, your fingers easing the hair over my ear, telling me how much you missed me and that I would get better soon. But when they then stood up I would see exactly how different they were to you, and then I'd feel ridiculous for taking refuge in my imagination. I'd try to settle back into the silence, torn between wanting another boyfriend to visit the dayroom and hoping the rest of the day would pass, flat and without sentiment.

Even when I spoke on the phone with Inessa and my father, they too felt like characters from another life; unable to relate to my current circumstances with anything other than feverish concern.

I thought of you, and desperately wanted to know what you were doing. I listened to the jazz CD that we used to play in your house. But despite these distractions, the nights remained very difficult. And, with the same sticky, taunting quality they had had just before I met Elizabeth, the dreams started to return.

At first they were only vague, distant affairs that reverberated into my awareness and then drifted away, leaving me alone in the sheets with the scent of something that should have long been forgotten still clinging to me. I was becoming my own worst enemy, because I wanted to explore those strange dreams further. In having the time to delve deeper into my memories and my fears I started to give those vague sensations life and strength. At first they were only bloodless and fleeting, but I made them strong and potent.

I began by dreaming about you and Catherine. About the nights that she described in her letters, when she would pull on a tight black dress and the two of you would steal out of the city in a taxi. As I lay immobile on the bed I felt as if I was a passenger in that taxi watching the two of you kiss, with haunting neon streetlights illuminating you every so often. In those dreams I was always invisible, but on the nights I did try to interfere I was dumb. When I tried to stop you holding hands you both laughed me off, and you looked embarrassed to see that I was there.

In the nightclubs you went to dance at I would linger around the edge of the bar, and when I looked down on myself I had no body, no reflection in the tiled mirrors that adorned the walls. I was a ghost, separated from the world around me by a screen I couldn't break through. Just watching you clasp her shining body against you, watching you find dark corners together, and then, finally, watching you leave together. I'd be unable to follow as you went into the night, to take a taxi back to one of your bedrooms.

As the nights in the hospital went on, the dreams heightened in intensity. My mind started to rake over the remnants of those letters that had lodged in my memory. It started to recreate, as accurately as it could, the moments when the two of you were sexually intimate.

As if I had been forced to film it, my mind's eye followed as Catherine pulled on stockings under your watchful gaze, as she buckled gold heels onto to her slim, elegant feet. It zoomed in on the moments when, her eyes wide with fear and excitement, she laced up a corset while you lay helpless at her feet. The images whipped around me as your bodies closed, or as you forced her to submit to your will. My mind would fixate upon the expression of pleasure on your face just as you found what you were looking for. Then I'd suddenly wake, my body covered in cold sweat.

I decided to fight back against my mind. If it was going to taunt me with details, then I decided I was going to overcome those details one by one. By the dim light of the car park, not daring to turn on bedside lamps and rouse the nurses, I began to list every detail I could remember about the erotic encounters described in her letters. I actually made lists, in handwriting I hoped was too small for Dr Ibarra to read. 'Skin-tight corset' might have been one entry on a list, 'black ribbons' perhaps another. And once I had made these lists, which I believed covered every detail of your sexual history with her, I started to write letters to you. I would tick off every item from the list in the contents of the letters, translating the items into my own words as I described what I intended to do with you. I tried to write the letters in a lovelorn, affectionate way, making the content gradually narrow to a sharp eroticism at the conclusion of each letter. At the start I would be genuinely writing to express how much I was missing you, but as I began to incorporate each item the missives became more concerned with these 'units of eroticism'. Through them I hoped to match every potent moment Catherine had given you, and then add more, to weld myself more deeply to you than she ever had. But late at night I think the mind labours for an objectivity it would quickly dismiss in daylight. I would wake the next morning, amongst the sterile light, having dreamt of more erotic detritus, more encounters I had to match. After a while I was no longer able to tell which items were from her letters, and which were feverish delusions, whipped up by a mind railing against itself. I told myself that if I couldn't see you, couldn't please you in person, then these letters would compensate.

In the cold light of day I never seriously considered sending them to you. It scared me to think what Dr Ibarra would make of them, and what, if they were ever analysed, they would reveal about me. I recall those letters now only as detritus from a sick mind, products of a trapped brain feeding back on itself. Obsessing on delusions that were neither here nor there.

During those dead, endless nights, the starched sheets and the smell of the hospital became overwhelming; an insipid, muggy smell that seemed to consist of overcooked vegetables and bandages. I could hear patients in other rooms, snoring and moaning and occasionally crying out in pain. I could hear the city outside. I would lie there and think of the times you had taken me to concerts down by the river. When you had led me down into the city's lights, where all the pleasures of the world danced on my face before you. I remember how it felt to have your proud eyes upon me as we walked home, faintly woozy with wine and music. But the memory would break the instant I caught my reflection in the window across the room. I saw a haunted, gaunt woman staring back at me. I tried to find within her the beautiful young woman who had walked with you down by the river, who had waited in the wings to perform as Giselle. As I did so, I felt tears well up in my eyes. I desperately wanted her back. Why could I not reach her? What had I done to lead myself here, to the point where I needed such protection from my own mind? To the point where my body no longer obeyed the simplest command, when it had once held audiences spellbound.

I remember one night in particular. It was around four in the morning, during the time that I was being eased off the morphine. As I lay in that bed every movement of my legs was causing pain so great that it made me want to scream. Despite this, I desperately needed to move so that my eyes could look at something other than the cracked white expanse of that ceiling.

I decided that the only way I could stay sane was by looking out of the window. At the very least seeing a hint of green, even if it was veiled in darkness. I told myself that the small patch of green visible from my window was the same patch of grass that bordered your house. That it was the field

I had walked around, full of trepidation, on the night before our first date.

I found a way to bring the bedside lamp to life, and I searched for my crutches. With the room now bathed in a dim blue glow, I tenderly looped my good foot under my bad one and gradually, inch by inch, eased my bad foot onto the ground. The moment weight was put on my bad foot it recoiled in pain, but I insisted that my body endure the discomfort. I had to set my eyes upon something else.

I leant against the crutches and hobbled, ever so slowly, over to the window sill. When I finally got there, looking out into the night, I felt as if I was searching for the Yelena that Erin and Eva had come to visit. In that state of late-night delirium I felt sure that she was somewhere out there. At this time of night she'd perhaps be awake, in her small bedroom by the quayside, worrying that the role she felt destined for might soon be taken by another. Her expression would be relatively light, for she was yet to encounter the wracking pain that was in store. But I would go out there and find her, and plead that she resist giving into her darkest fears.

I felt tears stream down my face. I tried not to make a sound, as I didn't want to be caught out of bed by the nurses. I felt hunger scrape the pit of my soul, because I desperately needed to see you. I needed to tell you that I was sorry for my act of madness. I needed to convince you that it had all emanated from love. And then a car went past, its headlights briefly illuminating that barely visible patch of grass, and for the first time I saw that that green was not the green of the field by your house. It was an untended piece of wasteland, on a bleak industrial estate.

I tried to wipe the tears from my eyes but a kind of hysteria took over my body. The reality of my situation was suddenly so apparent that I was unable to compose myself. To fight off the tears I turned back to the bed, but as I moved, my dead leg caught the base of the drip. Helplessly, I watched it swing back, that transparent bag shining in the blue light. I clawed out for it but it went out of reach and clattered into the wall. In the distance I heard an alarm go off, and for a few moments I stood there between the bed and the window. As I struggled to stay upright the pain in my leg grew enormous. I looked up and saw the concerned face of one of the student nurses as she entered the room. 'Are you alright Yelena?' she asked, as the light came on.

She did not indulge in my moment of embarrassment. She moved as if propelled by natural empathy, her small body bustling with professional concern. I felt her cool hands on my shoulders as she eased me back onto the bed, and between the sheets. I tried to get comfortable while she organised the magazines and books at my bedside, and as she did so I took in her face – the hazel brown eyes, the small freckles on her nose.

'Those gowns don't like to stay shut, do they?' she said, raising my head to place another pillow underneath it. She stood immobile for a moment, before leaning against the bedside cabinet. 'Do you feel more comfortable now?'

I wanted to reach out and connect with her, tell her exactly how I was feeling even though we had never met. At that moment, in the small hours of the night, she seemed just as vulnerable as me. Something prevented the young girl from leaving my side; perhaps she had somehow understood that I needed her to stay.

'What's your name?' I asked.

'Faye,' she said. 'Were you… trying to stretch your legs?' I could not decipher her expression. She started to smooth out the sheets at the side of the bed.

I nodded.

'I think we sometimes forget that as a dancer, you need to be on your feet. You must feel this big need to move about. Not that I know anything about it.'

'I wanted to look out of the window.'

She continued smoothing the sheets.

'There's not much of a view from here,' she said, and seemed to instantly regret saying it.

'It reminds me that there's something else,' I said. She looked up.

'We could just move your bed nearer to the window?'

I thought I could make out a slight smile on her lips, and I laughed.

'We could do that,' I answered.

'Then in the morning you can have a better view… '

'Of the car park.' I finished.

She laughed. 'I'm glad I heard you. The nights are hard, aren't they, when you're by yourself? I expect you sometimes just fancy a natter, or a cup of tea. It amazes me how much can be fixed by a cup of tea.'

'Are you on your own on the ward?'

'Yes.' Faye looked down at the bed. 'I mean, there's another orderly, who takes care of the domestic side of things, but I'm just sat at the desk, for the whole night.'

'Are you not tired yourself though?'

'It's not tiredness, it's something else. I don't think people are meant to stay awake all night. Sometimes, it doesn't seem right.'

'What do you do?'

'Nothing. I mean, I'm not sure what I'm supposed to do.' Her voice lowered. 'It's a bit like what I imagine purgatory will be like.'

'Do they not organise it so that you're with someone else?'

'Yeah, but it can be lonelier with them.' She was now looking at me, rather sheepishly. 'I don't find the night shifts easy. Sometimes I text my boyfriend, though of course he's asleep. It still makes me feel better, you know? To say something to him, even if he doesn't reply until morning.'

'I know what you mean.'

'Soon I'll be back on day shifts.'

My eyes trained on her features for a moment. 'Are you looking forward to that?'

The brown eyes looked blank. 'I don't know. Sometimes… I'm sorry, I don't know why I'm telling you this.'

'It's okay. It's just nice to natter, like you said.'

'It is, isn't it?' she said, looking a little relieved. 'The truth is, sometimes I don't know how to handle the day shifts either. They just go on for so long. Sometimes – and this is dumb – I actually go to the store cupboard and just hide there until I feel ready to go back out again.'

I laughed. 'I know where you're coming from. Sometimes, before going on stage I used to sit in the toilet and lock the door for a few minutes, just to get my head together. It seems ridiculous, but sometimes we do need to do these things, don't we?'

'I know. I know what you mean.' She paused. 'Obviously, I'm not glad you fell over, but a chat with a dancer made for a far more interesting night than I usually have, honestly.'

'I'm not doing a lot of dancing right now,' I said.

She smiled. 'I used to do ballet, until I was about twelve. But I started to feel ridiculous, seeing as I'm so short and graceless. So I did tap dancing instead.'

'You shouldn't worry about being graceful,' I said, trying to adjust the pillow under my head.

Faye immediately moved forward to help. 'Just sit up a minute, and we'll put it under you properly.'

'I'm hardly graceful right now.'

'The doctor says you're making good progress. They often give a bit of a negative prognosis, because they don't want people to be disappointed, but I'm sure you'll be up and about in no time.'

'And dancing about the ward?'

'Exactly. And when you are, perhaps you can show us a couple of your easier moves.'

I laughed. 'Thanks for coming in here.'

'You've got a bed to lie in. Think of me at this time of night, with my bum on an office chair, sat behind a desk.'

'I will,' I said, smiling once more. She touched my shoulder, and then moved to leave the room. As she did, she quickly waved goodbye.

After she left, the atmosphere in the room felt completely different. The fact that she had reached out to me, without any requirement to, transformed my state of mind. It seemed to signify that there was so much to life that I was yet to experience. It even occurred to me that life might still be worth living.

Love,

Yelena

Dear Noah,

After two weeks in the hospital Dr Ibarra insisted that I was immediately moved to a spare but deceptively warm respite home called The Cedars. He kept this from me until the end of a particularly confrontational session.

During our time together I had, on his insistence, delved back into my childhood and gradually plotted the events of my life that had led to the accident. Although it had been difficult to discuss the years I'd lived with Bruna, he pushed me to describe the worst occasions: the night Inessa was smothered, the self-harming, the wetting of my sheets. He wanted us to explore how my fear had led to me wetting myself during my first sexual experience, and how that might have affected my sexual relationships since. He seemed particularly keen to express how, as a result of this, I might have demanded complete psychological refuge in a lover, and how unrealistic that was. I eventually confessed my obsession with those letters and photos, and how they had affected me. Ibarra explained how unrealistic it was to try and objectify desire and love in such a way. In one sense his advice seemed obvious, but I was amazed how many problems seemed to vanish as soon as I shared them. Presented with many challenges, he said, my mind had created coping strategies which were not always helpful, and which now needed monitoring. For instance I had never before thought of my blood-letting as 'self-harming', merely as a private way of dealing with situations that had become overwhelming. Ibarra helped me see how the cutting had been a way of tricking myself into believing I had some control over challenging situations; but in so doing I had unwittingly been creating a new difficulty. But even with this realisation, I knew it would require much more than a single conversation to completely eradicate that tendency from my mind. Knowing in theory that it was dangerous to put a blade to my own skin was one matter, but avoiding doing so when a powerful urge arose quite another. Nevertheless, from that point on I possessed the tools by which to handle my problems without being self-destructive, and as time went on I used those tools more and more until they became second nature to me.

On that particular day I had been struggling to convey to him the pressure that I had put upon myself while dancing as Giselle. He had wanted to know all about the voice of Bruna that seemed to barge into my consciousness at times of extreme stress and worry. He suggested that over time I could replace her voice with an inner dialogue that was encouraging and nurturing. I had never considered this.

At the time I had seen his almost relentless advice as disruptive. Many of the sessions had taken on a combative feel, and I had often felt that he was trying to verbally out-manoeuvre me. Only now do I see that he was constantly questioning me to try and fully understand my mental processes. I see now how many perspectives he embedded in me, which I have been able to seek comfort from in time. As a consequence I felt slightly drained by the end of the session, though I quickly perked up when he told me that I was about to be transferred to a new residence. He promised he was going to keep seeing me regularly.

He told me the new residence housed a skilled multi-disciplinary team keen to accelerate my recovery. It boasted a swimming pool, a gym, and a team of chefs who would precisely cater to my demands. He would continue his visits, though they would gradually become less regular. 'There are psychologists there who can keep an eye on you, though I will still oversee your mental recovery from afar.' Shuffling his annotated notes, he added, 'I understand that your room overlooks a duck pond.'

'Why?' I couldn't help but ask.

'Because,' he said, standing up and placing his fountain pen in his top pocket. 'In Michael's eyes, you are an investment. And he is keen to protect his investment as best as he can, by giving you the best of everything.'

'And that includes ducks?'

Regardless of the description, I could not help but feel anxious about my temporary new home. Was I about to be fast-tracked towards dancing again, regardless of the long-term consequences? Although I had experienced great lows in the hospital, I had felt livened by the occasional visits from Eva and Erin, and the chats with Faye. The Cedars sounded like a halfway house for people with mental health difficulties. What sort of people would I be living alongside? I prepared myself for this new life by trying to purge my mind of everything that had plagued me in that hospital, an effort that began with destroying those strange, irrational letters I had written to you. Gradually, with careful monitoring and medication from Ibarra, I began to surface from the mist I had been submerged in. I gradually became able to talk about Bruna without hearing her first. Slowly, I started to uncoil with relief.

Set amongst a crop of trees a mere fifty metres from the sea, The Cedars certainly looked luxurious. As I unpacked in my spacious room, I longed for a few days of quiet in which I could compose myself, but a minute later I was surprised by an abrupt knock on the door. I heard a deep, chuckling laugh, and the door quickly swung open to reveal a portly African woman in a tight green uniform. She looked at me and smiled broadly. 'Our glamorous dancer – here to give a little razzmatazz to this godforsaken place!' I couldn't help but laugh.

'Hello,' I said.

'This is your new physiotherapist, Grace,' one of the hospital orderlies advised, squeezing around her.

'Nurse Polly, I can introduce myself,' she said, with a thick Caribbean accent. As she spoke she placed her fingertips on her not unsubstantial bosom, whilst fluttering her eyelashes with fake modesty.

'I thought you needed no introduction?' the orderly replied, prompting another booming laugh.

'You have been here two minutes, Yelena, and yet you have already decided this place is so bad that you must sit in darkness!' She swept the curtains open, allowing thick blasts of white light to douse the room in colour. 'I know that you ballerinas can be tortured sorts, but there will be no room for that if I am going to get you walking again. You are going to have to start working very hard for me, and if it takes me wearing a tutu in order to get you to do that, then I will. Won't I, Nurse Polly?'

Polly laughed, and looked at me. 'Please don't let Grace wear a tutu,' she said. 'No-one on the floor will get any sleep.'

'In five minutes I will come and call for you again my darling,' Grace said. 'First I must get you some decent crutches, and then we will see exactly how much work lies ahead of us.'

Grace took me to a gymnasium in the basement of The Cedars. I felt my heartbeat quicken as I took in the array of ropes, pulleys and exercise balls all around me. What exactly was she going to make me do? But the warmth of her hand on my shoulder quickly calmed my nerves. Grace began by sitting me down and asking me to stretch my legs and feet as much as I could. She then had me stand in front of her and sway gently from side to side without support. I could read my anxiety on her face, as she held out her arms and promised to catch me if I toppled over.

Over the course of the next few weeks she made me walk, again and again, injured foot first, down the winding corridors of The Cedars. She would stand one foot behind me, encouraging me as I made my unsteady progress. Those sessions reminded me of the time Uncle Leo taught me to ride a bike. He used to run a foot behind me as I pedalled away, shouting 'I'm still here!' so I knew that I would be caught when I inevitably fell off.

Quickly, Grace became the hub of my life. Occupational Therapists consulted with her before teaching me how to cook simple meals in their bespoke kitchens, as I couldn't carry anything with a broken foot. Dieticians bartered with her about which of my favourite foods I could eat. But after a while my natural fitness seemed to kick in, and I was delighted that I surpassed even Grace's expectations during the sessions we had together.

'I always push my patients hard,' she said, as I clambered in a frame towards the other side of the gym. 'But I am not used to them exceeding my expectations. You were obviously in peak physical condition when you had your accident, Yelena, you were far fitter than I have *ever* been. In fact I expect I was not as fit as you the day I left the womb, and it has all been downhill from there. You are doing great, you seem to have no pain barrier!'

And she was right, Noah. Grace had ejected me from the dark, lonely room that I had been living in, and prompted me to become the real Yelena again. A woman who drove herself, a woman who was pushy and ambitious.

'That is enough for today!' she would shout, when I had reached the other side of the gym. 'Why do you have to break every record going? As far as I see it, you should match your previous session and then do a tiny bit more. You do not need to charge the wall down!'

It delighted me to hear her speak like that, as it meant I was doing all that I could.

After that session, one of the orderlies brought us a cup of tea, but for once Grace did not rush me back up to my room. A mood seemed to have taken over her, and her demeanour was very different to the brash, vivacious one that I had grown used to.

'Why do you have to push yourself so hard, my darling?' she asked, as I sat down to catch my breath. 'You are like so many Western women,' she continued. 'Constantly pushing yourself towards the next achievement. But where is your quality of life? Pushing this hard is counter-productive if the journey itself always feels tortuous. Do you not ever ask yourself why you do it?'

'I don't know,' I said. 'I guess I just want to be better.'

'But, my darling, your sense of being better or worse does not come from what you do, or from what you achieve, it comes from how you feel about yourself. How can you like yourself, if all you do is endure? You need to be kind to yourself, Yelena. It's so important to be happy in your own company, and to not be fearful of your next demands.' She sipped from the cup of tea, whilst looking momentarily distracted. 'Where I come from, there is none of this perpetual testing, like there is here. Life is for living – for laughter, for food and for family. I apply effort to causes that are important to me, but I never strive just for the sake of it. Yelena, my dear, you have shared your wonderful gift with many people, but you must allow them in enough so that they can help you as well. Tomorrow we will take a break from this work. We will go out into the garden. We will enjoy fresh air and conversation. How does that sound?'

The next day, during our allotted time together, Grace and I walked through The Cedars' garden. It felt somehow audacious to step out of the therapeutic environment and just enjoy the bracing November air. Admiring the recently planted flowers whilst listening to Grace talk about her family, I felt myself take on aspects of her temperament. She seemed so calm, so accepting and so content to let time sweep her along its strange and convoluted path. Despite being acutely aware of how far I still had to go, that afternoon for once I truly felt comfortable in my own skin.

It was the following day when I received a postcard from Inessa. Though we had spoken briefly on the phone since the accident, given her naturally elusive nature I had not felt a sense of kinship with her over it. Though she'd sounded concerned for me, she was still as distant as ever. But the postcard suggested that something might have shifted in her.

Dear Yelena, it read. *It has been so long since we have been together, far too long. A lot has happened here, and for me, a change of scenery is now required. I would very much like to come and visit you. Message me to let me know if that would be alright. It would be wonderful to see you again. From your loving sister. Inessa.*

Coming from Inessa, I found the choice of sign-off particularly unusual. I called her to say I would be very happy to see her, and the cryptic and rather emboldened woman on the end of the phone could not have sounded more thrilled. We arranged for her to come and stay for a few days in the nurses' quarters. She didn't exactly say what had sparked this sudden resolve, only mentioning that she had been following my progress as a dancer over the last year, and that of course she had been extremely worried about my accident. Somehow I was not quite ready to accept that I was about to have the type of sister I had always longed for. Just before she arrived it occurred to me that in many ways, Inessa was a stranger to me, and yet the two of us were going to need to find a way to feel at ease with one another.

I was sat in the drawing room, in a chair overlooking the driveway, when I saw Inessa for the first time in many years. I was instantly struck by how tall and slim she was, dressed in an expensive-looking, fur-trimmed coat. She had grown a little into her face since I had last seen her, and she now looked refined, elegant even. Her high heels looked handmade, and the curls of hair that I could see burgeoning from her hat looked carefully coiffed. As she approached the door she caught my eye, and her pale face erupted into a childish smile.

I heard her asking the nurses urgent questions about my welfare, with a concerned manner that I didn't recognise. Seconds later she was upon me, kissing my cheek as I inhaled the scent of her designer perfume. 'Oh my goodness, it is so good to see you,' she said, her voice containing an intriguing new English inflection. 'I have missed you so much.'

'I must look pretty terrible to you,' I whispered.

'You look anything but. You have grown so beautiful. Though that's not a surprise. The nurses tell me you're recovering really well!'

'They do?'

'Yes. I've been on the phone to them a few times after you've hung up. Sometimes I even rang them back! You didn't think that I wouldn't ask after my sister's welfare?'

I paused. 'I don't know. What's with the expensive clothes, Inessa? I should have known you would make quite the girl about town.'

'Thanks. But I have none of the natural glamour of a *prima ballerina.*' She seemed to say the words with genuine admiration. I laughed. 'I helped negotiate the sale of Dad's business, and with the money I made, I started my own beauty retail company. But haven't I told you that already? So far it's going really well! But I don't need to sell myself to my sister. Dear Yelena. How did we fall out of touch for so long?'

Because you didn't help me fight Bruna, I thought. You weren't there for me. You were in another world. I looked up at her, making the effort to bite my tongue. She registered my silence, whilst seemingly absorbing my expression. I wondered if it caused her some pain.

'We're going out for dinner tonight,' she told me. 'I will

arrange us a taxi in a few minutes, and we can talk properly then.'

After a few effusive conversations with the staff, Inessa ordered us a taxi to a small Italian restaurant overlooking the coast. It was good to leave The Cedars, but I was rather disappointed when Inessa led me down a small flight of steps to the restaurant's candlelit cellar. I didn't protest as her body language suggested she had something to disclose, something which would perhaps not suit wide-open spaces. Nonetheless, this sudden intimacy slightly unsettled me.

Her lips remained pursed until we had ordered our meals. Finally, when the waitresses had left us alone, Inessa leant in conspiratorially.

'I wanted to come here to see how you are,' she started. I tried not to react. 'We are not good at looking out for one another in our family, Yelena. Dad is – I'm sure you know – very worried about you. But how could he bring himself to come right out and say it, let alone visit? He always was so poor at communication. He sends his love. I know he does, but you know as well as I that he could never put it quite like that himself.'

I smiled. I tried not to think of the loneliness I'd felt in those early days just after the accident. When even a card from my family would have meant so much. There had been nothing but silence from my father, and Inessa.

'I'm not sure I know him as well as you,' I said.

Instantly I felt transformed back to the fourteen year old who was envious of their bond. Her eyes darted between me and the table, in what seemed a spontaneous reaction of guilt.

'Perhaps,' she conceded. 'But if that's true, it's only because I stuck to him to keep me safe from Bruna. And I learnt a little more about him as time went on. What surprised me most was that he didn't even enjoy his work. The truth is, when Mum died his light was snuffed out. It all became too much for him. The only way he was able to get through each day was to get his head down and work. Working meant he didn't have to ask himself questions about how well he understood his daughters. But, what you've got to remember is that at the root of all that was a love for us. It's just that he turned that love into fear.'

I knew that inevitably this was only a compacted version of my sister's understanding of him, but it surprised me how shaken my perception of my father was simply by the language someone else used to describe him. I realised I might have been working from misconceptions and in time building them, making them more elaborate.

'I should have supported what you were trying to do before you went away, Yelena. I was young, yes, but you were right to try and bring Bruna to justice before leaving. You were right to push me to admit what she had done.'

I felt a powerful urge to speak, to remonstrate with her. Again I restrained, but I felt her sense my anger.

'What you have to understand is that Dad was my whole life, Yelena. You had your dancing, but I had nothing else.' There was a pleading edge to her voice now. 'Keeping him content and happy was all I had, and at that age, I wasn't ready to distress him by admitting the things that Bruna had done to us.' Her expression softened. 'But once the business was sold, I gained a little confidence. By then Bruna and Dad were, of course, separated. She'd moved back to… whatever rock she had crawled out from. Yelena, I have been desperate to tell you this,' she leant forward. 'After you left for the Vaganova I got in touch with a local police officer, and started to sound out how one would go about reporting a case of child abuse. Gradually, over the course of a many months I told her our story but I wasn't quite ready to submit an official testimony. I suppose I didn't think Dad was ready to confront the truth just yet and I didn't want to pull you back to Donetsk when you had only just got away. I suppose I let the trail run cold, to be honest. But then I had a call, a month ago, from the police officer I had first spoken to about Bruna. I had, for a long while, known that when the time was right I needed to bring her to justice, to make sure that another child was never at risk of abuse from her again.' I forced myself to stay silent. I told myself I had waited so long to hear her speak about this, that I must not interrupt her now.

'This officer,' she continued, 'was only a new recruit when I first brought our case to light. Now she is in a more senior position, and it just so happened that when she was promoted she became a senior officer in the district that Bruna now lived. One day she was asked to look into a woman who had recently been offered a position at a school, as a dinner lady. Unfortunately this woman's criminal checks had gone through, and without the charges having been pressed, the case had been dropped and Bruna was about to start working. However, her file had been brought to this senior officer as the policeman permitting Bruna's new appointment had been unsettled by some of the allegations he'd read about her, and had wanted someone above him look into it. Having found out about Bruna's current situation, the senior officer tracked me down and contacted me to ask if I was ready to pursue the charges. They needed me to testify, she said, if Bruna was going to be prevented from working in a school.'

I was sat bolt upright at this point.

'I engaged with her straight away,' Inessa continued.

At that moment a waiter bustled into our conversation. Hurriedly, I ordered red wine from him. Inessa, just as I had expected her to, took her time deciding.

'For God's sake tell me what happened Inessa,' I said, the moment he'd finally left.

'It seemed that my engagement with her was not quite fast enough. Bruna had already been working in the laundry department at this school for many weeks. This new post as a dinner lady had represented something of an advancement for her. An advancement, the senior officer told me, which had come about because of her new relationship with a teacher in the English department. A rather elderly and eccentric professor. Apparently a man of some controversy, who'd recently fathered a child with a former student of his. They'd had a daughter, who he now had custody of.

I felt as if my blood was about to freeze. 'Inessa,' I suddenly hissed, with an audible bitterness that shocked me. I felt years of frustration rise up inside me. 'How could you have been so cowardly? You had the perfect opportunity to put this woman behind bars, and yet you allowed her enough time to start working in a school?'

'Please, Yelena. You must allow me to finish.' Her hands trembled slightly as she poured out the wine. Her face had gone pale, and for the first time I wondered if this story would have a happy ending or not.

'The senior officer told me her sources indicated that until recently Bruna had been working as a maid for an elderly gentleman out in the countryside. She therefore thought it very unlikely that Bruna had had the opportunity to reach any children since she had fled from Donetsk. She assured me that this was most likely the first time Bruna had been at risk of offending again, and the moment she had become aware of the case, she had started trying to track me down.'

'Then what happened?' I snapped.

'Well, the clearance for the dinner lady post had taken a very long time to come through, given the allegations that had been noted on her record. Apparently Bruna started to suspect, according to the senior officer, that I was behind its delay. Though Bruna had been informed she'd eventually gained clearance, as soon as her file had landed on the senior officer's desk the clearance had quickly been suspended. But it still seemed she might have access to her boyfriend's new child. The senior officer knew she had to put Bruna behind bars. I didn't tell you about this at the time, Yelena, because it was in the week of your accident. The officer told me I had to move fast. I finally had the confidence to convince Dad to appear in court too. Reluctantly, Dad agreed. The charges were re-opened against Bruna, and it looked as though she was going to be sent to prison for a good stretch of time.'

'Going to be?'

Inessa's face darkened. 'This is where the story gets a little more… difficult. Along the years, Bruna had found a solicitor who not only cost very little, but who was also very good at his job. He was able to delay the proceedings in order to buy Bruna the time to mount a more rigorous defence.'

'And?'

'And because Bruna wasn't put immediately into custody, she had some freedom. The future was looking pretty bad for her, no doubt about it. Yelena she… she came to visit me.'

'She came to *visit* you? When?'

'Two weeks ago.'

Inessa's face had now gone completely white. 'She tracked me down. It couldn't have been very difficult, I should have been more careful to cover my tracks. It was the day Uncle Leo and I were clearing out Dad's offices, after the sale of his business had just gone through. I was taking boxes into the hallway, when I looked up to see Bruna waiting for me on the doorstep.'

'What happened?' I asked, barely breathing.

'Dad wasn't in,' she continued. I saw a painful memory flash across her face, and I wished I had been there. She suddenly looked very small, like my baby sister, little Inessa. Ambushed by the woman who had caused her so much pain. At that moment I loathed the world for the situations it sometimes handed us. I sat back, willing myself to let her speak.

'I was with Uncle Leo. He was in Dad's study, just behind me. We had been loading everything into the car so for once the front door was open, and Bruna was coming through the entrance, seemingly going towards the foot of the stairs. Her face was a little more wizened, more twisted than I remember it being. I think I quietly said her name, barely believing that it was really her. 'So you've not forgotten me yet then?' she roared. I screamed so loud that I felt sure it would shatter the hallway mirror. I heard an imperceptible shout from Leo, and Bruna grabbed me by the neck. I tried to wrestle her onto the floor. But she was stronger than I had ever imagined she would be. There was just so much anger in her.'

'Did she hurt you?'

At that point Inessa set down her glass of wine. I saw for the first time how much her long, pale hands were shaking. She reached down, and after looking carefully around her to ensure that we were alone, she unzipped the side of her dress to reveal a long, freshly stitched scar running down the side of her torso.

'Inessa!' I cried.

She looked me steadily in the eye. 'I thought I had her,' she said. 'I was just turning her over, when I saw the flash of a blade. I was terrified, but I somehow managed to wriggle free of her. But she panicked, and I felt the knife bury itself in my side. There was this awful feeling, Yelena, as it punctured the side of my body. I looked at her in disbelief, and she looked surprised too, surprised that she had actually done it. I kicked out at her, and she fell back onto the hallway table. Desperate to get away, I ran up the long staircase, but seconds later I heard her coming after me. It was then that I realised Uncle Leo had finally come out of the study, seen Bruna, and worked out what was happening. I heard him struggle with her at the foot of the stairs, but she somehow got free of him and charged up the steps towards me. I couldn't believe how much blood there was; I was almost shaking too much too defend myself, and Leo seemed so useless at preventing anything.

Bruna got to the top of the stairs, and backed me further down the balcony. Leo was right behind her, treading cautiously in her wake. I remember him repeatedly saying, 'Put the knife down, Bruna. This has gone too far.'

'It's her who's taken it too far,' Bruna hissed, and then she lunged for me. I fell onto my back, trying to use my feet to keep her at a distance. But with a shout, Uncle Leo pulled her off me. Bruna staggered back against the balcony rail. For a second I wasn't sure if she was going to fall over the rail or stagger back towards me. But then her eyes widened with shock as she realised she had suddenly lost her balance. The knife fell to the floor with a clatter, and then I heard this desperate scream come from her as she toppled over the side. A second later we were looking down on her. She was lying awkwardly on her back on the stone floor of the hallway, a small trickle of blood emerging from her mouth. Leo ran down the stairs, and a few seconds later he shouted that she was dead.'

At this point I saw that I was gripping Inessa's hand. It dawned on me that I hadn't held her hand for many years, and yet at this moment it felt so natural to do so. 'I think I passed out with the pain,' she continued. 'Uncle Leo called for an ambulance, and for a few hours it was just flashing lights, worried expressions and this terrible pain.' She pointed at the scar, and furrowed her brow. 'The major organs were unaffected, they said, but there were some minor internal abrasions that will take time to heal. But fortunately, after a few days I found my feet again. I wanted to phone you, but Dad insisted that you weren't told about it all until you were back on your feet. Leo wanted to phone you too, but I stopped him. I told him, once the wound had started to heal, that I would come to England and tell you myself.'

For a few minutes, neither of us were able to look at one another. Through the disbelief, we were merely two people trying to understand the chaotic plane that we were both living on. And beneath it all, I knew we were wondering if we had somehow caused all this, or at least allowed it to happen.

I held Inessa's hand. 'I'm so glad you're here. And that you're okay.'

I said it suddenly, for once speaking to my sister without trying hard to moderate my emotions. She clearly didn't know how to respond. She looked down on my hand, now gripping hers, and her eyes remained fixed on it.

'I am now. I am now that I've told you,' she said.

'Have you ever told anyone else, about Bruna?' I asked.

She looked up, and slowly shook her head.

'Dr Ibarra said I mustn't carry it alone any longer. He said it can destroy a person.'

Her eyes glazed over. 'I've no doubt it can. But I bet he hasn't ever had to wonder what to do with all the horrible things a person can put in your head. There's just nowhere for those thoughts to go. I think they take on a new life inside you, and eventually, if you kill them you kill a part of yourself too.'

I squeezed her hand tighter, desperately hoping something sincere would transmit through me and into her. I hoped that I could speak without being hindered with formality or self-consciousness, that I would speak just to heal my sister, who had never felt more like my own flesh and blood. And yet she also seemed so alien to me just then. Her mind so different in the ways it had coped with events, even events that had happened when we had been in the same room.

'Then maybe we can't do that,' I said. 'Maybe we just have to learn to live with them. And not lock them away.'

She looked up. 'How can I lock it away, Yelena? She obviously hated me so much more than you, because I was that bit closer to Dad. She used your love for me against you. How can I bring all that out in the open, find a way round it? She just… intrudes. Even dead, Bruna just intrudes on everything.'

'Do you… ever feel her intruding even now?'

Her eyes fell. 'All the time,' she said. 'I dream about her all the time, Yelena. And I hear her voice too.'

'I do too,' I said, as I clasped her hand. 'I didn't like him saying it at first, but Dr Ibarra says we can be fixed.'

'I hope he's right,' she said, and smiled. 'I'm so glad you're back on your feet, I prayed for you, you know. For weeks after the accident, and I don't even believe in God. I didn't know what else to do. I worried about how you were feeling when you were alone in the hospital.'

I felt something inside me move. Her voice began to break. 'I worried about how you were ever going to handle it, so far away from home. I prayed like I did for us when we were little girls, do you remember? I prayed someone would come in the night and keep you safe.'

Then her voice broke, my body moving into hers to protect her sob from the other guests. 'It sounds so stupid, I'm sorry.'

'Don't be sorry,' I laughed, gently. 'It means a lot to me.'

She smiled and wiped her eyes. I looked apologetically at the waiter, but in truth I was glad he had seen her tears. Strangely, I felt proud.

The rest of the dinner was spent in silence. The loud, somehow undignified clattering of cutlery behind us only accentuated the relieved silence that now bloomed between us. Two sisters, sat together in the dark, in the corner of a near-deserted restaurant. For once, I felt aware that anyone looking at us would know we were family. The way we moved into one another's space, the way we were so content to sit wordlessly.

Despite the horrors she had described, I didn't want Inessa to leave my side. I felt there was someone I needed to protect. That I had a responsibility. For the duration of that dinner, I also felt safe for the first time. Despite all that there was to still contend with, I felt happy.

That evening, Inessa went to bed early. I tried not to think how she must have felt, helping her older sister into bed before going alone into the nurses' home, where the bath was hand-pumped and the ironing boards were chained to the walls. I tried not to think of Inessa's own silences as she lay down on the bed, in a country where she knew so little.

After breakfast the next day, Inessa took me out to watch the new rose garden being planted. It encompassed a small square of earth, dug up by a gardener in a flat cap, who planted each small rose bush before carefully placing moist soil around its roots. Inessa asked him why the garden was being created now, and without looking up he said it was for the women on the ground floor, who had nothing to look at from their windows.

'We didn't get to see too many roses in Donetsk, did we?' Inessa said. It was still early in the morning, and the grass was wet with dew. Although it was Inessa who wheeled me out into the still, cold morning air I'd still felt a maternal feeling arise in me as she did so. That morning her face was scrubbed clean of makeup, and she looked untainted, innocent somehow. The night before I had wondered if, given the pain she had gone through, it was possible for her to ever fully live as others do. But watching her amongst the roses, as she touched and smelt them, I realised that of course she could. I could too. I wondered if in fact, because we had known such darkness, Inessa and I could now live more colourfully, more hungrily than anyone. I must have been smiling at that thought, because when Inessa caught my eye she smiled too.

'I'm moving to England,' she said. I looked up at her, and her smile persisted. 'I've made enough money from selling the business to leave the Ukraine, and I want to come and work here. I want to leave behind all that's happened and start afresh. I know I haven't been the best sister in the world but I do hope that there is still time. And if you like, once you're ready to leave here, I thought that perhaps you could come and live with me?' We both kept smiling for a few moments, until it grew ridiculous. 'Of course,' I said.

Honestly, Noah, the pleasure of that moment was such an unexpected surprise. During our time together so much that had been repressed for many years was finally expressed. I'm sure I would never have been so relieved to have first bonded with you had Inessa and I connected at a younger age. In a strange way I therefore felt as if I needed to tell you about what happened between Inessa and me when she came to stay. As I know only you understand how rare and precious such moments are to me.

With love from,

Yelena

Dear Noah,

During the remainder of the time Inessa stayed with me, our conversations were full of plans about our new life. From talking to her, I think my father also sensed a sea change occurring in the relationship between her and me. With her moving to England I think he saw that now was the right time to start resolving matters with me. Inessa made some tentative enquiries about him and me speaking on the phone, properly speaking on the phone, unlike the few, stilted conversations we had had during those early days in the hospital, and a few days later, he called me.

At first I didn't recognise the voice on the end of the phone. It seemed more ragged and timid than I had recalled it being. He asked about my recovery, asked what I thought would happen now with my career. We leapt between conversational islands, neither of us seemingly wanting to glimpse below at the raging torrent of questions that lay underneath. I felt slightly resentful of his sudden interest in me now that Inessa was drawing close to me, and yet the possibility of putting aside my bitterness towards him was liberating. Throughout the conversation I tried hard to remember just what Inessa had said about him, that at the root of all that was a love for us. I tried to connect that sentiment with the distant voice on the phone. At times I could sense that what she had said was true. If it was not enough to solve my reticence, then it did at least feel like somewhere to start.

During that time, Eva came to visit me. She told me that along with another Principal ballerina – one who had trained at the Bolshoi – she'd decided to start a new dance company in the North East. She said that once I had got back on my feet she would be very keen for me to become deeply involved with it. 'If we're going to put decent performances together I'll need input from as many experienced dancers as possible,' she said. She mentioned that she had employed a famous choreographer as a consultant for the new company, and she intended to learn the skills of her profession from her. 'You should join me, in being trained by her,' she said. 'But only if it would not feel too difficult to become involved with dancing again, of course.' I was surprised that someone who appeared so naïve had been able to coordinate a venture so detailed and ambitious. I was full of excitement at the prospect of being part of this exciting new company, and I realised that I'd underestimated the girl with the wide, innocent eyes and disarming manner. Her expressive, animated demeanour began to inspire me.

For some reason I didn't admit that in fact I felt strangely enlightened by the idea of not dancing again. At least being a choreographer would allow me to pursue my love of dance while avoiding making the sacrifices required to dance myself. I started to wonder if my accident had lit a vague path through the dark woods that I had ultimately found myself in.

Despite her enthusiasm, I did sense in Eva some concern about the psychological difficulties I had experienced. She kept making repeated references to 'your state of mind' and how 'of course, everything depends on that'. When I told her about my sessions with Dr Ibarra, and my plans to live with Inessa, she looked relieved. 'That all sounds very… helpful,' she said.

The sessions with Dr Ibarra seemed to be approaching a resolution. He mentioned that he thought I was almost ready to meet you again, and we finally discussed the possibility of you coming to visit me. He had come to believe that my 'psychotic episode' had most likely been a phenomenon caused by the many upheavals I had been experiencing. I felt as though I could look back on the place I was in prior to the accident, and feel sorry for the person I was. By confronting my fears, discussing and dissecting the very fabric of my life, I felt as though years of hardship were finally breaking away. The focal point of our sessions became my imminent discharge and assimilation back into normal life. Inessa's impending move to England seemed to give everyone the confidence that I would have the support to tackle life outside The Cedars. I would occasionally be visited by Grace and Dr Ibarra, and with them keeping an eye on me, and the skills I had picked up from our sessions, I felt I would be prepared to take on the outside world again.

Finally, after five weeks of intensive rehabilitation, I was deemed ready to see you again. I was barely able to contain my happiness, but by then I felt so deprived of pleasure that I daren't think it might actually happen. I was right to hesitate, because in the next breath, Ibarra told me that you were about to go away for three months on a European book tour. I couldn't help but feel crushed by the revelation; and I felt barely able to look at the crumpled piece of paper he handed me as he gave me the news. 'I have spoken to Mr Stepanov, Yelena, and he has asked me to pass this onto you. It's the addresses of everywhere he's staying for the next three months, with corresponding dates, until he's back in England.' I saw that the piece a paper contained a list of fourteen addresses of various hotels scattered across Europe. Peering over the edges of his spectacles, and lowering his voice he added, 'Write to him, Yelena. I guarantee he will write back. He has missed you just as much as you have missed him. He has inevitably suffered a great deal as a result of being apart from you. And, if I may say, I think writing to one another might be a good way for you to both come to terms with what's occurred between the two of you.' As I turned the piece of paper over, I saw that there was a small Polaroid picture attached to it. It was the picture of you and me taken at the launch party. I looked so young, and you looked so scared.

Despite my initial resentment, by that time I had grown to see Ibarra as something of a father figure. I'd never before had someone take the time to fully listen to what had happened to me and then make a reasoned judgement on how best I might conduct my life, and for that reason I remained grateful to him. With hindsight, I now question the logic behind him keeping you and me apart for so long, especially if he was aware of your impending tour. But he came into my life at a time when I craved guidance and direction, and he gave me both. So if he felt that we were finally ready to see one another, then I bowed to his judgement. After all, I had often worried that if we reunited too soon you might come to me with bitterness and reproach in your eyes rather than relief.

The next day, during physiotherapy, I saw Ibarra waiting for me outside the gym. When he spoke to me he was predictably brief, but his manner was also somehow apologetic. He asked if I would like you to briefly visit me before you went away in two days time. Drained from the session with Grace, I just nodded my approval. Though I barely dared to believe you would come.

And so the next day, after almost six weeks apart, you came to see me. For the first time since my accident, I made a real effort with my appearance. I didn't just want to look presentable; if possible I wanted to look attractive again. My skin was paler, and my hair less lustrous than it had been as I'd placed a silver tiara on it to dance as Giselle. When I brushed the smallest amount of rouge on my cheeks the result was a little startling. My cheekbones were more accentuated than ever. I could feel myself becoming uptight, but the tension was instantly dispelled when I looked behind me to see Grace laughing in the doorway.

'What's so funny?' I asked.

'I just find it hilarious that you think you have to make so much effort. He is just a man Yelena.'

I looked at her as if she was mad.

Still chuckling, she stepped into my room. 'However much of a catch he might be, he is still just a man. And he can't have much money, he is a writer for God's sake. And I find it very improbable that he is even half as good-looking as you. I think it must be the Eastern European diet that made you so trim, I'm sure if *I* had been brought up in Ukraine then *I* would have a figure just like yours.' And then she did a little dance, until I reluctantly cracked a smile.

When it was time, I pulled my black trench coat around me and made my way on crutches outside. To my surprise you were already stood at the gates, nervously waiting for me to appear.

There you were, your essence burning perceptibly behind your eyes as you approached me. The second before we made contact you smiled, then hugged me and kissed my cheek. I couldn't help seeking out your scent, and once I found it I felt both overwhelmed and relieved. You glanced at my face and then hugged me again, harder this time. I sensed a small movement in the curtains of the drawing room behind us, and I wondered if Grace was watching the whole event.

'It's good to see you,' you said. I felt something well up in my throat, but I turned it into a laugh. You held me at arm's length. At first your look seemed one of pride, and I was reminded of how handsome you were. Then the pride turned into something softer, a look that I had not seen since the last time I had lain in your sheets. 'Let's walk,' you said, looking up at the windows. You waved. I turned to see Grace waving back at you, shamelessly.

There was, inevitably, silence as we walked towards the rose garden. As if both of us were considering the next step on our convoluted and private path through all that had happened. 'I'm so glad you came,' I said, as we came to the edge of the garden.

'I've wanted to visit you for a long time,' you replied,

looking down at the frozen grass. 'But Dr Ibarra said… '

'I know.'

You tried to smile.

'I want you to know how sorry I am, Noah, for… '

You shook your head. 'From now on you must look after yourself. I mean… really look after yourself.'

'You can help me,' I said.

You looked back at the grass. 'I hope so. I mean, of course I will. Can you walk okay?'

'The bones will have healed by now. If I'm careful, I *can* walk without crutches. I'm just keeping them for a little while longer. To be on the safe side.'

'Good. This garden is rather beautiful.'

I looked around me. 'The gardener here is obsessed with planting roses for the women on the ground floor. But because the roses are out of season, he's worried they might not survive the winter.'

You touched one of them gently. 'If he keeps an eye on them… maybe.'

I suddenly felt all the silence of the last six weeks gather inside me. I felt the clinging, selfish emptiness I'd experienced in the room at the hospital. The poisonous hunger growing inside me during the nights when I'd missed you, when I didn't know where you were, when I had no idea what you were doing. The way every plane and feature of my room had felt like yet another place that my mind could not help but explore. I remembered the confusion that had lingered inside me for so many days, which had sometimes grown so powerful that I'd been barely able to speak. And I remembered the increasing sense of helplessness, and the sheer frustration at not knowing what to do with it. I remembered the surety I'd had that nothing could ever work out again, because I'd simply been through too much to now be able to believe in my own reasoning. I was suddenly aware of the emerging belief I had, that I would always fail in whatever I wanted to do because I was somehow marked. And lastly I remembered the way I had felt all my emotions bubble to the surface when Dr Ibarra had first tried to get me to open up, how difficult it had been to ease each feeling out of me, one by one. I wanted to tell you all about those feelings, but I knew it was too soon. You were looking down at the roses, and you weren't yet ready to even meet my eye.

The cold began to close around us. We decided to head back inside. It was then, during that brief, careful walk, that you suggested we write to one another while you were away.

'After all,' you said, 'far too much has happened when we have not been together. If we write to each other, we can learn about everything that we have missed. And… I do want to know it all.' You stopped. 'To be honest, Yelena, I think that I *need* to know it all.'

I knew I couldn't guess at your silences. Mine were labyrinthine enough, and I could only imagine at that point how solemn and elaborate yours might have become. Having begun to accept the thought of us being apart again, I found the idea of us exchanging confessional letters moved something inside me. I could see it hurt you to think of us being apart for three months this time. It was only later that I learnt why you'd agreed to the tour, to help yourself handle the possibility that we could be kept apart for even longer. Wanting to ease that expression from your face, I suddenly became determined to convince you that our separation could be of benefit.

'We can tell each other everything in these letters,' I said. 'Everything we have been unable to say in the last six weeks.'

'The next three months will be bearable if they are filled with letters in which we finally share it all with one another. And close the gap that's inevitably opened up between us.'

The way you looked at me, it was clear you felt sad that was the case. Sad that we could not immediately have a remedy for that.

'But our letters to one another could achieve much more

than that,' I said, as we lingered in the driveway. I saw one of the nurses tentatively begin to approach us, and I wished she would hold back. A certain spark seemed to have just reappeared in your eyes, and I wanted to help it ignite into something greater. 'I want these letters to like be maps of ourselves, Noah. Maps which… eventually lead us back to one another.'

You took a step back, but I sensed that a seed had been planted. You looked up and smiled at the nurse.

'I'll be back in three months, Yelena. Twelve weeks, that's all. It's really not long.'

'I know.'

'You have the addresses, don't you?'

'Yes,' I said.

'You shouldn't be staying out in the cold for too long, Yelena,' the nurse said.

'I'm taking her back inside,' you answered.

We hesitated for a moment. I felt rather limp and helpless on my crutches. You stepped closer to me and kissed me on the cheek. I felt your hands gather my hair, and then, as if unable to prevent yourself, you quickly kissed me on the lips.

'People are watching,' I said.

'Twelve weeks,' you said.

You smiled, and rather disconsolately turned to make your way out of the driveway. I didn't want to watch you fade into the distance; that would have felt so melodramatic. After all, there was little reason to mourn. I had these letters to write, with all their secrets, longing and regret.

Two days later, just as you were arriving in Strasbourg, I wrote my first letter. In which I told you about the recurring dream I'd had of when you first watched me dance.

With love from,

Yelena

Dear Noah,

I am still not quite able to accept that in three days' time you'll be back in England. I'm glad that the final European leg of the tour has not been too bad. I know you were worried about Russia after the visa issues last time. I'm glad to hear you're safe in France now, I know how much you love it there. When you get this, you'll be about to head north once more. I hope you're looking forward to coming home as much as I'm looking forward to seeing you.

Five days ago I moved out of The Cedars and in with Inessa. It's surprised me just how differently I see the world now that I have been allowed back into it. In the past I just accepted that the world whirled around me. It felt full of distractions and obstacles. I never took the time to appreciate its colours and vibrancy. Anything I couldn't immediately contain I saw as a threat. I see now how that mindset would always struggle in a world of such glorious chaos, in which so much of our happiness is contingent not on expectation, but on perspective. The chaos that I previously feared, I cannot help but now enjoy. It feels reckless and bold to do so, and that encourages me. My months of denial have given me a hunger for life that I now cherish.

After a couple of weeks of haggling, Inessa and I secured an apartment not far from the quayside. It caters to Inessa's cultural pretensions well, but I also find it pretty homely. I think you will approve of it, Noah. It is next to a music venue, and we hear the strains of distant melodies late into the evening. Inessa has filled it with modern sculptures and reproductions of paintings and already the air is constantly filled with the unique fragrances of her experimental cooking. She is trying to brush up on English culture. Last night we watched Dickens adaptations and had fish and chips. I've never seen her so happy. She keeps taking photos of us undertaking relatively mundane activities, and then texting them to God knows who in the Ukraine.

I enjoy the ordinary pleasures of this fragmented and sumptuous world so much. This morning I went shopping, and I loved being amongst that array of colours, being pulled in by the boisterous cries of the market traders and then sampling exotic dishes from around the world. I particularly love the walk from the Monument down to the quayside – the misty site of so many of our delirious adventures. At night I savour the experience of watching the moving water and the glittering skyline. In the dark, the city seems to breathe with laughter and possibility. It feels incredible to be able to walk amongst it all again.

Still, I have to ease myself gently back into the pool of life. I sometimes wonder about how to live, about what the rules are. To be honest, I still have no idea how I am expected to conduct myself on a daily basis. I know it sounds strange as I was only away for six weeks, but I sometimes wonder how long it is reasonable to stay in a shop for, how long I can sit alone in the square without looking odd. It all makes me wonder how you gained the confidence to live a life governed by its own rules. Due to your profession, we both now seem well acquainted with the interiors of the cracks in society. We must just be cautious enough not to become caught in them.

I found your last letter very soothing. You stated that there were no rules on how to conduct your life. I will get used to that ethos. Any difficulties I currently have adjusting are overpowered by my new hunger for experience. It's already led me to enquire about night classes, to go out into the city for drinks with Inessa, to sit in diners and watch the city shake off its shroud as evening gently arrives. Inessa and I are both learning to seek out enjoyment together. I feel as if the wounds of the past are being gradually treated.

This brings me to our letters. When we first began exchanging them we hoped that they would function as maps of ourselves, maps which would lead us right to the heart of one another. The first few, we agreed, would probably be successful only as rough outlines and each progressive missive would hopefully fill in more details, plot uncharted territories, and define vague boundaries. But as the date of your return draws closer it occurs to me that as a consequence of these letters I now exist. I've realised that although I can credit you for that development, I must now start to see beyond you. I understand now what a pedestal I put you on; how I saw you as I someone I always needed to please and keep close. But now I am starting to understand that another person should never be needed in that way, and that I should look only to myself for comfort.

When the letters began, in the real world I felt like something of a non-entity. I was physically weak, practically lost, and emotionally damaged. But through words and letters I gradually rebuilt myself, and I feel proud of my act of reconstruction. If someone held all of the letters I've sent to you in their hands, they would be holding the real Yelena. Far more than they could if they ever tried to lovingly gather up this bag of bones in their arms. In justifying and detailing myself to you, I became flesh and blood. How strange it is that such thin, weak slips of paper can become durable pillars of a person's being. And so I can never thank you enough, for provoking me to write these letters. We always feel that those lonely, cold moments that we experience will continue to exist just inside us; that they will never be brought into the light for consideration by others. I am glad to see now how untrue that is. The world applies suffering to us in whatever rational and wild methods it sees fit, and yet by chronicling each act of suffering, though it is not always easy, those dark moments cease to be yours alone.

These letters were intended only for you, and yet now they have been written anyone could read them. Through the exquisitely intimate act of letter writing, my fears have been ventilated one by one. And so I see why people guard their letters so furiously, because in the end they contain blueprints of themselves.

For my part, I do not feel a need to protect them. They were meant for you, and after that I feel too much gratitude towards them to feel I have a say in their future.

For my part, I must admit that your letters have worked very effectively as maps of you as well. In those crisp, hidden missives, I firmly believe that there enough shards of Noah that I could put back together, with care, the shattered mirror and present you with your own beautiful reflection. It may surprise you to know that I find the Noah in your letters a beautiful proposition. The Noah in your letters – particularly in the ones describing the darkness of your working life before you found writing – is a very different Noah to the suave, earnest man I was introduced to at the launch party. In your letters I have often found you alone, frightened, disappointed and cynical. I take it as no small achievement that I remain more willing than ever to stand by your side despite that, that in fact I feel more closely bonded to you for it.

When we were finally reunited in the rose garden, we were like foreigners to one another, with no common language. But through this exchange I now feel that we have developed our own language, and our own comprehensive maps to which we can always refer for the other. How few relationships have that starting-off point? Has it ever occurred to you, Noah, that when we next meet we will be building from the very place that every couple strives towards? All we have to overcome now is the social awkwardness that's arisen due to a few months' separation. Something both our cultures might tell us is hard to overcome, but a challenge which you and I, with our private reservoirs of courage, both know is relatively small. Finding our way to one another for the first time was by far the most difficult part. The next and perhaps final step, I think we both know, will be far easier.

If, for that reason, this feels like a moment of revelation, or celebration, then I am glad. But something occurred to me last night, when I awoke from my usual recurring dream of the first time you saw me dance. That it's not the journey we described in the letters, which was where the greatest hardship took place. The hardest part was getting to the point where the journey began. I realised, in the dead of night, that I always recall the moment you first saw me dance in my subconscious because that is the moment I was first discovered. That was the moment that the hardest chapter of my life drew to a close. I was able to describe my loneliness so precisely from then on, because no matter who separated us or what country you were in, I was never alone.

I feel I have learnt solutions to problems only a few are familiar with, and am already more confident. I feel ready to take on the world by myself, on my own terms, not looking to another for guidance. Instead drawing from all that I have learnt and now become. By coming to terms with my past I have began to build a secure base for myself from which I can explore the world.

I hope you get to write to me again before you return. I am so excited to see you, Noah. Even if getting to know one another again is a little awkward, knowing how we can be together makes the challenge all the more worthwhile.

With love from,

Yelena

Dear Noah,

I understand you are now in La Rochelle. Thank you for your postcards, they are now pinned to our new fridge, which hums with domestic joy. It gives me pleasure to see how each progressive postcard resembles my current surroundings more and more, as you draw closer to home.

Going to the theatre on the Sunday of your return sounds like a lovely idea. However, I cannot help but think of Dr Ibarra's advice, that I adjust slowly to life and do not expect too much of myself. But the production sounds wonderful, and I would love to go to the theatre again, as it is has been so long. Wait for me there on Sunday night and if I do feel up to meeting you, then rest assured that I will. There is just so much to adjust to right now!

With all my love,

Yelena

Dear Noah,

I just wanted to send you a brief note. Firstly, to say how glad I am that I did decide to come and meet you on Sunday, and that we are now ready to include one another in our lives again. Secondly, to say how wonderful your company was, and how much I enjoyed the theatre. And lastly to say, given what happened afterwards, this will most probably be the last of the letters I will need to write to you.

With all my love,

From

Yelena

Dear Margaret,

I'm sorry it has taken me so long to reply to your letter. The truth is, when I received your package I instantly dropped everything and started to read my mother's letters immediately. After a few days of gorging myself on them it feels like only now I am coming up for air.

I can't thank you enough for handing these letters over to me. When reading them, at times, I finally felt close to my mother. How can I ever explain the value of that to anyone? It was not always easy to read about the hard times she endured, but it was a very necessary journey for me to undertake. I became able to understand, given the pain she experienced as a young person, why she found it quite so difficult to be close to me during her lifetime. I have started to stop blaming myself for not being closer to her, now that I have seen the bigger picture. The letters also allowed me to understand where my name came from, from the one woman who I think first gave my mother hope during her life. I like to think she named me Natalya because when I was born I represented hope to her too.

Reading the letters I was in fact struck by how fortunate my mother was to have met Mr Stepanov. If she had not, I think she most likely would have gone through life without ever opening up to anyone. I feel fortunate to have been given this legacy. How often do people strive to completely capture themselves in the written word? There were good reasons why my mother felt she had to do this. Fortunately, they eventually were of great benefit to me.

Had I known in advance the important role Mr Stepanov played in her life, I would have taken the time to properly thank him when I briefly had the chance. I hope that when he passed away he understood that he had offered me something I had craved for many years. Nevertheless, his offer would have been meaningless without your support. Between the two of you, you have given me an understanding of where I came from, and who I am now. It is rare indeed for us to experience such clarity in life. I feel it has cleansed me, invigorated me. Allowed me to lay the past to rest. In all honesty, I suspect even if my mother had taken the time to speak to me she would never have been able to communicate as candidly as she did in her letters. The wait has been worthwhile, because it has belatedly allowed all my questions to be fully answered. These letters have allowed me not just to get to know my mother, but to make my peace with her too.

With my warmest regards to you and your family,
Natalya

Guy Mankowski was raised on the Isle of Wight before being taught by monks at Ampleforth College, York. After graduating with a Masters from Newcastle University and a Psychology degree from Durham, Guy formed a Dickensian pop band called Alba Nova, releasing one EP. After that he started working as a psychologist at The Royal Hospital in London. Guy is currently undertaking a PhD in Creative Writing at Northumbria University and writing his third novel, entitled *How I Left The National Grid.*

In 2011 Guy was awarded a Research and Development Grant by the Arts Council which allowed him to travel to St Petersburg and research the lives of the young ballerinas there. He worked backstage at the famous Mariinsky Theatre and was one of the few English people to ever be granted unmitigated access to the prestigious Vaganova Academy.

Guy was also a Writer in Residence for the North East based Dora Frankel Dance company, and is currently working with them as a Dramaturgical Consultant.

Acknowledgements

In writing this book I was grateful to be able to draw upon the experience of English and Russian ballerinas, dancers and choreographers who gave me their time and knowledge. In particular I was fortunate to interview the exceptional Isabella McGuire Mayes, the only British ballerina to have been accepted into St. Petersburg's Vaganova Academy, and I am very grateful for her input. I am also grateful to Stephanie Gordyniec for facilitating this. I am particularly indebted to the choreographer Dora Frankel, who let me interview her at great length. Her dancers Holly Irving and Natasha Kowalski were generous in offering me their insights. Beth Loughran kindly allowed me to sit in on her professional ballet classes at Dance City in Newcastle.

I would like to extend special thanks to Christine Chambers at Arts Council North East for her guidance and support. Much of the research and development time for this novel was funded by a grant from the Arts Council, to whom I am thankful. Their support allowed me to travel to St Petersburg in Russia to research the novel. Whilst there, thanks to Alexey Fomkin, pro-rector of the Vaganova Academy, I was allowed to tour their prestigious ballet school and spend time with the ballerinas. Masha of St Petersburg Tour Guides served as an excellent translator for me, even in the face of questions of considerable and sometimes questionable detail. She gave me an illuminating insight into the cultural heritage of St Petersburg and its ballet.

I would also like to thank my family – Vivienne, Andrew and Oliver Mankowski and Shirley and Stanley Firmin, who have been very supportive.

I would also like to thank the publicist Lucy Boguslawski and the director Tom Chalmers at Legend Press, a company it's been great to work with. My editor Lauren Parsons-Wolff was instrumental in developing the novel and I am particularly grateful for her help.

I would lastly like to thank Sarah Assbring, whose music as El Perro Del Mar first inspired Yelena.

This is dedicated to Professor Graham Beaumont,
with thanks for his support.